SOUL
KITCHEN

SOUL KITCHEN

a novel

POPPY
Z. BRITE

THREE RIVERS PRESS
NEW YORK

Published in the United States by Three Rivers Press, an imprint of the Crown Publishing Group, a division of Random House, Inc., New York.
www.crownpublishing.com

Three Rivers Press and the Tugboat design are registered trademarks of Random House, Inc.

Library of Congress Cataloging-in-Publication Data
Brite, Poppy Z.
    Soul kitchen : a novel / Poppy Z. Brite.—1st ed.
        1. Cooks—Fiction.   2. Restaurants—Fiction.
        3. New Orleans (La.)—Fiction   I. Title.
    PS3552.R4967S68   2006
    813'.54—dc22   2006005039

ISBN 13: 978-0-307-23765-1
ISBN 10: 0-307-23765-6

Printed in the United States of America

Design by Ruth Lee-Mui

10 9 8 7 6 5 4 3 2 1

First Edition

Soul Kitchen was completed the night before Hurricane Katrina hit New Orleans. In the aftermath of the storm, it soon became obvious that I must dedicate the book to the readers and friends who kept us afloat during impossible times.

To them, and also to Buddy Diliberto, Big Chief Tootie Montana, Joseph Casamento, Mary and Ernest Hansen, Clarence "Gatemouth" Brown, Marisol, Commander's Palace, Angelo Brocato's, Crystal hot sauce, Christian's, Camp-A-Nella's, Dixie Beer, Mandina's, Restaurant Mandich, Camellia Grill, Liuzza's, Dooky Chase, Adam's BBQ, Willie Mae's Scotch House, Ruth's Chris on Broad, Charlie's, Crescent City Steakhouse, Wagner's Meat, King Roger's Seafood, the Circle Food Store, Bruning's, Sid-Mar's, Rocky & Carlo's, Campo's Marina, and everyone and everything else we lost in 2005. Some will be back; some won't. All are irreplaceable.

What is soul food? I say, tell me where your soul is, and I'll tell you what kind of food you want.

— Leah Chase, New Orleans restaurateur

Sic volo, sic jubeo.
(As I wish, so I command.)

— Motto of the Mistick Krewe of Comus

PROLOGUE: TEN YEARS AGO AT THE TOP SPOT

THE first argument Milford Goodman ever had with Eileen Trefethen was about the slogan she wanted to print on her menus: *More Art Per Square Inch Than Any Other Restaurant in New Orleans!* He hadn't taken the head chef job so people could come and look at art. He wanted them to pay attention to his food.

"Oh, don't be such a prima donna," Eileen said, breathing smoke in his face. She was a tall, slender white woman who wore strenuously creative outfits and way too many pins in her water-color-auburn hair. "People know the food is going to be good. I've worked hard amassing this fabulous art collection, and I want people to know about it. Besides, I'm the owner, and I make these decisions. You're the chef, and you stay in the kitchen."

To Milford, the fabulous art collection looked like a bunch of kindergartners' paintings and strange coathooks you could put an eye out on if you weren't careful. It swarmed all over the walls of the dining room and into the pass; he figured it would invade the kitchen unless he guarded against it. But he knew he had to choose his battles at the Top Spot. He was one of only three or four black executive chefs of fine-dining restaurants in the city, the youngest of the bunch at thirty-three, and Eileen never hesitated to remind him of that fact when he expressed any frustration.

"You were a line cook when I discovered you," she liked to say, "and you could be a line cook again, so just remember who butters your cornbread, Milford."

He hadn't been simply a line cook at Reilly's, the hotel restaurant that had previously employed him; he'd been lead PM cook in charge of a crew of thirty. But there was no point telling that to Eileen. She already knew it. She just had a gift for revising history to suit her purposes.

After the more-art-per-square-inch argument, the feuds came thick and fast between them, but somehow they forged a working relationship anyway. Milford liked the money Eileen paid him and the creative control he had over the food. Eileen liked Milford's cooking, and even more than that, she liked bragging about him to her rich Uptown customers.

"Where ever did you find him, Eileen?"

"Oh, I rescued him from an awful turn-and-burn place on Canal Street. No one had ever heard of him, of course, but really I think that's ideal, because we can create a reputation together . . ."

And thanks to his talent and Eileen's ability to generate publicity, people began to hear about the Top Spot. The *Times-Picayune* gave it a four-bean review. *Gourmet* included it in a roundup of New Orleans restaurants serving Creole food with a dash of originality—but no more than a dash—the template that the rest of the country expected from the city they loved to call the Big Easy, though locals never did. The restaurant drew a fashionably mixed crowd: the black political elite Eileen knew from her days as a civil rights worker; the artists whose daubings and coathooks hung on the walls; Carnival royalty from the Garden District. Milford wasn't famous yet, nowhere near the level of a Paul Prudhomme or a Lenny Duveteaux, but he was considered a Promising Young Chef, one to watch.

On his last night at the Top Spot, Milford made dinner specials of crawfish Clemenceau, pork tenderloin with oyster dressing, and whole roasted red snapper. It wasn't a very busy dinner shift, and after they shut down, he decided to give the kitchen a thorough cleaning. The dishwashers helped him take up the rubber mats, mop the floors, wipe down the glass doors of the coolers, and scrub all the surfaces. When the job was done, he bought a round of drinks for the crew and sent them on their way. He was standing in the kitchen enjoying the unusual spotlessness when Eileen came in, glanced around, and said, "I thought you said you were really going to clean things up tonight."

Milford knew she hadn't had a good evening. Eileen liked to think of herself as a hands-on hostess, personally booking all the reservations and greeting the customers at the door. Of course that meant when there was a problem, she took the brunt of it. Tonight a party of ten's reservation had disappeared; either they thought they'd called but hadn't, or Eileen had forgotten to write it down. She found them a table anyway, but they had to wait in the bar for a while, growing increasingly restive, refusing her offer of free cocktails; they were from Utah and didn't drink. A thing like that could make Eileen mighty tense, and when Eileen was mighty tense, you wanted to stay out of her way as much as possible. So Milford just said, "It looks pretty clean to me."

"Are you serious? Are you?" She strode across the floor, nearly tripping over the mop bucket he still needed to empty. "Milford, when I say clean, I mean *clean*. Look at all this crud underneath the cooler. Just look at it! Come here!"

Cautiously, Milford bent over and peered under the cooler. The cement floor was stained and discolored, but he didn't see anything that qualified as crud.

"Where, Eileen?"

"There, around the legs. Look how it's all caked up." She poked at the short metal legs supporting the old-fashioned cooler. "There must be half an inch of dirt around them—it's disgusting! I want you to touch that! Put your finger in it!"

With one large forefinger, Milford scratched at the floor around the cooler leg. "It's just stains. You don't wanna see it, maybe we should get one of them nice new coolers sits flush with the floor. Bet you'd save on the light bill."

At once he knew he'd said the wrong thing. When Eileen was in one of her moods, you didn't suggest that she drop a big chunk of change on something, even if it would save her money in the long run.

"Oh, that's your answer for every problem in this restaurant, isn't it, Milford? Tell Eileen to throw money at it! Eileen's wealthy, isn't that right? Eileen's just holding out on you because she's such a mean bitch! Everything would go better around here if Eileen would just loosen up the purse strings! Well, let me tell you something. I know you grew up poor, you don't have any understanding of how these things work, but that's not how you run a business, Milford. If I spent money on every little thing you ask me to . . ."

She was off. Milford leaned back against the steel countertop and listened to her rant, trying to let the words roll over him without registering in his brain. If he listened to her, he'd get mad, and if he got mad, they'd end up hollering at each other again. There had been too much of that lately. He knew the waiters were gossiping about it, saying he was going to quit or Eileen was going to fire him every time they had a blowup. Eventually, one thing or the other would probably happen. He wasn't going to let it happen tonight, though. He'd just gotten his paycheck, tomorrow was his day off, he was in a good mood, and he was going to go have a drink somewhere—not the Top Spot—and then go home and get some sleep.

"Eileen?" he said when she paused for breath.

"What?"

"Good night."

He picked up his knife roll and walked out of the kitchen. She could empty the damn mop bucket herself, or the sous chef could do it when he came in tomorrow morning.

•   •   •

Eileen stood in the dining room trying to calm herself down. Everyone else had left the restaurant, and she would lock up and go home as soon as she felt capable of driving. Right now her hands were shaking and angry tears still stung her eyes.

She knew she was going to lose Milford if she kept blowing up at him. He'd be incredibly foolish to quit; this job was an opportunity of the sort he'd never be likely to see again, but he was a man, and men did all sorts of foolish things if you abused their fragile egos.

Never capable of apologies, Eileen decided she would do what she always did when she was afraid she'd pushed Milford too far: put a twenty-dollar bonus in his next pay envelope. She firmly believed that, if given the choice, most chefs would prefer money over respect.

Behind her, a steel sculpture of a tree covered with dozens of sheet-metal "leaves" jangled softly. It always did that when somebody opened the front door. She turned, expecting to see Milford;

perhaps this time *he* thought he'd pushed *her* too far. But it wasn't Milford. A shiver of fear touched her heart.

"Oh," she said. "It's you. Listen, I told you not to come here anymore."

· · ·

An hour after he left the Top Spot, Milford was sitting in Audubon Park watching the moonlight play on the dark waters of the lagoon. He could hear the traffic on St. Charles, and now and then a night bird would call out, but otherwise the park was peaceful. Not up for the noise and smoke of a bar, he'd stopped at a Time Saver, bought a couple of Miller High Lifes, and come out here to drink them. They had gone down smooth, and he felt better. He'd just run by the bank machine and deposit his check before heading home. He reached into the pocket of his houndstooth check pants, feeling for the pay envelope, and came up empty.

"Aw, shit!"

Now he remembered: Eileen had handed him the envelope when he was in the middle of sautéing the brabant potatoes for the crawfish Clemenceau, and instead of putting it in his pocket or his knife roll, he'd absentmindedly stuck it on the shelf above his workstation. He thought about just getting it tomorrow, but his rent was due and he really needed to make the deposit tonight. He hoped Eileen had already left: he'd just let himself in with his key and grab the check.

Irritated with himself but not really upset thanks to the beer, Milford drove back to the restaurant, parked, and walked up to the front door. A light was still on inside, and the door swung open at his touch. Shit. Well, he'd just tell Eileen he was sorry if he'd made her mad; he felt mellow enough not to care.

He didn't see her in the dining room. Hell, maybe she was in her upstairs office and he could get in and out without having to see her at all. She didn't usually leave the door unlocked when she was alone up there, though. His basic decency overrode his desire to avoid her, and he called out, "Eileen?"

Nothing.

"Eileen?"

Behind him, he heard something dripping. He turned and saw a dark droplet fall from one of the sharp metal branches of the tree sculpture into a spreading puddle on the floor.

"Eileen!"

He turned the corner of the bar and there she was. A painting of magnolias more colorful than any found in nature had been smashed across her back. A ceramic plaque shaped like a human ear lay shattered near her face—no, partly *in* her face. And he could see that other, even more terrible things had been done to her.

A small, stealthy sound came from the direction of the kitchen. Milford burst through the swinging doors just in time to see a familiar figure disappearing through the rear exit. That was when he knew his situation was hopeless.

Nevertheless, he ran back to Eileen. Before he could even lift her wrist to see if a pulse still beat there, red and blue light splashed through the glass door and bathed the dining room in its unearthly glow.

"YO, BUDDY, WE SEE YOU IN THERE," said an amplified voice. "PUT YOUR HANDS OVER YOUR HEAD AND GET YOUR ASS OUT HERE RIGHT NOW."

PRESENT DAY
AT LIQUOR

1

MARDI Gras morning dawned dank and cold. The four cooks had already been at the restaurant for a couple of hours, preparing a krewe breakfast for Rickey's mother's truck parade.

Truck parades are a Carnival Day phenomenon unknown outside New Orleans. Rather than the ornate and glamorous confections boasted by the bigger, richer krewes, their floats are basically giant wooden boxes pulled by tractor-trailer cabs that blast their air horns incessantly as they roll through the streets. Each float's riders select a theme—Louisiana Sports Legends, say, or Favorite Desserts—and decorate their trailer in foil and crepe paper to reflect it. If they are feeling flush, they might invest in theme sweatshirts too, but many of the beads, cups, and trinkets they throw are caught from other parades earlier in the season or even the previous Mardi Gras. Truck parades are a part of blue-collar Carnival seldom seen by the tourists who frequent Bourbon Street, but a certain segment of the citizenry cherishes them.

John Rickey and Gary "G-man" Stubbs were not a part of that segment, at least not today. Because they owned a popular restaurant, Rickey's mother had convinced them to put on a breakfast buffet for the Krewe of Chalmatians, so named because most of its members were from New Orleans' Lower Ninth Ward or the neighboring suburb of Chalmette. Rickey and G-man had grown up in the Lower Ninth Ward, but moved away when they turned eighteen, a little over a decade ago. The only vestiges of downtown that remained were their gritty Brooklynesque accents and a certain reluctance to take any shit off of anyone, be it a lazy line cook, a purveyor delivering inferior produce, or a diner with an unjustified complaint about his meal.

Having cooked together for fifteen years and lived together for the better part of that time, Rickey and G-man knew each other's kitchen habits by heart and worked together as efficiently as two hands washing one another. To fill out their crew this morning they had recruited Tanker, their dessert guy who was secretly a crackerjack sauté cook, and Marquis, who was young but learning fast. He'd started out as a salad bitch, but now they let him work the hot line on slow nights. Today he would be in charge of keeping bacon, sausage, and toast coming out of the oven, topping up the water in the rented steam tables, and cutting celery for the Bloody Marys.

Tanker had reheated the big pot of crawfish étouffée they'd made last night and was now working on a giant batch of grits. G-man, Rickey's co-chef and the true workhorse of the kitchen, was adding clarified butter to egg yolks in a double boiler to make hollandaise sauce for Rickey's eggs Sardou. Tall and rangy, with short dark hair tucked under a purple New Orleans Hornets baseball cap, G-man scowled at the sauce through the dark glasses he habitually wore in any bright light. He had tried to talk Rickey out of this fussy and time-consuming dish, but Rickey had insisted on it. The restaurant's name, Rickey pointed out, was Liquor. All their dishes contained some form of booze, a perfect concept for New Orleans. Of course they weren't sticking to the gimmick for this breakfast, but Rickey felt that at least one dish should pack an alcoholic punch, so eggs Sardou it was: poached eggs with artichoke hearts, hollandaise, and an Herbsaint-laced spinach cream.

"Splooge," Rickey muttered as he tasted the spinach. Not as tall as G-man and a little paunchy from a lifetime of sampling his own dishes, he was handsome enough to have been anointed a glamour boy by the national food press, but his features were sharpened by a nervous tension that seldom left him even when he was drunk or sleeping. "Baby food. All this fucking shit is baby food. It's giving me flashbacks to when I had to work hotel brunch."

"So why'd you sign up?" said Tanker. "More to the point, why'd you sign *us* up? Nobody said you had to make breakfast for three hundred."

"It's not three hundred. I mean, they got like three hundred people in the krewe, but not all of them are gonna show up."

"You hope," G-man said.

"My mom made a signup sheet, OK? We got one-eighty coming in. We scoop it and poop it, they eat it, everybody's happy."

"Yeah, but why'd you agree to it in the first place?" Tanker persisted. "I mean, you're a prima donna, Rickey. You hate this kinda shit."

"I know it." Rickey pushed the blue bandanna up on his forehead and thumbed a stray drop of sweat out of his left eye. "But it's my *mom,* dude. She never asks me for anything."

"Except a couple grandbabies," G-man said. Rickey's mother had been doing her best to ignore G-man's role in her son's life for years now.

"Yeah, well, you know she's never getting 'em, so I figured

we could do this for her. Besides, these clowns are paying pretty good."

"I think my momma wishes she'd *quit* getting grandbabies," said Marquis. "My sister, she just done had her fifth."

"Jesus."

"And the daddy don't help her out nohow."

"Same one for all five kids?" Tanker asked.

Marquis glanced up at him, seemed to measure whether such a fatuous white-boy question deserved any response at all, said, "Nah, dawg," and went back to laying out strips of bacon on a sheet pan.

G-man, the youngest of six children from an Irish-Italian family, silently counted himself lucky that his parents already had an even dozen grandchildren. Otherwise, his mother probably would have been pushing him and Rickey to get a kid from some-where or other despite her strict Catholic beliefs. Of course, own-ing a restaurant was a lot like having a five-hundred-pound baby that never grew up. Originally financed by local celebrity chef, multimillionaire, and all-around shady businessman Lenny Du-veteaux, Liquor was running under its own steam now, and they hoped to buy Lenny out with some money Rickey had inher-ited under strange circumstances the year before. Most of the in-heritance was tied up in a piece of Texas property, however, and Lenny still owned twenty-five percent of Liquor. Fortunately, he was busy with his own two successful restaurants and mostly left Liquor alone.

Rickey put the spinach cream in the lowboy refrigerator at his station and headed back to the walk-in cooler to get a case of eggs. The other cooks had begged him to use a powdered mix for the scrambled eggs—it would have made his life far easier this morning, and if Rickey's life was easier, theirs were too—but such a shortcut simply wasn't in his nature. He might be a bit of a whore, he supposed, but he was no shoemaker. He would scramble the eggs slowly and gently in a double boiler, adding a knob of butter now and then, until they took on the perfect creaminess that was the only acceptable consistency for scrambled eggs as far as he was concerned. If the Chalmatians just shoveled the eggs into their hungry maws, too drunk to notice the difference, he would still have the satisfaction of knowing he had done them right. That satisfaction was one of the major things he lived for.

In the three years since it opened, Liquor had become not just a popular restaurant but a trendy one. Between Lenny's machinations, food-press enthusiasm, a prestigious James Beard award, and a couple of healthy doses of controversy, it was now one of the best-known new restaurants in New Orleans. (In a city where several eateries had been in business for a century or more, it would remain a "new restaurant" for at least a dozen more years.) Rickey had very mixed feelings about this trendiness. Because of it, and because of what *Food & Wine* had once cringe-inducingly called "his dissipated-fratboy good looks," he had been subjected to all manner of hype that had nothing to do with the backbreaking day-to-day business of running a world-class kitchen.

Agreeing to do this breakfast had been one of his little ways of reacting against the hype. Most hot chefs would probably turn up their coke-encrusted noses at the idea of cooking splooge for a hundred and eighty working-class yats. Rickey still considered himself one of those yats, and while he wasn't exactly proud of the food itself, he liked how aggressively déclassé such a breakfast was.

Lost in his thoughts, he nearly tripped over some large object that had been left on the floor of the walk-in. Peering down in the dim light, he saw that it was a burlap sack of oysters. At the krewe's request, they'd set up a makeshift oyster bar in the dining room for those perverts who considered a dozen icy-cold raw mollusks dipped in ketchup, horseradish, and Tabasco part of a nutritious breakfast. (Rickey liked oysters on the half shell just fine, but not at seven o'clock in the morning.) Marquis was supposed to have lugged the oysters up front and dumped them on ice to await the shucker's arrival, but apparently he had forgotten.

Rickey started to holler for him, then decided not to. Marquis was getting to be a decent cook, but he was easily distracted. If he left his station now, he'd probably burn the bacon or worse. Instead Rickey bent to hoist the fifty-pound sack onto his shoulder. As soon as it came off the floor, he knew he'd lifted it badly, and an instant later he felt something give deep in the small of his back.

"Owwwwww*fuck*!" he yelled. His hands instinctively wanted to go to the injury, but he knew if he dropped the oyster sack now, he wouldn't be able to lift it again. Instead he got it the rest of the way up and stood holding his breath, waiting to see how bad the pain was going to get. It flared, twisted through his spine like a hot wire, then settled down with the air of a visitor that had found a comfortable spot and was planning to stay a while.

●   ●   ●

While Liquor was something of a trendy restaurant, its dining-room décor had little in common with that of most hot spots: no dangerous-looking metal sculptures, lipstick-red walls, glass floors with saltwater lagoons underneath, giant paintings of fruits and vegetables, or Arabian fantasies. Rickey, who micromanaged every aspect of the restaurant, had been far more influenced by the look of New Orleans' old-line joints, and so the dining room was a dark green, softly lit, clubby space accented with rich wood trim and small mirrors.

On a typical night, the dining room was full of men in suits or sports shirts, women in cocktail dresses, the clink of cutlery on plates and ice cubes in glasses, the aromas of fine food and fresh bread. This morning, it was packed with people in pink sweatshirts bearing the legend KREWE OF CHALMATIANS and the krewe's logo, a spotted cartoon dog with a bouffant hairdo. The dog was supposed to be a Dalmatian, a pun on the krewe's name, but looked rather more like a Chihuahua with chickenpox. Most of the women had hairdos that rivaled the dog's. Most of the men were balding. At 6:45 A.M., the krewe members were already well-lubricated, happy, and yakking up a storm.

"Raymond! Hey, Raymond! I hope you don't getcha hand stuck in there again—"

"Aw, Marie, hush up about dat."

"How you makin, dawl? I ain't seen you since Friday, maybe Saddy—"

"Bud-DY! Where y'at?"

"We gotta good team! Dis is gonna be da year!"

At the bar, Mo—Tanker's girlfriend and Liquor's head mixologist—dispensed mimosas and poured Bloody Marys and screwdrivers from huge pitchers she had mixed early that morning. The waiters circulated, clearing dirty plates and topping up the buffet. The shucker, who had finally received the contents of the fateful burlap sack, slid his short flat blade between shells, severed connective muscles, nestled oysters by the dozen into platters of crushed ice.

At the center of the hubbub was Rickey's mother, Brenda Crabtree (she had retaken her maiden name upon her divorce a quarter-century ago), resplendent in a fresh Copper Penny dye job and cat's-eye glasses with a dusting of tiny rhinestones at the corners. At her side was her gentleman friend, Mr. Claude, listening meekly as was his habit in life. "This is my son's place!" she told anyone who would listen. "My boy, he's a famous chef! He got him a write-up in Bone Ape Tit Magazine!"

Back in the kitchen, the famous chef winced as he bent to retrieve more eggs. A small hiss of pain escaped him. G-man, who was now cooking French toast, heard it even over the sizzle and bang of the kitchen. "Dude, what's wrong with you?" he called. "You been gimping around all morning."

"Nothing," Rickey said. "Just twisted my back a little. I'm fine."

In fact, the pain had increased so much that he felt a little nauseated. He wasn't about to say anything, though. He might tell G-man what had happened later, after the shift was over, but cooks in the kitchen didn't cry about their injuries. Burned yourself? Consider the weal a badge of honor, like the tattoos most of them had. Sliced your finger open? Slap on a bandage or some duct tape, maybe Superglue it if it's really bad, and get back to work. Most of them had cut off at least one fingertip during the course of their careers, and all had ladders of burn scars on their forearms, hot-fat spatters on the backs of their hands, and feet that looked as if somebody had worked them over with a hammer. It was a painful line of work, but in the hyper-macho pirate crew atmosphere of the typical restaurant kitchen, complainers were apt to be mocked without mercy or hounded right out of a job.

G-man looked searchingly at Rickey over the tops of his shades, but said nothing; to challenge Rickey on this point in front of their crew would seriously violate the rough etiquette of the line.

"Anyway," said Rickey, "we only got a couple more hours. The Chalmatians gotta stage way the hell down on St. Claude, so they'll all be out of here by eight-thirty. We can break it down and get gone by nine."

"Y'all gonna watch the parade?" said Tanker.

"Aw, I don't know. My mom wants us to," (G-man rolled his eyes at that *us*) "but there's gonna be all that Zulu traffic."

"Just go on down Broad Street," said Marquis. "You can cut over to St. Claude after Jackson. Zulu don't go no farther than that."

"I know, I know. I been getting from Uptown to the Lower Ninth Ward all these years, I guess I can do it on Fat Tuesday. But it's gonna be a huge clusterfuck, and there'll be no place to park, and—"

"And *waa, waa, waa,*" the other three cooks and the dishwasher chorused. Rickey frowned, then grinned reluctantly.

"Go see your momma," Tanker advised. "Live it up a little. Catch you some beads."

"Just what I need. I don't even like Mardi Gras, and we still got three garbage bags of 'em in the attic."

"All New Orleanians gotta have at least three garbage bags of beads in their attics," Tanker said. "It's, like, the law. Otherwise you're some kinda Communist."

•   •   •

As it turned out, nobody got out by nine; after a morning of serving up splooge to drunk Chalmatians, they needed a few drinks themselves. Cooks and waiters alike congregated in the bar, where Mo opened beers and poured bourbon over ice. She was dead on her feet, but as long as she didn't have to see another mimosa or celery stalk, she was happy.

"I think that was my worst shift since Escargot's," said Rickey, sipping his Wild Turkey. Escargot's was the hotel restaurant where he'd worked as a saucier before he and G-man began developing the Liquor concept.

"Hell, it was my worst shift since *Tequilatown*," said G-man. He and Rickey had worked together at this French Quarter tourist trap and been fired, along with the rest of the kitchen crew, for drinking on the job. It was this indignity that had spurred Rickey to come up with the idea of a restaurant where the food would actually encourage drunkenness.

"Worst job I ever had was at a place called the Nouvelle Orleans," said Tanker. "It was actually a revival of this old-line restaurant from the 1800s, where this famous gangster, Golden George Costello, used to hang out. Owners always pronounced 'Orleans' the French way, you know, Orly-AWN, and they'd yell at you if they heard you say it different."

"What was so bad about it?" asked Marquis.

"Well, it started out OK. It was, like, Mediterranean food with a Creole influence. I was sous chef, and we couldn't go too wild seeing as it was in the Quarter, but we got to be a little creative. Did some garlic shrimp with black rice paella, lamb tagine, that kinda stuff. We reviewed well, got a good customer response. Then management started getting scared. 'It's too weird! This ain't how Golden George liked to eat! We gotta get back to our roots!' Pretty soon it was crawfish étouffée and chicken Pontalba, just like every other damn restaurant within a two-block radius of Bourbon Street. You know why I finally left?"

"Why?" said Mo obligingly, even though she knew the story.

"The GM found out old Golden George used to hide diamond rings in ladies' food, right? Like if he had some ho he wanted to impress? So they started this contest where they'd stick cubic zirconias in the desserts. If you found one, you got entered in a contest to win a real diamond. I quit after the second fancy Uptown dame broke her tooth on a fake rock. Figured they'd be sued into oblivion pretty soon anyway."

"Man," said Rickey. "Once in a while I get to worrying that our gimmick is dumb, but we're fucking geniuses compared to that."

"Our gimmick's not dumb," said G-man, finishing his second beer. "It *could* be, but as long as the food's good, we got nothing to be ashamed of."

Rickey nodded. Then, thinking of the food they had served today, he gulped the rest of his drink.

•   •   •

When the truck parade rolled at noon, Rickey and G-man were on the downtown riverside corner of the neutral ground at St. Claude and Tupelo, just as Brenda had instructed them to be. They'd ended up parking at G-man's parents' house, only a few blocks away. The day had warmed up nicely, with enough cloud cover to keep the heat down but no real threat of rain. The crowd milling around the corner was as varied as it got in New Orleans, black and white, young and old, costumed and uncostumed. People didn't mask on Mardi Gras as much as they used to, but here and there were skeletons, drag queens, distinctly unsavory-looking baby dolls, and one sinister character in a rubber Nixon mask.

St. Claude was an avenue that had seen better days, but a few grand old oak trees still stretched their gnarled branches over the fly-by-night car repair shops and dilapidated corner groceries. As the trucks rolled, some of the beads flung by the riders caught in the branches, where they would hang for months or possibly years. The air horns seemed to split the day in half. Between them and the cacophony of the crowd, it was impossible to make oneself heard to the krewe members, but Brenda knew where they were. The theme of her truck was "What's Cookin'?" and she and her fellow riders were dressed in white aprons and chef's toques. They deluged Rickey and G-man with fancy beads: long metallic ropes, beads with blinking medallions attached, a huge pair of pink pearls decorated with plastic shrimp and white shrimpers' boots. Brenda also managed to paste G-man right in the face with an unopened package of beads that weighed more than two pounds, bending one earpiece of his glasses a little, but he charitably allowed that this had probably been an accident. Getting creamed with a whole package of beads was just one of the many hazards of Mardi Gras.

They went back to the Stubbs house for a late lunch and another round of drinks. G-man's parents, Elmer and Mary Rose, were watching Mardi Gras on TV. The various news channels had reporters on the scene at the major parades, on a Bourbon Street balcony, along St. Charles where families were having cookouts on the streetcar tracks. After lunch, Rickey and G-man tried to sneak out without their beads, but it was no good. "You boys gotta take them beads with you," said Mary Rose. "We already got seven bags in the back room."

By the time they reached their little shotgun house on Marengo Street, it was early evening. G-man found a basketball game on TV. Rickey stretched out on the sofa to rest his still-throbbing back and fell asleep halfway through the second quarter. When he woke up, the game was over and G-man was flipping through the channels. He paused on WYES, the public broadcast station, where a glittering Carnival ball was in progress.

"Aw, not this shit," Rickey moaned sleepily. "It's so boring.

Nothing but a million debs getting presented to Rex and Henri Schindler talking about how Carnival is a butterfly of winter."

"No, look, they're finished with the debs. They're about to have the Meeting of the Courts. This part's kinda cool."

"About as cool as my left asscheek," Rickey said, but he settled down to watch the pomp and circumstance. It really could suck you in if you let it.

Here was Rex, the King of Carnival: a rich and well-connected New Orleanian transformed for a day into an actual monarch, a golden Arthurian legend. His identity was kept secret until Fat Tuesday morning, when he and his court paraded from Uptown to the French Quarter, then held their ball at the Municipal Auditorium that night.

Comus was the darker face of Carnival, not a king but a god. He wore a smiling mask that was designed differently every year, and his name was never revealed, though he was generally known to be an even richer, better-connected citizen than Rex: the power behind the throne, as it were. The most ancient of the old-line Carnival clubs, the Mistick Krewe of Comus had ceased parading in 1993 after a city council ordinance forced all public organizations to integrate. Rather than suffer the possibility of a black man in their midst—in a city that was three-quarters black—they had withdrawn from the streets. Now they only held their ball. The two courts met at midnight to declare Carnival over for another year.

Rickey and G-man watched with tired eyes as Rex in his white tights and gold crown approached the throne of Comus. Comus stepped forward and lifted his silver cup to toast the monarch, and because gods outranked kings, Rex bowed.

"I know who that is!" Rickey said, sitting bolt upright.

"Duh," said G-man, "it's Alfred Gremillion. His picture was

on the front page of the *Times-Picayune* this morning, just like Rex always is."

"Not Rex. Dude, I know who *Comus* is."

G-man glanced around the living room a little nervously. Comus had always struck him as a sinister figure, and the refusal to integrate hadn't helped any. "Nuh-uh," he said. "That mask and wig, all those weird-ass capes and shit? He could be anybody."

"No, man. Look at how he kinda slumps over and holds his left arm up. That's Clancy Fairbairn."

Clancy Fairbairn was one of those New Orleans business-men who seemed to have an interest in every moneymaking local company without being strictly associated with any of them. He was on the directors' boards of Entergy, the Downtown Development District, the Pot O'Gold casino boat, the Audubon Institute, and just about everything else that was currently turning a profit or overseeing someone else's profits in New Orleans. He was also a regular at Liquor, the type who always demanded that the chef make an appearance at his table, and so Rickey knew that he had a withered arm as a result of a childhood bout of polio. He'd also seen Fairbairn lifting a cup or two.

"I guess it might be," G-man admitted as the camera panned over Comus' face. "Those kinda look like his eyes. Mean and smart."

"Dude, it's totally, definitely him. Comus eats at our restaurant. Far fucking out."

"Big deal," G-man said. "Most of the rich bastards in town have probably eaten at our restaurant."

"Yeah, but Comus eats there like once a month."

"Quit calling him Comus, would you? You're not supposed to know who Comus is."

"What difference does it make?" Rickey stood up, then paused, winced, and put a hand to the small of his back. "It's not like he can hear me."

"I know it," said G-man, but his eyes flicked around the room again. His Catholic upbringing had inclined him to worry in the presence of gods, even once-a-year ones. "Hey, you never told me why you were gimping around in the kitchen, and now you're doing it again. What's the matter?"

Rickey explained about the oyster sack. Of the two, G-man was usually inclined to be more lenient with the crew, but he scowled at Marquis' negligence. "That damn kid. He shoulda took care of his business."

"Aw, it wasn't his fault, G. I mean, he left it there, but it's not his fault I lifted it bad. I'll be fine in a couple days. C'mon, turn this shit off and let's go to bed."

As he thumbed the remote, G-man caught one last glimpse of Comus' mask before the slanted eyeholes and slyly grinning mouth dwindled away to darkness. *Clancy Fairbairn?* he wondered, then pushed the thought away. He really didn't want to know who Comus was.

2

THE next day, a couple of the cooks and several waiters came to work with smudges of ash on their foreheads. Among the penitents was G-man, who'd gotten up at eight o'clock to attend early Mass. He had left the Church at sixteen, but over the past year or so he'd started going to Mass on holy days of obligation, and sometimes other days as well. Rickey didn't like it one bit; as far as he was concerned, the Catholic Church and most of its adherents could go to hell in the same handbasket they'd presumably condemned him to. After a couple of arguments, it had become one of the few things they simply didn't discuss. In every long-term relationship are a few pockets of deep and dangerous water into which one can step unaware if not careful. Eventually, somebody drowns or the interested parties post warning signs around these pockets. This was one of their no-swimming areas.

Rickey was in his tiny office back by the walk-in roughing out next week's schedule. He didn't usually do it until Friday or Saturday, but this week was difficult because they were short a cook: their old friend Shake Vojtaskovic, who'd been at Liquor since the beginning, had snagged a plum sous chef job at a new restaurant on Magazine Street. Rickey and G-man had worked with Shake back in the mid-nineties at the Peychaud Grill, where a bad-tempered, insanely talented chef named Paco Valdeon transformed them all from half-assed kids into hardcore line cooks. Shake was a slob and kind of a dick, but Rickey hated to see him go.

A bunch of applications had come in, but nothing Rickey could use; most of the applicants couldn't even complete his basic quiz, with no-brainer questions like "What is mise-en-place?" and "Name the five mother sauces." (One twenty-year-old high school dropout had written, "Gravy, red gravy, clam, steak, Tabasco." He wanted to start at ten dollars an hour.) So everybody was picking up extra hours, even getting overtime, which they loved but which raised hell with the payroll budget. Rickey and G-man had talked about trying to get away for two or three days after Mardi Gras, but that was on indefinite hold.

He cursed as he realized he'd scheduled Terrance, his grill cook, for Sunday dinner. Terrance was currently dating some holy-roller babe who liked him to spend all day in church with her, then come eat a big dinner with her family. Of course Rickey thought it was bullshit, but Terrance was a solid worker and didn't ask for a lot of favors. That meant he'd have to schedule Marquis, which meant Marquis' two days off would be split for the third week in a row and he'd probably get pissy, but Sunday was a busy night and it couldn't be helped.

Absorbed in the dull but necessary task, only vaguely aware of the pain that still throbbed in his back, Rickey didn't notice at once when someone entered his office. When he finally did look up, he got the feeling that the guy had been standing there waiting for him to do so. "Help you?" he said.

"I's hoping you might remember me."

Rickey took a closer look at the guy, a dark-skinned, heavy-set black man who appeared to be on the rough side of fifty. His face was deeply seamed, the whites of his eyes threaded with scarlet. His hands were sufficiently nicked and callused to make Rickey certain he was a cook, but he didn't look familiar . . . or did he? Rickey suddenly pictured him about twenty pounds heavier, a lot healthier-looking, and at least ten years younger. "Holy shit," he said. "Not Milford Goodman?"

"The one and the same."

Rickey got up from his desk and came forward to shake hands. Milford hesitated, then grasped Rickey's outstretched hand and gave it one determined pump before pulling away.

"Where you been, man?" It wasn't the right thing to say, but it was something to ease the moment.

"Angola." Milford shrugged wearily. "Where else I'm gonna be?"

"All this time?"

"Till last week. Rode the Greyhound into town on Thursday, been lookin for work since. With Carnival goin on, thought I might be able to pick up some dishwashin at least, but nobody wants to know nothin."

"Dishwashing!"

"Yeah, I figure I can make a little money that way."

"No, I mean . . . dude, that's like Kevin Garnett working as a ball boy or something. You don't need to be washing dishes."

Milford smiled a little. "Thanks. Always thought G was the hoops fan."

"Well, you know, it rubs off."

"Not saying I *want* to wash dishes, mind you. Just figured

that was the best I could hope for right out the gate. You got cooks' work for me, believe me, I'm jumpin on it."

Rickey didn't usually make his hires without talking to G-man. He hadn't hired a convicted felon before, and he most certainly hadn't hired anyone who had served a decade in Angola Prison for murder. But he'd never known anyone else who could cook like Milford Goodman, which was why he didn't even hesitate before asking, "When can you start?"

Milford's tired and somehow watchful face broke into a huge smile. It looked a little strange, as if he wasn't accustomed to the expression. "Any time. Today, if you want me."

"You got a place to live?"

"I been stayin with my sister. She about the only family I got left—my momma died while I was up there."

"Tell you what. Why don't you come eat here tonight? My treat. Give you a chance to see what we're doing." This was true, but Rickey also wanted a chance to show off for the older cook: last time Milford had seen him, Rickey had been a twenty-year-old punk with barely enough chops to work the dinner shift hot line. "If you like our food well enough to work with us, you can start tomorrow."

• • •

"So who's this new hire?" said Terrance, buttoning his white chef jacket across his massive chest and swiping an arm across his huge, gleaming head. Though Terrance sweated over the grill more than any other cook Rickey had ever seen, he never complained, and he seldom got in the weeds even during the craziest rushes. Right now things were still slow and Milford hadn't come back in yet.

"Milford Goodman. Me and G used to work with him like twelve years ago." A ticket came chattering out of the machine at Rickey's expediting station, and Rickey paused to call out the order: "Marquis, ordering three green salads, one terrine. Terrance, ordering one ribeye, mid-rare, one pork. G, ordering two redfish."

The three cooks called the orders back to him, confirming them. Terrance bent to slide a pork shank into the oven at his station. He didn't usually fire entrées as soon as they were called out, but the pork took a while to finish.

"Anyway, yeah, we worked with him at Reilly's. Crappy old chestnut of a downtown hotel restaurant. We were just kids, but Milford was already in his thirties then. He's about forty-five now, I guess."

"Kinda old for a cook," Marquis commented.

"You tell him that after he cooks circles around your ass," said G-man, who was pawing through the lowboy at his station. "He's probably one of the best cooks ever to come up in New Orleans. Rickey, you seen my tequila brown butter?"

"I made you a batch this morning. It's not in there?"

"No, dammit . . . wait . . . here it is."

"It was a dog turd, you woulda stepped in it."

"Well, I don't usually keep it in a fucking Rex cup."

"I ran out of Tupperwares," Rickey said, smiling a little guiltily as G-man held up a purple plastic cup printed with a picture of Rex, King of Carnival. "We had plenty of those and I was in a hurry."

"Was it clean, at least?"

"No, it had an inch of rancid daiquiri mix in the bottom. Course it was clean."

"What about this guy Milford?" said Marquis, who sometimes tired of Rickey and G-man's banter. "How come nobody ever heard of him if he's such a great cook?"

"People *were* starting to hear about him." Rickey came over to Marquis' station and glanced at the baby greens he was using to make the salads, picked out a couple of leaves that looked less than fresh. "Not too long after we left Reilly's, he got hired away by this lady Eileen Trefethen. White lady. Back in the sixties she was some kinda big wheel in the local civil rights movement. A few years later she opened a restaurant Uptown. The Top Spot. Real nice Creole place, kinda artsy, used to get write-ups in the food press. Her first chef moved to New York or something, and she wanted to hire an unknown local guy, turn him into a star. She almost managed it with Milford."

"So why she didn't?"

"Hard to make anybody a star once you get murdered," said G-man.

"Somebody killed her?" said Terrance, trimming a sliver of fat off the ribeye steak he would soon put on the grill. Of course the steaks had already been trimmed, but Terrance had a thing about steak fat and insisted on removing as much as he could. Sometimes customers even complained that the steaks were too lean, and Rickey had to bitch at him about it.

"Somebody killed her in the restaurant, and they pinned it on Milford," G-man said.

"He didn't do it?"

"He pled innocent, and he never struck me as a real violent type," said Rickey. "Eileen was raped, strangled, had her head bashed in on some piece of artwork. Besides, what'd he kill her for? She gave him his big career break. Her and Milford used to go round and round, though. He came back to see us at Reilly's a couple times, and he'd tell us what a righteous bitch she could be. She was this big civil rights type, but she had an all-black kitchen crew and supposedly treated 'em like it was old plantation days. Milford said sometimes he'd get fed up and fall on his knee in front of her, start hollering 'Yes, Massa, I's sorry, Massa, how this nigga ever gonna please you, Massa?' Course then she'd really get mad."

"So they used that to pin it on him," said Marquis, who despite his tender age had seen this sort of justice in action a time or two.

"Well, it sure didn't help any. At the trial, I heard they had waiters testifying that Milford hated Eileen—he always said the waiters were her little bitches—and that he'd threatened her and all this shit. But the stuff they were repeating, it was just, like, kitchen trash talk. You know, 'One of these days I'm gonna kill that bitch.' Y'all probably said the same about me before."

"I say it every day," said G-man.

"So Milford got a dipshit public defender, and the prosecution stacked the jury with old white people who managed to forget how they probably used to call Eileen Trefethen a niggerlover, and they sent him up the river to Angola."

"What's he doing here now?" said Marquis.

"Well, see, one day he read about this little thing called DNA. He wrote to some activist types in New York—the Innocence Project, I think he said—got them to dig up the physical evidence from his trial and test it. Miz Trefethen's underwear or something, I guess."

Marquis made a face.

"So Milford got a new trial, and this time they found him innocent. They let him out a couple weeks ago, gave him a check for ten dollars, and cut him loose. Dollar per year of his life they stole. Nice, huh?"

"Wait a minute," said Tanker, who'd been listening from his dessert nook. "You mean to tell me Louisiana wasn't testing for DNA in trials, what—ten years ago?"

"Not always, I guess, and not when the victim was a rich white lady and the defendant was a black guy with a public defender. We figure DNA evidence has been around forever because of all the forensic TV shows and shit, but even now, Louisiana's like eight years behind on DNA tests."

"You expecting too much from the system, Tank," said Terrance. "You think they gonna miss a chance to fry a big black buck for killing a white lady just cause the evidence don't match up?"

Rickey turned and looked at him. It was about the only bitter thing he'd ever heard Terrance say. "You OK, man?"

"Yeah, sure. I just seen this shit too many times. White people always talking about how race relations are so great in New Orleans because they can hold a conversation with black folks in the Wal-Mart. Black man gets railroaded into prison, they just shake their heads and blame the public schools and the welfare system."

Everybody nodded, because they knew it was true. "Yeah, you right," said G-man.

"So who killed the lady anyway?" said Marquis.

"Nobody knows," Rickey told him. "Whoever it was, their DNA wasn't in the database. They found out one thing, though— it probably wasn't even a black guy."

A depressed hush fell over the kitchen, and for a few minutes everyone went about his work with only the most minimal talk.

"Well, don't everybody act like the guest of honor at a funeral,"

Terrance said at last. "Ain't like we're to blame. Hell, you're help-ing the man out in his time of need. I bet nobody else wanted to give him a job."

"That's what he told me," Rickey said. "And when you taste his cooking, you're gonna see how fucking stupid all those other restaurants were."

•   •   •

Milford Goodman sat at the bar with a plate of food in front of him. The maître d' had offered him a table, but he thought he would feel more comfortable in the bar. He wasn't sure that had been a good decision. The bartender was very pretty, her dark auburn hair rolled at her neck, a dash of red lipstick on her no-bullshit mouth, her white shirt and black pants snug in a way that made him want to look at her for hours and run out of the restau-rant all at the same time. After ten years with scarcely a glimpse of a woman, he was hungry for the sight of them but not at all com-fortable in their presence, and he could imagine what this one would think if she heard what he was supposed to have done. So far she'd been very nice, refilling his Coke twice without being asked, but what if she knew who Eileen Trefethen was? In prison, Milford had received hate mail from angry patrons of the Top Spot. He bet plenty of people still remembered the case.

He dragged his eyes away from the bartender's pert ass, picked up his fork, and took a bite of his dinner. First Rickey had sent out an oyster tart with Vidalia onions and gin-scented crème fraiche, and he'd eaten that right up because he was hungry. Next had come a mushroom-cognac soup with a dollop of rich, salty duck confit set afloat on a crouton in the middle of the bowl, like a little raft. Now he was eating a piece of redfish with grilled Gulf shrimp and tequila brown butter. Though he hadn't tasted anything like these dishes before, his near-instinctive grasp of culinary principles made him see the coherence and the talent in them. He could also see how at least one of them might be improved—the crouton in the soup was a distraction; it got in the way without adding any real flavor—but of course he wouldn't mention that to Rickey yet.

He appreciated the food, but he wasn't used to so much richness at one time. Until recently his diet had consisted of gristly meat, tasteless starch, and Jell-O. Prisoners could buy candy from the commissary, but he'd never had much of a sweet tooth; his favorite snacks had been the summer sausages and sharp cheese that were sometimes available. They weren't much good, but they beat hell out of the cafeteria slop. Trying to eat this meal after getting used to that was a lot like consuming several sticks of butter at one sitting. Milford hoped there were some Tums back at his sister's house.

More than the food or the pretty bartender, though, his discomfort was caused simply by sitting here and being treated like anyone else. For ten years he had been told what to do and when to do it. A man didn't like that kind of treatment, but he got used to it after a while. So much freedom all at once was unsettling. It gave him a wild, uncontrolled feeling, as if he really was the dangerous killer they'd made him out to be, as if he should holler a warning to the people around him. His stomach was always aflutter, his throat always tight. Sitting here at this shiny zinc bar, among these fancy people, just made the feeling worse.

A hand landed on his shoulder. Milford cringed, hating himself for it but unable to stop himself.

"Hey," said Rickey. "Hey, sorry. You OK?"

"Yeah," said Milford. "Least I think so. Just startled me is all."

"How you like the food?"

Milford turned a little on his barstool and looked at Rickey. He remembered working with Rickey on the line at Reilly's. Even as a raw kid, Rickey had had a way of imposing his will on people. He'd look at them with those intense blue-green eyes, beam that smile at them, and say, "Sure, Chef, I know we always done the salads that way, but if we make our dressing from scratch, it actually costs out cheaper *and* the plates come back empty." Stuff most young scrubs never thought or cared about. It worked Milford's nerves sometimes, but it was the way a cook got ahead. Milford wasn't surprised that Rickey had ended up with his own restaurant, and he wasn't surprised that G-man was in on it: Rickey needed somebody to boss around, and it had always seemed to Milford that G-man needed to be bossed.

"It's real nice," Milford said. "Fancy, but not just for the sake of bein fancy. Some places, they worry about they decorating, they presentation, whether they got the right people comin in. By the time you get to the food, it seems like an afterthought. You know?"

Rickey was nodding vigorously. "It's true. I mean, I put a lot of thought into the look of the place, the service—you know how in a lot of restaurants, the waiters unfold your napkin and lay it across your lap?" Milford didn't know, but he nodded anyway. "Well, I don't let my servers do that. I think it's tacky. Intrusive. So I do kinda micromanage this place, but the food comes way ahead of everything else."

"Like it oughta."

"Right. Listen, I gotta get back to it. What you think, Milford? You want to work here?"

"Course I do. Y'all doin great food, and it's not like anybody else beatin down my door. I wonder, though . . ."

"What?"

"You think I could eat the rest of this here dinner in the kitchen?"

Rickey looked puzzled for a moment; then he seemed to understand. "Sure. Sure you can. There's no place to sit back there, really, but you can eat at my desk or just pull up a milk crate—"

"Milk crate be just fine." Milford nodded to the bartender, picked up his Coke and his plate, and followed Rickey back to the kitchen.

•   •   •

Rickey got Milford settled back by the walk-in, where he could see the action of the kitchen without being in the way. Then he pushed the blue bandanna up on his forehead, checked the front of his jacket for any particularly offensive stains, and headed back out to the dining room. The waiters had let him know that some regulars were in the house, and so he had to make his rounds.

Some chefs would probably refuse to set foot in the dining room during service even if the governor, the pope, and Michael Jordan were all dining at the same table. Others spent an hour or more each night swanning around the tables, schmoozing, fishing for compliments on the food, showing off how pretty they looked in their tall hats and spotless jackets. Rickey didn't like either kind. He wasn't crazy about dining-room rounds, but he knew what a kick some people got from having the chef appear at their table, and it wasn't a lot of trouble.

He wished the waiters would get their shit together, though. As he approached the table of one of his most devoted patrons, Dr. Frank Lamotte, he saw that Lamotte was dining with Clancy Fairbairn. Rickey hadn't been aware that the two men knew each other and wouldn't have minded a heads-up about Fairbairn's presence. He could just see himself saying something like "So, Mr. Fairbairn, how was your Comus, I mean, how was your fish?"

Of course he would do nothing of the sort. *Be cool,* he admonished himself as he approached the table. *You got ice in your veins, take it easy, be cool.* The men looked up at his approach, smiles spreading over their faces but not quite touching their eyes.

Dr. Frank Lamotte was an orthopedist who'd been dining at Liquor for a couple of years now. He had an oily complexion and a little slicked-down fringe of black hair out of which his scalp seemed to poke like an island rising from a sea of Brylcreem. He was not a fat man, at least not by New Orleans standards, but his round face and the plump hands poking from the ends of his sportjacket sleeves gave the impression of fatness.

Clancy Fairbairn was tall and thin, with luxuriant silvery hair and a face as impassive as an iguana's. Rickey wondered if the perpetually smiling mask of Comus had felt strange to him. He kept the withered hand tucked close to his chest most of the time, but for some reason he liked to drink with it, and he had it wrapped around a cocktail now. A Ninth Ward Iced Tea, from the looks of it—one of Mo's specials. Fairbairn was an aggressively unadventurous eater. Once he had bragged to Rickey about a meal he'd had at the Polonius Room a couple of years ago. Despite its stuffy name, this was an envelope-pushing restaurant in one of the fancier downtown hotels; its tasting menus were laden with gelees, foams, savory cotton candies, and other experimental fare. Fairbairn ordered a bowl of seafood gumbo, a steak, and a bottle of 1890 Lafite Rothschild. The wine had cost nearly four thousand dollars, he said, and the gumbo wasn't very good.

Lamotte was pulling the last shreds of meat off the thick

bone of his pork shank. Fairbairn's plate bore traces of the redfish; he always ordered either that or the filet. Rickey shook their hands, asked about their meals, accepted their praise. It didn't mean much to him, since he didn't believe either of these men was serious about food, but it was part of the game.

"How was your Carnival?" said Lamotte.

"Spent it right here working. How about yourself?"

"Went to a ball or two. Mostly I was busy with my boat."

"Fishing?"

Lamotte laughed. "Not hardly. I'm a partner in the Pot O'Gold, the casino boat out by the lake. We're talking about starting up a fine-dining restaurant there. Something several cuts above the usual buffets and snack bars. You think it'd work?"

"Sure," said Rickey. He could imagine few things more hellish than trying to run a fine-dining restaurant amid the tacky cacophony of a casino, but there was no point in bursting Lamotte's balloon. "How bout you, Mr. Fairbairn?"

"Carnival?" Fairbairn said as if he'd never heard the word before. "Oh, yes. I took the wife skiing in Vail."

Rickey tried not to look at him. "Well, nice seeing y'all, thanks for coming in—"

"Hang on!" said Lamotte as Rickey turned away from the table.

"Yeah?"

"You hurt yourself, Chef? You're moving like one of my eighty-year-old patients."

"Aw, it's nothing. I just wrenched my back a little."

"Well, we can't have that. C'mon into the office when you get the chance—I'll take a look at it."

"No, really, Doc, I don't—"

"I insist. No charge. You can buy me dinner next time I come in, if you want."

Rickey thought it would be rude to refuse after that, so he took the doctor's card and promised to see him soon. As he bent over to pluck a piece of trash off the floor on his way back to the kitchen, a new, previously-unheard-from pain shot through his lower spine, and he figured maybe the appointment was a good idea after all.

●   ●   ●

When Milford had finished eating, G-man called him over to the sauté station and showed him the setup. "See, I got this six-burner stove, but I hardly ever need all the eyes. If we're running a pasta dish, I keep a pot of water at the boil so I can dunk it. I got my sauces in this bain-marie. I don't use this little oven much—I know oven braising's supposed to be the big thing right now, but I'd rather do it on the flattop. Feel like I got more control."

"Y'all ever serve cornbread?"

"I don't think we ever have. We get most of our bread from La Boulangerie."

"I was workin this station, I'd keep a pan of cornbread cookin in that oven whenever I could. People love to find it in they breadbasket, and it don't take no time at all. I got about two hundred cornbread recipes."

"Two hundred!"

"Yeah, I been collectin 'em all my life." Milford shrugged. "I mostly worked in fine-dinin places, but what I really love is soul food. Learned to cook it from my grandmomma."

G-man peeked over the tops of his shades at the big man, trying to imagine him as a little boy standing at his grandmother's stove. It made him sad to imagine what Milford had been through over the past ten years, and also curious. He wanted to know what prison was like, just as he would want to ask questions of a friend who'd traveled to a foreign country, but *Did you get raped?* and *Didn't you just about go crazy when they locked the gates behind you?* were a far cry from *How was the food?* Instead he just said, "Yeah, my mom taught me to cook. She's Italian, so I was making lasagna, stuffed eggplant, all that wop shit way before I ever set foot in any fancy kitchen. What'd your grammaw cook?"

"Well, she was like me—she could make just about anything. One time when she was real old, her church group went to New York City and somehow she ended up in a Thai restaurant. Had these real spicy noodles with shrimp, cloud ear mushrooms, I don't know what all. Two weeks after she got back to New Orleans, what you think? She made the dish for us. Real good, too. I never did find out where she got the ingredients."

"Out East, probably." There was a large Vietnamese community in eastern New Orleans, with quite a few restaurants and Asian groceries. "That's cool. So you can do that too? Just taste a dish and figure out how to make it?"

"Sure. Hell, most of the time I can just smell a dish and find out does it got too much salt in it. I try not to brag much, but I got a talent for that kinda thing."

"I don't. I can come up with some pretty good dishes, but my palate's nothing special. I wouldn't know much of anything if it wasn't for Rickey . . . speaking of which, would you hand me that chervil from Rickey's station? If he's gonna spend all night in the dining room, I guess I'll just garnish these plates myself."

"I'm right here," said Rickey, coming back into the kitchen. "Everybody wanted to tell me about their damn Carnival. I couldn't get away." He plucked the chervil from Milford's hand, lifted two orders of redfish from G-man's station, and finished them with the herb sprigs and a dash of deep green olive oil.

"Yo, Milford, you want some dessert?" said Marquis. He was handling the dessert station, since it was Tanker's night off.

"Nah, thanks anyway. I guess I'll be goin if y'all don't need nothin else. Rickey, you want me to come in tomorrow?"

"Yeah. Plan on getting here about three—you can shadow me and G while we do our prep, then maybe work the cold-apps station to get used to the flow of things."

Privately, Rickey doubted Milford would have any trouble getting used to the flow of things and hated to make him work an easy-ass station like cold apps, but Thursdays could be busy. Better to err on the side of caution than end up flailing in the weeds.

Milford left. There was another little rush of business at the second turn; then the evening waned and they began breaking down the kitchen, storing perishables in the refrigerators, calling in their orders for tomorrow. As they drove home, G-man told Rickey about Milford's vast collection of cornbread recipes.

"That's a great idea," Rickey said. "Cornbread in the bread-basket—it'll add a homey touch. See, I knew he was gonna work out well."

Rickey had occasion to remember this statement later, from a rueful distance, but if he had it to do over again, he wouldn't have taken back his words. Though the hiring of Milford Goodman would end up causing them any number of headaches, Milford himself just wanted to cook good food, and Rickey would never regret giving him a chance to do it.

3

TWO and a half weeks later, with Milford working out like a dream and Tanker in temporary charge of the kitchen, Rickey and G-man set off for their brief vacation. They'd have their cell phones along in case of emergency, but would otherwise be absolutely untethered from the restaurant, something that had only happened a couple of times since they opened the place. Rickey wasn't in as good a mood as he'd hoped to be, but he was getting over it. The source of his irritation was a phone call he'd received at the restaurant that morning when he went in to get things squared away before they left:

"Hello, is that Chef John Rickey?" said a girl who sounded about sixteen.

"Yeah."

"Please hold for my producer, Sylvia Chow."

"What? No, listen, I'm here for twenty more minutes. If you got somebody wants to talk to me, put 'em on now or tell 'em to call back next week."

There was an abashed pause, a series of whispers and scuffles; then another, far more savvy-sounding woman spoke. "Chef

Rickey? Sylvia Chow. I produce the award-winning show *Switcheroo* on the Clean Air network. Perhaps you've seen it?"

"Can't say I have," said Rickey, who rarely had time for TV beyond sports and the occasional *Iron Chef* rerun.

"Not a problem. I'll run down the premise for you: we take two young, attractive, fairly high-profile professionals and have them switch jobs for a week. Naturally, hilarity ensues." Rickey took the phone away from his ear and stared at it for a second: had she actually said *Hilarity ensues*? He was pretty sure she had. "Now, what we have in mind for you is a trade with a Dallas exotic dancer, Dirk Dagger. No worries if you've never stripped in public before—that just makes it wackier."

Rickey closed his eyes and visualized a knife chopping an onion into match-head-sized bits at lightning speed. This was a mental trick Lenny had taught him, and he found it much more effective than counting to ten. "Miz, uh, Miz Chow? Are you actually suggesting that I let this Dagger guy run my kitchen?"

"Well, yes, that's the point of the show. He does the cooking for a week—with the help of your staff, of course—and you perform at his club." Rickey heard papers rustling. "It's called the Leather Angel. Very upscale, not a sleazy place at all. We pay each of you a thousand dollars, plus it's great publicity for your restaurant."

Rickey's imaginary onion went flying off the cutting board. "Great publicity for my restaurant," he said in what G-man would have realized as a dangerously quiet voice. "To let some bimbo leather queen with zero kitchen experience come waltzing into my kitchen and cook for my customers. Is that the kinda publicity you think I need?"

"Well . . . honestly, we thought if you had any problem with the proposal, it'd be because of the stripping."

"Yeah, I'm not too fucking crazy about that either. In fact, I'm not too fucking crazy about ever having gotten this call. And you know what else? *I fucking hate Dallas!*"

"I assume that's a no," Rickey heard the woman say, crisp as ever, just before he slammed the receiver into its cradle.

Rickey had stewed about the call, resolving not to tell G-man, who was home packing. That resolve lasted until he actually got back to the house, where it all came spilling out. They'd never been any good at keeping things from each other. G-man had sense enough not to start laughing right away, though Rickey could tell he wanted to.

"I mean"—Rickey started ticking off items on his fingers—"the ad offers are bad enough—there's been the clothes, the cell phone company, the knives—"

"You probably should've done the knife ad. That was nice money."

"I hate Centaur knives. They get dull if you look at 'em wrong. Anyway, those offers were stupid, but at least they weren't completely humiliating. *This* shit . . ."

"Hey, at least they thought you had the ass for it."

Rickey looked up quickly, but G-man was throwing toiletries into a plastic freezer bag and Rickey couldn't determine the expression on his face. Nonetheless, he began to see a tiny bit of the humor in it. "You saying I don't?"

"I'd rather look at your ass than some stripper's."

"That doesn't answer my question."

G-man lost it then, and snorted laughter. After a moment, Rickey reluctantly joined him. So he'd gotten an embarrassing offer. Big deal. He'd put the TV woman in her place, and now he was going on vacation for three whole days.

They headed out of town on Claiborne Avenue, passing

through their old neighborhood and into the neighboring parish of St. Bernard. They were bound for Shell Beach, a tiny spot on the south shore of Lake Borgne, an estuary that spilled into the Gulf of Mexico. Their friend Anthony Bonvillano had a fishing camp there and a buddy with a boat. Of such humble components were great Louisiana vacations made.

Towns flashed by: Chalmette, Meraux, Violet, Poydras, each smaller and more haphazard-looking than the last. They passed oil refineries, old broken-down plantations, Catholic churches, little wooden houses with their Mardi Gras decorations still up. At Reggio they turned off the main road onto a narrower one flanked by swampy canals and thick green vegetation. Not long after that they crossed an old-fashioned drawbridge over a bayou lined with shrimp boats and oyster sheds, and then they were in Shell Beach. It was rather a ramshackle place, with abandoned hulls of boats settling slowly into the bayou and eternal-looking trash heaps accumulating in people's yards. Nearly everyone on the docks raised a hand in greeting, and a man unloading oyster sacks with a small forklift backed out of the street to let them pass, gesturing them extravagantly by. They could scarcely have felt farther from New Orleans, yet the whole trip had taken just under an hour.

Anthony's camp was on a narrow road that wound along an arm of the bayou, went past Campo's Marina, and dead-ended at the lake. They saw all this because they missed it the first time and had to turn around. When they drove slowly back up the road, Anthony B was standing in the front yard beside the skeleton of a wrecked pirogue, waving at them. In the front yard of the next house (roughly six feet away) was a large hand-painted sign that read MR. CONGRESSMAN—MR. PRESIDENT—PEOPLE OF U.S.A.—HERE "R" YOUR SHRIMP WHERE "R" OUR LEVEES.

"Anthony B!" said Rickey, climbing out of the car. "Where's the shells?"

"For that matter, where's the beach?" said G-man.

"Aw, we don't got nothing like that down here. I couldn't even tell you why they call it Shell Beach, unless it's because they used to pave the roads with oyster shells."

Anthony Bonvillano was a narrow-headed, balding man with a perpetually worried expression. A cook by trade, he'd opened a little bar on Tchoupitoulas Street in New Orleans several years ago and loved it so much that he'd never been tempted to return to kitchen life. Rickey and G-man had developed much of their boozy menu at the Apostle Bar before opening Liquor.

Like most of its neighbors, Anthony's camp was set several feet above the ground on pilings, so they had to climb a flight of splintery wooden steps to reach the front door. As they entered the main room, Rickey blinked twice, then gazed around in awe. "Jeez, Anthony. I thought I was a Saints fan, but this is ridiculous."

Nearly every inch of the place was decorated with some sort of paraphernalia advertising New Orleans' perennially luckless football team. There were Saints blankets and pillows on the sofa, Saints beer lights and autographed team pictures on the walls, Saints helmets and dolls and drinking glasses on the shelves. Everything had a fleur-de-lis on it. All the fan slogans that had come and gone over the years—CHA-CHING; DOME PATROL; WHO DAT SAY DEY GONNA BEAT DEM SAINTS?—were represented. The room was a tacky paradise of black and gold.

Sheepishly, Anthony rubbed his hand over the thinning hair on top of his head. "Aw, you know how it is. I used to have a lot of this stuff in the bar, but after the '96 season, I took it all down and was gonna throw it away. I didn't have the heart to, though, so I brung it out here. And people keep giving me stuff. You get it, Rickey. I know you love 'em."

"Well, I'm not wearing a pope hat in the Dome every Sunday or anything, but I guess I'm a little bit of a Who Dat. This is a fucking *museum,* though. They ought to give you some kinda award."

Even more sheepishly, Anthony indicated a plaque on the wall that bore the legend SAINTS-SATIONAL FAN AWARD and a picture of himself, clad in a team jersey and holding a parasol, his face painted black and gold, surrounded by cheerleaders.

"Jeeesus," Rickey said admiringly.

G-man just shook his head. He had caught Saints fever a time or two over the years, but all in all, he considered basketball a much more refined sport.

They stashed their bags in one of the two bedrooms, grabbed some bait and sandwiches at Campo's, and took off across the lake with Anthony and his friend, a hard little twist of a man who introduced himself as Captain Alan. Rickey wasn't familiar enough with boats to know what kind this one was, but like most people who'd grown up in south Louisiana, he and G-man both knew how to fish even though they had never pursued it as avidly as many locals did. They baited their hooks, Rickey with a live shrimp and G-man with a lure Captain Alan had given him, a fluorescent yellow thing with a chartreuse tail. Captain Alan said it was called a Speculizer. Everyone dug into the cooler and settled in for a day of drinking and fishing. Rickey's back twinged as he leaned against the hard metal strut of his seat, and he felt a small warm thrill as he remembered the bottle of Vicodin Dr. Lamotte had prescribed for him, waiting in his overnight bag back at the camp. It wasn't so bad to be in pain if you knew you'd be able to ease it later and enjoy a pleasant high at the same time.

"Anthony, you gave up drinking for Lent again?" he said, watching Anthony drain off half a bottle of Dixie. Anthony was a lifelong liquor drinker, and only switched to beer when he had made a Lenten vow.

"Yeah. I didn't quite make it last year, so I thought I better try again."

The day was diamond-bright, the air just a little cool. Pelicans cruised by like World War II bombers, dark and unwieldy, then splashed down near the boat hoping for a handout. G-man hooked the first fish, a twelve-inch speckled trout with silvery sides and a black-tipped tail. "That's good eatin," Captain Alan said approvingly. "I told you that Speculizer gonna have beaucoup trout jumping on your line."

They returned to the launch four hours later, sunburned and salt-lipped, with a cooler full of specks and redfish. Everyone had caught them but Rickey, who had only managed to pull up sheepheads, also good to eat but a holy pain in the ass to clean. He threw them all back and vowed to switch to the Speculizer next time out. They cleaned the trout at the marina and took their share back to Anthony's camp, where they breaded the filets with egg, corn flour, and Tabasco and fried them in bacon grease. With a bag of pork rinds and a couple of cans of Blue Runner Creole Cream Style red beans, it was a heavenly feast.

"You know what this reminds me of?" G-man said with his mouth full.

"Whuh?" said Anthony.

"All the people we've ever known who wouldn't invite us over for dinner because they were scared to cook for chefs, and they got no idea we'd be happy to eat like this every damn day of our lives."

Rickey laughed. "Yeah, they think we're at home stacking

salads into towers and bamming the edges of plates in our own kitchens."

"Eating caviar and foie gras every night," said G-man.

"Chefs got the worst eating habits of anybody I know," said Anthony. "They live on burgers and junk food, and most of 'em are fat. No offense, Rickey."

"Jeez." Rickey patted his gut. "I put on a few pounds since I turned thirty, I guess, but I'm not *fat*."

"You're comfortable," said G-man.

Anthony got up abruptly and started clearing the plates. "Well, I better get going pretty soon. I told Laura I'd try to take over for her by eleven."

"You're driving back tonight?" G-man asked, surprised. Rickey kicked him under the table and rolled his eyes.

"Yeah, I couldn't get anybody else to work the late shift at the Apostle. I'll sleep all day tomorrow. Y'all stay as long as you like— just lock up when you leave. Key's hanging on that hook by the door."

"What hook? All I see is a fleur-de-lis."

"It's shaped like a fleur-de-lis, but it's a key holder." Anthony saw that G-man was kidding him and grinned. "I went a little overboard on the Saints stuff, huh?"

"Not at all. They ever make it to the Super Bowl, you can put all this shit on eBay and be set for life."

Soon after Anthony left, they finished cleaning up the remains of dinner and went to bed. The mattress was thin and sagged in the middle like the one on the bed they'd had when they first moved in together. "You know why Anthony left before bedtime, right?" said Rickey.

"No, why?"

"The walls are pretty thin in this place. He was scared he'd hear us doing perverted stuff."

They had known Anthony Bonvillano for more than a decade, but only when they'd worked for him a few years ago had he realized that they were a couple. Even then, his first words had been "A couple of what?" He'd never been nasty about it, but he had never quite seemed to adjust to it either; apparently Rickey and G-man just didn't fit his idea of gay people.

"Well, he might have, huh?"

"I don't guess we would've if he'd stayed. I mean, it'd be kinda rude. But now, sure."

For the first week or so after Rickey hurt his back, their sex life had been much more sedate than usual. Ever since Dr. Lamotte had given him the pills, though, things had been better. They relaxed more than just his aching spine; they turned off the constant aggravated gnawing in his mind and his heart like nothing ever had before. He'd had the same prescription once before, when he broke his ankle, but had nearly forgotten how good it felt. Now it all came back to him: the spreading warmth, the disappearing pain, the diminished importance of things that had previously griped his soul.

Dr. Lamotte had taken a cursory look at his back, made him bend over and lean from side to side, had him fill out a survey rating the pain from 1 to 10 (Rickey circled 6). "I could do an X-ray," the doctor said, "but from what you told me it sounds like you just strained it. I'll give you something for the pain, and you can let me know if it gets worse. Say, you ever done any consulting work?"

"Yeah, I redid the menu for a Dallas restaurant last year. Why?"

"I told you about the restaurant we're opening at the Pot

O'Gold, right? I'm looking for a chef who has a reputation in New Orleans, somebody locals will take seriously. We have somebody like you design the menu and train the staff, we're halfway to bringing in local business before we even open."

"Wow, I'm flattered, Doc, but I just don't think I could take on something like that right now. I'm awful busy with my own place." In truth, the slow summer season was coming up, but Rickey didn't like the idea of a restaurant in a casino boat now any better than he had when Lamotte first brought it up on Ash Wednesday.

"Understood. Well, if you know anybody who might be good for the job, have 'em give me a call. Here's your prescription. Don't let reception try to charge you—you're all settled up."

Since then, Rickey had maybe been hitting the pills a little hard; it was an enormous bottle and they made the pain in his back melt right away. He didn't take them at work, of course, but it was easier to get through dinner service knowing he could have one when he got home.

G-man was worried at first: "That's a pretty strong drug, huh?" In their younger days, they had sampled almost any illicit substance that came their way. That was just how restaurant life tended to work when you were in your twenties. In recent years, though, they'd settled down to a level of drinking that might have seemed excessive elsewhere, but was pretty much normal in New Orleans, and little else beyond the occasional joint.

"It's medicine. The doctor prescribed it. It won't do me nothing bad."

"Well, I don't know," G-man said doubtfully. But he liked the way it smoothed out Rickey's sore muscles and rekindled his sex drive, and so he hadn't mentioned it again.

Now they were tired and a little drunk from their day on

Lake Borgne, but no matter. Afterward, G-man went right to sleep. Rickey felt the first dull fingers of pain returning deep in the small of his back. *What the hell, I'm on vacation,* he thought, and got up and took another pill.

"Whuzzdoing?" G-man said fuzzily as Rickey came back to bed.

"Nothing. Go back to sleep." Rickey crawled under the covers, into the pool of their shared warmth. He wrapped his arm around G-man's chest and pressed his face into G-man's back. Because of his Sicilian blood, G-man had tanned rather than burned out on the lake; his skin was a pale golden-olive and tasted slightly salty. The warmth of the pill began to spread through Rickey's gut. They still had two days here, during which they could go back out with Captain Alan or fish from the rocky shoreline or do nothing at all. He didn't even wonder how the restaurant was doing before he slept.

4

TANKER wasn't having a good day. Though he had held positions of kitchen authority up to and including chef de cuisine at one of Lenny Duveteaux's restaurants, his first love was desserts. Most hardcore chefs didn't take desserts very seriously, but Tanker had always been captivated by them, and they were what Rickey had hired him to do. He'd invented a great many liquor-based sweet dishes, including a chocolate Napoleon death mask filled with brandy mousse that had become Liquor's signature meal-ender.

He struggled constantly with an urge to push his dishes beyond the boundaries of weirdness Rickey found acceptable, and now, in Rickey's absence, he was pretty sure he'd overstepped himself. The dish in question was made of very thinly shaved Charentais melon with a sauce of Opal Nero Sambuca, a jet-black liqueur that tasted like a licorice jellybean. In his mind it had been a witty trompe l'oeil of squid-ink pasta, but in reality it had turned out gray and horrible-looking, and it didn't taste all that great either.

Tanker wondered glumly what had made him think New Orleans diners would even *want* a dessert that looked like squid-ink pasta. If he didn't quit reading about Ferran Adrià, José Andrés, and other crazy Spanish chefs who could actually get away with making stuff like this, he was liable to innovate himself right out of a job. He knew Rickey wished he'd back off the desserts and work the hot line more often, but the thought of sautéing fifty redfish filets every night made him insane with boredom . . . and Liquor's menu was one of the more innovative in the city.

Not for the first time or the hundredth, Tanker wondered if he ought to get out of New Orleans for a while, go cook in DC or Chicago or anywhere that had a slightly less fossilized food scene. People here weren't unwilling to try new things, but they invariably returned to their fish topped with crabmeat, their pannéed veal smothered in red gravy, their eternal gumbo.

Palming sweat from his forehead, he could have been a model for an aspirin ad: a tall, bone-thin young man dressed for a glamorous but stressful profession, a look of weary disgust on his face. Only the scrap of bloody toilet paper stuck to his jawline spoiled the picture. He wondered whether Mo had been using his razor to shave her armpits again.

The phone rang. With some measure of relief Tanker turned away from the grainy-looking gray dish and answered it. "Kitchen."

"This the chef?"

It was probably a sales call; he'd refrain from taking a message and save Rickey some trouble. "Yeah."

"Y'all let that murdering nigger keep working for you, somebody else gonna get hurt."

The accent wasn't New Orleans: though the voice was muffled, some stretchiness of inflection made Tanker think the speaker might be from Mississippi or north Louisiana.

"Now wait a sec, what—"

"Y'all open for dinner tonight with him cooking, you might close down sooner than you think."

"Why don't you come in here and say that, you fucking chickenshit?"

The line went dead. Tanker replaced the receiver and stood staring at it, his failed dessert forgotten. After a few minutes he picked it up again, dialed *69, and connected with the number the mechanical voice reeled off. It rang ten, fifteen, twenty times. Just as he was about to hang up, he heard the receiver lifted on the other end. "Who dis?" said a voice, obviously not the one that had spoken to him before.

"Uh, I'm trying to figure out who just called me. What number is this?"

"Dis a pay phone."

"Whereabouts?"

"Yo, why I'm a tell you where I'm at? How I know what you be tryna do?"

Tanker rolled his eyes. All the pay phones in the city, and he had to get one frequented by KKK types *and* crack dealers. "Well, listen, you see any redneck-looking motherfuckers skulking around there?"

"Doin what round here?"

"Doing anything."

"I ain't see no crackers nowhere. Don't want to, neither. Now quit tyin up my bidness phone."

For the second time in five minutes, Tanker found himself listening to a dial tone.

•   •   •

"I should call Rickey," Tanker said to Terrance.

"Well, go ahead and call him then."

"But he's on vacation. He and G-man haven't had a vacation for, like, two years. I'm supposed to be in charge—I should deal with this myself."

"So deal with it."

"But what if some nutcase really means to do us something? What if they put a bomb in the men's room or some crazy shit? Rickey would rip my nuts off and stuff 'em down my throat if that happened and I hadn't told him about the phone call."

Terrance was silent. He knew Tanker would probably go back and forth several more times before coming to a decision. For about ten minutes they worked without speaking, Terrance prepping his meats, Tanker dipping pretzel rods in melted white chocolate, then rolling them in multicolored sugar. These would be used to garnish the popular "Margarita" dessert, scoops of tequila-lime and Triple Sec sorbet served in a sugar-edged martini glass. It had been off the menu for a while, but had recently returned by popular demand.

Finally Terrance asked, "You gonna say anything to Milford?"

"Aw, no. Poor bastard already seems freaked out. The other day I was showing him how to do the terrine and he asked me could he go to the bathroom. I mean he asked my *permission* to take a piss."

"That's prison for you. He tried to go without asking there, probably got a nightstick in the balls."

"Shit."

Tanker fell silent again, and Terrance knew he was still thinking about the phone call. "I wouldn't worry too much about that call," he said. "Nineteen out of twenty race-hatin sons-abitches is all talk and no action."

"Yeah, but what about the twentieth one?"

Terrance shrugged.

"You know what I'm gonna do?" Tanker said in a burst of inspiration. "I'm gonna call Lenny. See what he thinks."

"Oh Lord."

"What?"

"You call Lenny, next thing you know we gonna have ten big motherfuckers in here name of Rocco and Rico and Tony the Eyeball."

"Lenny's not even Italian."

"You know what I mean."

"Well, I hate to bother Rickey, but I don't feel right doing nothing. We get Rocco and Rico and Tony the Eyeball, at least we'll have a little protection."

• • •

As he answered the phone, Lenny Duveteaux glanced down to check the red light on his tape recorder, but both light and recorder were gone. Until last year, he had taped all his telephone conversations as well as those that took place in his office. This had come very close to earning him an indictment, and his lawyer had finally talked him into quitting, but old habits died hard.

"Yeah?" he said.

"Lenny? It's Tanker."

"Tanker! How's my favorite pastry puff?"

Tanker usually rose to this bait, at least with an amiable "Fuck you" or "Suck my ass," but today he didn't even seem to hear what Lenny had said. As Tanker described the phone call he'd received at Liquor, Lenny's frown deepened until his bushy black eyebrows nearly met over his considerable nose. Scowling into the phone this way, he didn't look like a multimillionaire or one of America's most famous chefs; he looked like a thug.

"Just sit tight," Lenny said when Tanker had finished. "I'll have some people over there by the time your dinner service starts."

"Jeez, do you really think that's necessary? I don't want a bunch of tough guys hanging around all night."

"No tough guys. They'll look very respectable, I promise. But if anybody tries something funny, they'll be equipped to deal with him."

"Deal with him as in he goes to jail, or as in he leaves in the coroner's van?"

"I suppose that depends on what he tries."

Tanker sighed. "You really think somebody might pull something?"

"Probably not. But I have the resources at my disposal. Why not use them?"

"I guess you got a point there."

"Of course I do. Try not to worry."

"You think I should call Rickey?"

"Christ, no. He'd come flying back to New Orleans like a bat out of hell, probably beat up anybody who looked cross-eyed at one of your black employees. You can fill him in when he gets home. Just let me handle it for now."

Lenny hung up and sat thinking for a moment. While he knew Rickey and G-man were grateful for all the help he'd given them, he also knew they hoped to buy him out someday. So far they hadn't managed to get the money together. Lenny rather hoped they wouldn't, not because he doubted their ability to run the place themselves but because he took a genuine interest in Liquor. It was different from his own two restaurants, Lenny's and Crescent. Lenny's was a classic, pricey French Quarter joint that mostly pulled the tourist trade. Crescent on Magazine Street was trendier; his current chef de cuisine called it "New Creole." He knew both restaurants were very good, but he also felt that both bore the stamp of someone Not From Here. That was how the locals said it; you could hear the capitals. Lenny was from Portland, Maine, and while he'd been cooking in New Orleans for more than twenty years, he still believed there was some mysterious local quality his food would never be capable of embodying.

Liquor's menu was far less Creolized than either Lenny's or Crescent's, but Rickey and G-man themselves were local to the core, the kind of New Orleanians who called themselves yats and couldn't imagine living anywhere else. Lenny, beloved in the city but still something of a stranger in a strange land, envied their unshakable sense of place. He supposed there was a certain condescension to this—the big bwana admiring the purity of the unspoiled natives—but it wouldn't hurt them as long as they didn't know it.

At any rate, he wasn't about to let some race-baiting wingnut mess with them for hiring a good cook who needed a job. Lenny picked up his phone again and started making calls.

•   •   •

Terrance had expected mobbed-up types, but Tanker knew the Mafia hadn't really had a serious presence in New Orleans since the eighties, when the Marcello family had begun to die off. They were still here, but they didn't run much of anything these days. Instead of wiseguys, Lenny seemed to have sent over most of the on-duty police force. As the acting manager, Tanker had to decide whether to feed them for free. He had no idea if Rickey let cops eat on the house, so he called Lenny again. Lenny, now busy expediting at Crescent and sounding slightly exasperated, just said, "What the hell do you think?"

So they gave away something like two dozen free meals over

the course of the evening, and since most of the cops' tastes ran to the unexotic, they ran out of redfish and steaks. By the time dinner service ended at ten-thirty, nothing sinister had happened. Tanker guessed maybe all the gratis meals had been worth it; if his afternoon caller had come around, the ranks of cruisers in the parking lot must have scared him off. He was about to say as much to Terrance when one of the last remaining cops, a detective whose nametag barely contained the name CATTALONOTTO and whose blue shirt barely contained his gut, shouldered through the steaming, pot-slamming clutch of dishwashers at the back of the kitchen and beckoned to Tanker. "Yo, Chef, something you might wanna see back here."

"Back where?" said Tanker as he followed Cattalonotto through the kitchen and into the rear hall.

The cop smacked the pressure bar on the back door. "In the parking lot."

They exited by the Dumpsters, and at first the day's accumulated garbage was all Tanker smelled. A moment later a breath of gasoline and charcoal touched his nostrils. "What? Somebody burn something?"

Wordlessly, Cattalonotto pointed at a corner of the parking lot so far away it was almost a part of Toulouse Street. Tanker couldn't see anything there at first; then a weakly glowing ember caught his eye. He walked over and examined one of the smallest, wimpiest crosses he had ever seen, less than knee-high and apparently made out of Popsicle sticks. This construction had been set on fire, sort of. Shreds of gasoline-dampened rag, or possibly toilet paper, still clung to it. Most of the sticks hadn't even burned through.

"What the shit is this supposed to be?" he said. "A warning to quit buying the competitor's brand of ice cream?"

The cop laughed. "Y'all employ any midgets? Maybe it's a warning not to hire 'em."

"Seriously, man, you ever seen anything this lame before?"

"Oh, I pray for lame. Every day I fall on my knee and pray for the crooks to be real lame and my life to be real boring. It's when things get interesting that you gotta worry."

"I guess." Tanker started to kick the cross over, then thought better of it. "Should I leave this thing for, like, evidence?"

"Yeah, we'll dust it and see if we can match the fingerprints to the Good Humor man. Nah. You wanna knock it down, be my guest."

Once he had done so, Tanker scuffed at the little pile of sticks looking for live embers, but the fire was pretty much out.

"Course, I still gotta file a report."

That meant Rickey would have to be told. It was probably just as well; Tanker knew Rickey and G-man had a right to know about everything that had gone on in their absence. He didn't look forward to Rickey's reaction, though, and he especially didn't look forward to what Rickey would say when he found out Tanker hadn't called him right away.

Hope you're hooking some big fish, buddy, he thought as he walked back toward the restaurant. Terrance's large form now filled the back door, and Tanker could see most of the rest of the kitchen crew behind him. Great; now everybody could go home and tell their friends and family a cross had been burned in Liquor's parking lot. *Yeah, I hope they're really biting, cause I got a feeling you're not gonna get away again for a long time.*

5

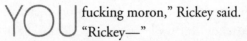YOU fucking moron," Rickey said.
"Rickey—"

"You dumb motherfucking moron. I thought you knew how to run a restaurant. I thought I could leave you in charge and trust you to let me know if anything went wrong. Instead I come back to find out there's been death threats on my customers, my employees, God knows who else, a fucking *cross* burned in our parking lot, and you didn't even call me. You dumb shit!"

Tanker slammed his knife down on the cutting board where he'd been chiffonading mint. "Look, I know you're pissed off and maybe you got a right to be, but I've heard about enough of that crap. I was in charge. A problem came up. I talked to Lenny and I took his advice."

"This isn't Lenny's restaurant."

"Well, excuse me if I'm wrong, but I kinda thought he was still paying a lot of the bills. Seems to me that gives him a say in what goes on around here."

"Yeah? Seems to *me* you got no idea what you're talking about. Lenny doesn't pay the bills here. We turn a profit. And you know why, Tank? You know why? Cause I care about this place and I handle every aspect of it. I micromanage it."

"No shit," Tanker said under his breath.

"How I'm supposed to do that if the guy I leave in charge doesn't even tell me when there's a fucking bomb threat?"

"It wasn't a bomb threat—"

"You didn't know what it was, asshole. You didn't talk to me and you didn't even have the courtesy to talk to the target of the threat. Milford said the first he heard of it was when you came back in after the fire."

"I didn't see any need to worry him."

"Yeah, you make decisions for everybody, huh? You know it all. I'm surprised you didn't fuck up my menu with a bunch of stupid trendy shit while we were gone, maybe a deconstructed sweet potato–bourbon pie or some kinda shrimp cocktail in an atomizer—"

"OK, that's it." Tanker grabbed his knife roll from the rack above his station and slid his knife into it without even bothering to wipe the chopped mint off the blade. "I know G-man lets you talk to him like that, and I guess the young kids think you're some kinda badass, but I'm too old for it."

"Where are you going?"

"I quit."

Tanker walked away from his station. Rickey caught up with him and grabbed his shoulder, but Tanker shook him off. "Rickey, think about what you're doing. You wanna kick my ass? You're a Lower Ninth Ward boy and I'm from Covington. It would be no contest. So is that who you are now? The screaming asshole who cusses out his best cook, then slugs him for walking off the job?"

Rickey was speechless. Tanker turned away again, stomped down the hot line, turned a corner, and disappeared from view. Rickey wanted to follow, to somehow take back everything he'd just said, but even now there was no apology in him. This was his restaurant, the only thing he'd ever been in charge of; after three years the place was like an extension of him. He knew everything that went on here; it couldn't run without him. And yet he had gone away for three days—three lousy days!—and Tanker had hidden something from him, something that had almost escalated into a disaster.

The cross-burning had made the paper: there was a little story in the Metro section of this morning's *Times-Picayune*. In fact, that was how Rickey had found out about the whole thing: as he and G-man were driving home from Shell Beach yesterday, a reporter called to get his reaction to "the racial incident at Liquor." Rickey barely had the presence of mind to stammer "No comment," then hang up and dial the restaurant. The only person in the kitchen—or at least the only person who would talk to him—was Marquis, who hadn't been working that night but managed to give him a garbled version of the events. He finally reached Lenny and got the whole story. That was one good thing about Lenny; he understood that to run a successful restaurant you had to be a control freak, had to know everything that was going on. Rickey would almost have suspected Lenny of alerting the paper to the story—it was the kind of thing he'd do for pub-licity's sake—except that Lenny wouldn't have done it without making sure Rickey knew all about the incident first.

It *had* drawn some pub, Rickey had to admit. His maître d', Karl, reported that regulars and strangers alike had been calling all day to offer their support; there were already a hundred and five reservations on the books for tonight and seventy-five more for tomorrow. No one seemed to care that the cross was such a pitiful little construction; their affront could scarcely have been greater if it had been twenty feet tall, wrapped in a Nazi flag and lighting up the night with its evil glow. One party had even requested that Milford Goodman cook their meals personally, as if he might work all the stations from salads to dessert.

Dessert: that brought Rickey back to Tanker. What the hell was he going to do without Tanker? He and G-man were rollers, and the rest of the crew was damn good, but Tanker was the crazy genius of the kitchen. He lent the menu a sense of controlled abandon, not just in his desserts but in his occasional dinner specials and the suggestions he made to Rickey. He knew more about food than anyone else Rickey had ever met. The kitchen would be bereft without him.

And yet he had betrayed Rickey's trust. Tanker had failed to let Rickey know when the restaurant was in danger, and Rickey couldn't live with that. He refused to entertain the idea that his own inability to back down might play any part in this decision.

A low, pulpy throb began deep in the base of his spine, and he mentally calculated the hours until he could get home and have a pill. There seemed to be way too much time between now and then, but he supposed he would get through it. He was a little disturbed to realize that if he had any here at the restaurant, he would take one right now. Maybe just half a one. It would help him forget the bullshit and deal with the things he needed to deal with.

Wearily, he wondered how angry G-man was going to be when he learned that Rickey had hounded Tanker into quitting. It took a lot to make G-man angry, but Rickey figured this would probably do it. He turned the stock he'd been making down to a low simmer, went up to the bar, and poured himself a shot of Wild Turkey. After considering for a moment, he picked up the soda gun and added a spritz of club soda, but only a small one. Today he needed the full effect.

•   •   •

Tanker was in Rickey's office sorting through a stack of cookbooks, several of which belonged to him. He set aside Ming Tsai's *Blue Ginger*, Thomas Keller's *The French Laundry Cookbook*, Fergus Henderson's *The Whole Beast*, resenting the fact that Rickey wouldn't buy his own copies of such esoteric compendiums. In his heart he knew that was unfair—while Rickey might not be the world's most innovative chef, he did have an insatiable curiosity about food—but right now he didn't give a damn.

He hadn't liked being cussed out, but he could chalk that up to Rickey's hysteria. What really struck a nerve was Rickey's remark about fucking up the menu with trendy shit. In truth, Tanker had tried out a couple of fairly experimental dishes while Rickey and G-man were gone: a carpaccio of gorgeous, translucent tequila-cured snapper with a sorbet of kaffir limes and black pepper; a savory sea urchin parfait with vodka crème fraiche and foie gras beignets. The crew grumbled about the unfamiliar ingredients, and though the diners who ordered the carpaccio loved it, they were few and far between. Worse, the sea urchin parfait got skunked: in two nights, nobody ordered a single one. He ate a couple himself, urged one on Mo, and threw the rest away. Sea urchin wasn't cheap, either.

So he'd really been in no mood for Rickey's tirade, and now he realized he was glad to be out of here. Liquor wasn't a bad joint as New Orleans restaurants went, but there had always been something of the little Hitler about Rickey.

G-man entered the office. In an instant he took in Tanker's stack of cookbooks, Tanker's knife roll, Tanker's pissed-off expression. "What's going on?"

Tanker told him.

G-man blew out air in an exasperated rush and leaned against the corner of the desk. "He's just freaked out and mad at everybody. It's not your fault. You know that, right?"

"Yeah, sure. But it doesn't—"

"Come right down to it, you probably *should've* called us. I know you thought about it. Hell, you could've called my cell, told me what was up—I'd have figured out how to break it to Rickey."

"Why do you coddle him like that?"

G-man spread his hands as if the answer was obvious. "Because we wouldn't be here without him. I don't know where you'd be at, but I'd still be working on the line in somebody else's restaurant. I know Rickey's a pain in the ass sometimes—"

"Sometimes!"

"—but he made this place happen and he keeps it going. And it just about eats him alive, you know that. Any time I can take some of the stress off him, I'm damn well gonna do it."

"Well, I can't help it, G. If he's gotta cuss people out to take the stress off, he can find somebody else to cuss."

"No, course he shouldn't have done that. But has he ever cussed you out before?"

"No," Tanker admitted.

"You ever heard him cuss out any of the other cooks?"

"No. He's pretty hard on some of the newbies, and of course he bitches at waiters, but I never heard him rank any cook the way he did me just now. And yeah, I should've called and blah, blah, blah. It doesn't matter now. I don't think this is the place for me anymore."

G-man took off his shades and looked steadily at Tanker. Tanker made himself look back, but that myopic gaze had never been so hard to hold. G-man's blunt, honest face was sorrowful, and Tanker realized how much he would miss working with this sweet-natured, fundamentally decent man.

"Well," said G-man, "maybe you're right, but I hate to see you go. We gonna lose Mo too?"

"Mo makes up her own mind about where she works."

"Yeah, but are things gonna be weird between you two if she stays on here?"

"Not at all. She likes this job, and I know Rickey's never said a rude word to her."

"That's something, anyway." G-man shook his head sadly and put his shades back on. "Look, you need a reference, put my name down. I don't like you quitting without notice, but I understand why you did it."

"Thanks, man."

They stared at each other. Tanker wondered if he should give G-man a hug, and thought G-man might be wondering the same. He guessed that kind of thing wasn't any easier for gay guys than it was for straight ones—harder, maybe. Finally he stuck out his hand, and G-man shook it. A handshake didn't seem adequate for all the heat and inspiration and drunken camaraderie they'd been through together, but it would have to do.

As he walked out to his car, he hoped Mo would still be at home. She wasn't due at work until later, but she'd said something about running a few errands, and he didn't feel like trying to explain all this on a staticky cell phone. He hadn't been completely honest with G-man: while he had no intention of pressuring Mo to quit her job right away, he did plan on trying to convince her to leave New Orleans with him. Unlike most natives, Tanker didn't thrive on heat and humidity, didn't feel that his basic human rights were being violated if he couldn't drink on the street, and wasn't unhinged by the idea of living elsewhere. It was time for a big change in his life. The heady wine of freedom coursed through his veins. By the time he was halfway home, he'd just about convinced himself that Rickey had done him a favor.

•　　•　　•

As G-man came back into the kitchen, Rickey tried to make himself intensely busy with his stock. Unfortunately, there wasn't much to do but skim it, which didn't require a great deal of concentration. He felt G-man's eyes on him. At last he said, "What?"

"What do you mean, what?" said G-man.

Rickey glanced up, and G-man wasn't looking at him at all: he was poking through the lowboy at his station, getting ready to replenish his mise-en-place, the assortment of prepared ingredients that would get him through the night: chopped herbs, sea salt and cracked black pepper, minced garlic, clarified butter, olive oil, and the like.

"I kinda thought you were gonna yell at me."

"What? About Tanker? No, I'm not gonna yell at you. You let him walk, I figure you must have a plan. You *better* have a plan"—here G-man permitted himself a deep breath, but did not raise his voice—"cause otherwise we're fucked to the moon."

"Well," Rickey said, trying to gather his thoughts. "Well, actually, yeah, I do have a plan. I'm gonna promote Milford to Tanker's job."

"I didn't know Milford could do desserts."

"Dude, forget the desserts. We'll hire a pastry cook. You know we didn't pay Tanker the fat money to do desserts. We paid him because he knew how to work every station, make dinner specials if we needed them, even run the kitchen if we took an extra day off. Milford can do all that. He's rusty on purchasing and costing out, but otherwise he's an even stronger cook than Tanker, and he won't try to sneak in any of that goofy shit."

"I thought you said that goofy shit added a necessary zing to our menu."

"I never said 'a necessary zing.'"

"You did so. We were all drinking in the bar one night, and Tanker thought some dish he'd made was too weird, and that's what you told him."

"Well, I wouldn't have said it if I was sober. Anyway, fuck him. He's good, but he's not as good as he thinks he is. When I met him, he was making sundaes."

Rickey had hired Tanker from a failed venture of Lenny's, a restaurant called Sundae Dinner where all the food was served in parfait glasses and made to look like ice cream confections. Steaks tortured into the shape of banana splits and crabmeat mousse topped with raspberry beurre blanc were among the least of the atrocities. It was Lenny's idea of avant-garde cuisine, and though Rickey had seen Tanker's genuine talent shining through the dreck, he never quite forgot that Tanker had been willing to make such ridiculous food. Had even been willing, as chef de cuisine, to put his name on it. Every cook had to make food he didn't believe in from time to time, but Sundae Dinner was extreme.

"Uh huh," said G-man, "and your exact words were, 'We gotta hire this guy.'"

"That wasn't because of the sundaes. That was later, when he came by the test kitchen and made the perfect salad."

"Yeah, he sure did make some gorgeous salads."

They lapsed into a gloomy silence, beginning to realize the true magnitude of their loss. That was how Milford found them when he arrived an hour later.

"What's goin on?"

"Tanker quit," Rickey said.

"You serious? He been with y'all since the start, ain't he? Aw, no, I bet this had somethin to do with that damn cross in the parking lot."

"Yeah, it did," Rickey admitted, "but don't worry about it, Milford. It was all my fault."

"Ain't none of this your fault. Not Tanker's neither. I brought nothin but bad luck to your restaurant. Ought to be me quittin."

"You do that, we're really fucked. I was gonna offer you Tanker's job."

Milford stopped pulling mise-en-place ingredients out of the reach-in and turned to stare at Rickey. "Offer me his job? You'd do that after what happened, the fire and all?"

"Fuck the fire!" Rickey smacked the metal countertop so hard that the pots hanging overhead rattled. "I'm sick of everybody acting like the fire matters. Yeah, I got pissed because Tanker didn't let me know what was going on—I should've been in the loop. But do you people honestly think I'm gonna start running my restaurant based on what anonymous assholes think? *Do* you? Have you ever *met* me?"

"Here we go," G-man murmured.

"C'mon, Milford, you're the best cook we got and the only one I know can handle the kinda responsibility Tanker had. You want the job or not?"

"What about Terrance? He's been here a lot longer'n me."

"Terrance was washing dishes three years ago. He's turned into a great grill guy, but he doesn't have the experience to be a lead cook. Look, if you don't want the job, I guess I'll put an ad in the paper. Hire some twenty-two-year-old hotshot with a culinary degree from Delgado. Next thing you know we'll be serving coconut shrimp with Brie and blueberry sauce."

"Ugh," said G-man, genuinely appalled.

"Now stop all that crazy talk," said Milford. "Course I want the job, if you wanna give it to me. I just hope you know what the hell you're doin."

"I always hope I know what the hell I'm doing," said Rickey. "As far as promoting you, though, I got no doubts. You feel like celebrating with a dinner special?"

Milford didn't hesitate. "What kinda Gulf fish we got? Snapper? How about a nice snapper with a sun-dried tomato crust? We marinate the tomatoes in vodka and Tabasco, call it a Bloody Mary crust."

Rickey and G-man looked at each other, blinked, looked back at Milford. In three years of making liquor dishes, they had never thought of a Bloody Mary crust.

So long, Tanker, Rickey thought rather smugly. *Here's your toque; don't let the door hit you in the ass on the way out.*

6

RICKEY sat in Dr. Lamotte's waiting room flipping through a
two-year-old issue of *Louisiana Fishing* that featured the Grand
Isle Tarpon Rodeo. The pictures of sunburned, grinning people
holding up big fish reminded him of his vacation in Shell Beach.
That seemed impossibly distant now, though it had only been
about a month ago. Had he really spent those crystal-blue days
out on Lake Borgne, eaten speckled trout so fresh it just about
swam down his throat, slept with a tanned, salty-skinned G-man
in Anthony's uncomfortable little camp bed? He supposed he
had, but it was hard to believe somehow.

Last week, low on pills, he had called Dr. Lamotte's office
and asked for a refill. Instead of saying, "I'll have him call your
pharmacy," as Rickey had hoped, the receptionist said, "Oh, your
name is flagged—the doctor wants you to come in." So Rickey
made an appointment, and now he'd been out of pills for three
days and his back was killing him. He wondered when his pain
tolerance had gotten so low. Cuts, burns, bruises from lifting
heavy boxes and slamming into the edges of countertops—none
of them bothered him, but this thing with his back was just about

enough to make him break down and cry sometimes. It was a more *personal* sort of pain, somehow.

After cooling his heels for half an hour, he was ushered into the warren of offices and examining rooms that was Dr. Lamotte's inner sanctum. When the nurse made him step on the scale, he saw that he'd lost seven pounds since Mardi Gras, when he had weighed himself at the Stubbs house. Among other things, Vicodin was a pretty good appetite suppressant. The nurse stashed him in one of the examining rooms, where he waited for another ten minutes without even a copy of *Louisiana Fishing* to pass the time. At last the doctor walked in, the top of his bald head oily with sweat, the cuffs of his lab coat rolled up to his elbows, managing to convey the impression that he was a fantastically busy guy who'd generously squeezed a few minutes into his hectic day for Rickey. "So, Chef! How you doing? How's the restaurant business?"

Rickey shrugged. "Crazy. But I got a new cook who's a genius, so I can't complain too much."

"Goodman?"

"Uh, yeah. How'd you know?"

"I think Clancy Fairbairn must've mentioned something about it. Said he remembered the guy from the Top Spot, back before he had all that trouble."

Rickey didn't want to get into that. There hadn't been any more anonymous threats, but he had fielded a few calls from aggrieved patrons who couldn't believe Liquor would employ a cook with such a sordid past. Rickey figured that just went to show how little they knew about cooks. Most cooks hadn't served time for murder, but criminal records weren't uncommon in the business, usually for small-time stuff like drugs, shoplifting, assault. It wasn't a life that naturally tended to attract upstanding citizens. Rickey tried to be polite to these callers, but he told them exactly what he told Dr. Lamotte now: "He served his time and he's a damn good cook. The rest of it's none of my business." *Or yours,* he would sometimes add if the caller was particularly obnoxious, but he didn't say it to Lamotte. He wasn't here to get into an argument.

"Hey, I'm impartial. Long as the food's good, I don't care if you got Jeffrey Dahmer working for you. How's the back?"

"Still hurts. Look, I can't afford to keep getting worse—you think we should do an X-ray?"

"That depends. *Is* it any worse?"

"No, but it's no better either. If I—"

"See, Chef, the thing about the human spine is it's just not real well-designed. There's only so much we can do to fix that. Hell, people go under the knife and we still can't tell what's wrong with their backs. We take X-rays, it's gonna cost you a couple hundred dollars and probably show nothing. Best thing is to rest it and treat the pain."

"Yeah, I guess maybe it'd get better if I could take a month off, but that's not gonna happen, so—"

"Want some more Vicodin?"

"Well, sure, if you think—"

"Oh, say, I meant to ask you. Remember I mentioned I was opening a restaurant on my casino boat? The Pot O'Gold, out at the lake? Well, we found a chef-consultant, but he bailed on us at the last minute. Left us high and dry." Lamotte considered this for a moment, then seemed to decide he'd made a joke and laughed at it. "High and dry! On a boat, see? Anyway, we're looking for somebody else, but I wondered if maybe you could just take a one-time look at it? Just see what you think of the space, see if you get any ideas about the menu? We'd pay for your time, of course."

"Well, I—"

The doctor picked up his pad, scribbled on it, and clipped a prescription to Rickey's chart. From the corner of his eye, Rickey could see that it said x60. Sixty pills, twice as many as in his last prescription. "You think about it, huh? I'll call you in a couple days—we can set up a time. I sure would appreciate it. Clancy would, too."

"What's Comus got to do with it?" Rickey said. Then, realizing what had just come out of his mouth, he felt himself turning bright red.

Lamotte just laughed. "Secret's out! Don't worry, they don't really take you behind the Municipal Auditorium and shoot you if you figure out who Comus is. Half the time, the guys leak it themselves—people know you were Comus, it sure doesn't hurt your standing in the business world. Old Clancy doesn't need much help in that department, though. He's got a finger in just about every pie in New Orleans. The Pot O'Gold isn't a big thing for him—more like a toy—but we'd be up shit creek without his backing, that's for sure. Anyway, I'll call you soon."

Rickey knew he had been dismissed. "Say, Doc?"

The doctor half-turned on his way out. "Yeah?"

"Should I, like, be worried about taking this stuff? I mean, is it addictive?"

Lamotte waved a plump hand. "Vicodin's small stuff. I got little old lady patients who take it like candy. It can get its hooks in you, sure, but don't worry. You gotta take it for months and months before you're looking at a problem. We'll get you fixed up by then."

How, if you never even take an X-ray? Rickey wondered. But he thought of the calm place he'd found in himself, the place he never knew existed before the pills, and he was silent.

"Talk to you real soon," said Dr. Lamotte, ushering him out. Rickey went up to the desk and waited while the receptionist glanced over his chart.

"There's no charge today, Mr. Rickey. Did the doctor want you to make another appointment?"

"I'll let you know," Rickey said.

•   •   •

Tanker had made a classic seafood stock. He'd boiled shrimp heads and shells with onions, celery, herbs, and peppercorns; he had strained and chilled the resulting flavorful broth; he had reduced it to a syrupy consistency and chilled it again. All this was fine. Now, however, his heart sank, because his classic stock was about to become part of a ridiculous dish.

Mo hadn't wanted to leave New Orleans. Had, in fact, nixed the idea quite vehemently. "You think I never deal with shit from Rickey?" she'd said. "Hell, he gets all up in my face if he thinks I'm not using enough swizzle sticks." Liquor's signature swizzle sticks were topped with a little martini glass that mirrored the restaurant's logo, and Rickey believed people kept them as souvenirs, which reminded them to eat at Liquor again and again. Apparently he reprimanded Mo if he thought she was forgetting to use them in each and every drink, though Tanker hadn't previously heard about it. "But you know what I do? I just let it roll off my back. I've had plenty of asshole bosses, and Rickey's a baby Easter lamb compared to most of them. If you want to get into a dick-measuring contest with him and walk off the job, that's on you. I like my job and I like New Orleans."

For about a minute, Tanker had considered leaving anyway, but the hard truth was that he loved Mo more than he loved the idea of cooking the kind of adventurous food he wanted to make. He wasn't ready to go back to his journeyman-whore days of cooking at places like Sundae Dinner, though. He'd give Liquor that much: it had raised his standards. He made a list of New Orleans restaurants where he'd be willing to work, and came up with four. The first had no kitchen openings. The second and third couldn't afford him. The fourth was the Polonius Room, which hired him as garde-manger.

In a kitchen run on the traditional French system, the garde-manger was responsible for every cold item on the menu: salads, pâtés, terrines, galantines, even some desserts, which was what had attracted Tanker to the position. In practice, he had a couple of salad bitches and a cold-apps guy to help him, and of course the Polonius Room employed a world-class pastry chef. It said so right on the menu: "Our world-class pastry chef, Martina Jesus-Vasquez, has prepared a selection of desserts to tempt your mind and palate." Her current masterpiece was called "Degustation of the Forest Floor": a selection of chocolates and caramels fashioned to look like rocks, leaves, bark, pine needles, and other natural debris haphazardly scattered across a big square plate. The head chef had promised Tanker that he could contribute a dessert or two—particularly if he was willing to reprise some of the more popular ones he'd created for Liquor—but so far Martina, a lanky, intense Brazilian woman, had allowed him nowhere near her air-conditioned alcove.

The Polonius Room had begun life as a steak-and-chop joint in the d'Hemecourt, the city's most expensive hotel. A couple of years ago, when the owners got wind of the fact that hotel restaurants were trendy, they'd fired the entire kitchen staff and brought in a chef from Amsterdam to overhaul the menu. Tanker wasn't previously aware that the Netherlands were a hotbed of culinary revolution, but this chef, Jaap Noteboom, apparently believed he was northern Europe's answer to Ferran Adrià. Now he was one of New Orleans' many crosses to bear.

That wasn't fair, though: Jaap was talented and wildly creative, and Tanker winced only a little when he reflected that this was exactly the sort of food Rickey would have expected him to end up cooking. Foams. Peculiarly flavored ice creams. Aerosols that were sprayed into the mouth. And, dearest of all to Jaap's wintry heart, gelees.

Oh, the gelees.

Jaap's ire had been kindled a couple of years ago by some rich guy who'd come in and ordered a bowl of gumbo, a steak, and a super-expensive bottle of wine. "I'll make sure no one can ever have that sort of meal here again!" he had raged, or so the other cooks told Tanker. Now the steak was cut into infinitesimal strips and served in a sort of log-cabin stack with mashed potato foam, and after racking his brains for a way to destroy New Orleans' most beloved dish, Jaap invented a gumbo gelee topped with two small scoops of ice cream. One was sassafras, in a nod to the traditional filé powder. The other, even more horribly, was roux.

Tanker liked the idea of unconventionally flavored and even savory ice creams. His signature Napoleon death mask dessert at Liquor contained a scoop of Camembert ice cream, and he thought some of the other ones Jaap did—sweet corn, white asparagus, Guinness stout—were excellent. The sassafras, though, was distinctly odd—a disturbing gray-green lump with a dusty, mossy flavor—and the roux was just as appalling as it sounded.

"Dude, nobody wants burnt flour ice cream," Tanker had said when the cold-apps cook told him about it.

The guy just shrugged: "Jaap does what Jaap wants to do. Don't take real kindly to suggestions, neither."

Sighing, Tanker layered shrimp, king crabmeat, and okra in a terrine mold, dissolved sheets of gelatin in warm water, mixed them with his shrimp stock, and carefully poured the resultant liquid over the layered items. This would solidify into something that could be sliced to show a cross section of the ingredients and served on a plate with the horrible ice creams nestled on either side: a good-looking dish as long as you didn't actually put any in your mouth. It really resembled an aspic more than what most people thought of as a gelee, but "gelee" was apparently Jaap's favorite word in the whole world, judging from how frequently he used it on his menu.

Here came the chef now, a perfectly groomed specimen of blond manhood who always made Tanker feel unshaven and degenerate. He patted Tanker on the shoulder and peered at what he was doing. "How's the gelee? Nice?"

"Oh, real nice," said Tanker. "But, you know, it really shouldn't have okra *and* filé. Most seafood gumbos have one or the other."

Jaap's handsome face darkened alarmingly. "I know that! In this case the diner has a choice: he can avoid the okra or he can ignore the ice cream. Or he can have both. Did you imagine I wouldn't have thought of that?"

How the hell can he avoid the okra? Tanker wondered. *It's right there in the middle of the damn dish, big as life and twice as ugly.* But he didn't say so, and he decided not to mention that king crab was all wrong for gumbo, either. Instead he said, "There was a restaurant here in New Orleans that served an app called 'Deconstruction of Gumbo.' They had a plate with one shrimp, one okra, and a little heap of flour—"

"I HATE deconstructions!" the chef roared. Tanker felt a tiny fleck of saliva hit the back of his neck. He hoped none had gotten in the gelee.

"Uh, that's cool. I was just gonna say—"

"The deconstruction technique is show for the sake of show. These chefs take a dish down to its components, but it's pointless. They add nothing and they prove nothing. 'Deconstructed Cheese Sandwich!' 'Deconstructed Glass of Wine!' Nonsense! I'd like to serve them a Deconstructed Shot of Scotch: a pinch of barley and a square of peat. You think they'd like that? Eh?"

Tanker laughed.

"Maybe your former chef would like it, eh? Carry on the liquor theme? Or is it too daring for him?"

"It'd be too daring, all right," Tanker said. "Rickey thinks the heyday of New Orleans cuisine happened round about 1873."

Jaap snorted. "Small minds worship the past. Great ones travel into the future. So how are you doing? Are you happy working here?"

"Sure," said Tanker. "I mean, I'm still getting used to it. But I gotta admit it's nice not having to think of some way to put liquor in everything."

"More nonsense! A gimmick, just like deconstruction. All right, then—carry on."

"Think maybe I can make some desserts pretty soon?"

"I'm working on Martina," Jaap promised. "For now, after you finish the gumbo, remember we need a batch of chlorophyll sorbet."

"You got it, Chef."

Tanker started to perk up a little. Working with chlorophyll was labor-intensive but deeply fascinating to him, just the sort of thing he'd never have been allowed to do at Liquor. To get pure chlorophyll, he pureed raw spinach and strained it through cheesecloth. The resultant juice didn't taste like spinach at all; it tasted pure green and could be made into sorbets, foams, or, of course, gelees. The only thing he couldn't do was cook it: heat dulled its color and destroyed its grassy flavor.

As he headed back to the walk-in to get a box of spinach, he heard voices: Eddie and Dejuan, a couple of PM line cooks. They were behind a row of bread racks and couldn't see him. "You prepped up them baby turnips yet?" said Eddie.

"Yeah, they lookin good. I got the new garde-manger to show me how Chef wants 'em—you gotta cut, like, six sides."

"Who—that older guy?"

"Yeah, him."

"He cool?"

"He all right for a white boy. Listens to rap and shit . . ."

They walked off, still talking. Tanker stood paralyzed by what he'd heard. *Older guy?* He was thirty, a year younger than Rickey and G-man. They'd had young cooks at Liquor before, most recently Marquis, but Tanker was used to being about the same age as his coworkers. In the Polonius Room's kitchen, though, everyone besides Jaap and Martina was young, black, and steeped in ghetto culture. This might have seemed unusual to diners who assumed their food was being cooked by stereotypical fancy French chefs, little round-bellied guys with pencil mustaches and bad tempers, but in fact it was perfectly normal; Liquor's slightly older, more experienced crew was the exception, not the rule. The crew here talked endlessly about cars, clubs, pussy, and hip-hop bands Tanker had never heard of, though they were impressed that he listened to Snoop Dogg.

"*Older* guy," he muttered as he hauled crates of tomatoes out of the way to get to the spinach. This walk-in was the most poorly organized he'd ever seen. "Older guy! They think I'm so goddamn decrepit, why don't they come move this shit out the way for me? *Older guy!*"

All the joy had gone out of making chlorophyll. As he dropped double handfuls of spinach into the Robot Coupe and pressed the button to puree it into oblivion, he caught himself wishing he was back at Liquor, where he was allowed to make desserts, where he was not considered venerable.

·　　·　　·

G-man added more lime to the margarita mousse he was making. Then he added more sugar. Then, in desperation, he added more tequila. Nothing he did made any difference: it still tasted like shit. Disgusted, he slung the whole thing into the trash. This was his third try, and the first two had been even worse.

It turned out that Tanker hadn't shown Marquis how to actually make the desserts, only how to plate them for service. Rickey and G-man didn't know how to make them either; in fact, though G-man could turn out a decent coffee cake, they didn't know how to make *any* desserts to speak of. The typical line cook tended to believe desserts were somehow unworthy of his manly skills, that the people who made them were "pastry puffs." Rickey and G-man had bought into this attitude wholesale, and now they were paying the price. Even Milford only knew how to make peach cobbler, banana pudding, and the like: good homey stuff, but not the sort of thing people wanted at a high-end restaurant.

Since running out of whatever Tanker had made, they'd been borrowing prepared desserts from Lenny's and Crescent. Of course most of these didn't carry out the liquor theme, and customers were bitching.

Karl popped his head around the edge of the dessert nook. "G? Got another applicant for the pastry job. You want to talk to her?"

"Sure, I guess. Rickey back from the doctor yet?"

"I haven't seen him."

"You got this chick's application?"

"Right here."

G-man scanned it: four years' experience, positions in several decent restaurants. He went out to talk to the applicant, a plump young white woman who said she'd grown up in Chalmette. "I see you worked at Porterhouse Charlie's, Riesling, Fourchette d'Or," he said. "You got much experience designing desserts?"

"Um, not really." The girl picked at a cuticle. "But I make a real good bread pudding. I can make it in seven flavors."

Inwardly, G-man sighed. "What else?"

"Well, let's see . . . flourless chocolate cake, pecan pie, cheesecake, crème brûlée, caramel cup custard . . . I guess those are the ones I do best."

If he had wanted to be rude, G-man could have recited the list right along with her. They were the same six desserts served in almost every restaurant in New Orleans, along with a few fancy renegades like bananas Foster and cherries jubilee. Totally traditional, and wholly inappropriate for Liquor. He talked to her for a few more minutes just to be polite, then said, "Thanks for coming in—we'll call if we can use you."

Rickey showed up half an hour later. "Everything OK?" G-man asked.

"Yeah, sure. It was kinda weird, though—Lamotte wants me to come look at that casino restaurant of his."

"You tell him no?"

"Not exactly."

G-man glanced over at Rickey, who was taking a box of phyllo pastry out of the reach-in cooler. "How come? I thought you said you were never gonna do a consulting job again."

"Well, he didn't exactly give me a *chance* to say no. He said he'd call me, get my answer in a couple days. And it wouldn't really be a consulting job—he just wants to get my opinion of the space, and maybe the preliminary menu."

"Sounds like a consulting job to me."

"You think I shouldn't do it?"

G-man considered. "I guess not necessarily. So you had a bad time in Dallas—if a horse throws you, you're supposed to get back on, right?"

Rickey grimaced at the Texan-sounding metaphor.

"Sorry. But, I mean, consulting's a nice little sideline. Look how much cash Lenny makes off it. I don't think you should automatically turn down any offer that comes your way. But I *do* think"—G-man tapped his knife handle on the counter to emphasize his point—"that clown Lamotte needs to give you some answers. What's wrong with your back? How come it still hurts? Did he take an X-ray this time?"

"He says an X-ray would be a waste of money. Says I oughtta rest it."

"Good luck with that."

"Yeah, I know. But at least I got some more pills."

G-man looked up ready to speak, even opened his mouth, then shut it again and went back to what he'd been doing. The pills scared him a little, but he knew they did something for

Rickey besides take away the back pain, and he wasn't sure he should question that. If it went on much longer, maybe he would, but not yet. Things were stressful enough right now without the two of them fighting. Rickey was a big boy. He had handled himself more or less wisely through the years of excess growing up in New Orleans, and he could handle himself now.

7

AFTER a long period of prohibition that would surely have shocked Mark Twain and his poker buddies, riverboat gambling was relegalized in Louisiana in 1991. Since then, a number of "floating casinos" had come and gone. The Pot O'Gold had been in business for about five years. Though it was lumped in with the riverboats, it was actually moored on Lake Pontchartrain. Originally all boats had been required to leave their docks and cruise several times a day. None of them wanted to, since gamblers disliked being stuck on the boat for an entire cruise and would disembark before it set sail. Because the law allowed them to remain in port if sailing conditions were dangerous, the captains came up with all sorts of creative threats to their vessels: mysterious debris in the lake, approaching hurricanes as late as Christmas, large flocks of pelicans and other, even more fearsome seabirds. Eventually the boats were allowed to drop anchor permanently. Now, except for their flashy retro-paddlewheel décor and the occasional glimpse of gray surf through a window, they were indistinguishable from land-based buildings.

Rickey left his car with the valet and entered the casino. He was immediately assaulted by a sensory blitz of noises and odors:

electronic bells, sirens, clinking coins, explosions, cigarette smoke, bad food, ancient liquor spilled on cheap, stale carpet. He'd only been in casinos once or twice before, and now he remembered why. If he had to work in this environment every day, Rickey thought he'd probably go nuts and start stabbing people with his chef's knife as they stood feeding greasy dollar bills into the slot machines.

As he wound his way through the brightly lit aisles, he took note of the poorly dressed, unhealthy-looking patrons and wondered how in hell Lamotte expected this place to support a fine-dining restaurant. Rickey was no fashion plate himself, but these people looked as if they might consider Wal-Mart a little too upscale for their tastes. He accidentally brushed the shoulder of a tiny old lady hooked up to a portable oxygen tank. "Watch it!" she snarled, shrinking closer to her Wheel of Fortune slot.

"Sorry."

Yeah, this joint definitely rubbed him the wrong way. He'd just find Lamotte, give the kitchen the once-over, and get the hell out of here. It was no place for serious food.

The weird angles and mirrors receding into infinity threw him off a bit, but eventually he found his way to the VIP bar where he was supposed to meet Lamotte. He saw the doctor sitting at a table with another man who had his back to Rickey. As Rickey approached the table, both men turned to look at him, and he saw that the second one was Clancy Fairbairn. Rickey hadn't recognized him at first because he was dressed so casually: a striped sports shirt, a baseball cap with a country-club logo pulled down over that luxuriant silver mane. He clutched his drink in his withered hand and offered the good one to Rickey. "I hope you don't mind me joining you. I had to stop by to pick up some papers and I happened to run into Frank."

This was obviously a lie—if Clancy Fairbairn needed papers

from the Pot O'Gold, he'd have them delivered by courier—and equally obvious that neither man cared whether Rickey believed it. For whatever reason, Fairbairn had wanted to be present when Rickey checked out the Pot O'Gold's would-be restaurant, and Rickey decided it didn't really matter.

"Course I don't mind. Good to see you." Now everybody was lying. All restaurateurs liked a rich customer in the abstract, but Rickey couldn't honestly say that the sight of Clancy Fairbairn ever gave him any pleasure.

"Your partner holding down the fort?"

"We're closed today." G-man was at home catching up on his backlog of TiVo'd basketball games. Rickey would have preferred to be right there on the sofa beside him, but when Lamotte had called yesterday, he'd found himself saying, "Sure, Doc, I guess I could come take a look at the place."

"Oh, right," said Fairbairn. "I forgot, since I never go out to eat on Mondays anyway. That's the night our Lainie makes her famous red beans and rice, just like her mother used to. They've been our domestics for years—almost like part of the family."

I just bet they are, Rickey thought, but all he said was, "She put sausage in 'em, or pickled pork?"

"Both."

"That's the best way, I think."

"Y'all are making me hungry," said the doctor. "Sit down, Chef. Have a drink. Honey! Hey, honey!"

This last turned out to be directed at a cocktail waitress, who hurried over to their table. "Bring us some snacky things," the doctor told her. "Not a bowl of stale nuts and pretzels, either. Real food."

"What kinda food would you like, sir? I could have the kitchen make you a sandwich, maybe a quesadilla or—"

The doctor waved a hand, cutting her off. "I said snacky things. You figure it out. And hurry up, we don't have all day."

Rickey didn't believe in coddling his wait staff. Though he tried to be more evenhanded now that he controlled both sides of the house, years of kitchen work had imbued him with the firm belief that the front of the house generally made three times as much money as the back of the house for half the work. He would take a certain amount of shit from his cooks and even his dishwashers, but none from his waiters. Once, after warning a waiter to quit chewing gum on the job and then seeing him masticating a great wad of the stuff the very next day, Rickey had smacked the back of the guy's head so hard that the gum flew out of his mouth and stuck to the opposite wall. Waiters couldn't be treated too gently or they would walk all over you, but he didn't think they should be wantonly abused, either, and he wouldn't have allowed a customer to speak to one of his staff the way Dr. Lamotte had just spoken to this cocktail waitress. But the girl only said, "I'll see what we can do, sir," took their drink orders, and walked away, a sad little rim of fat jiggling above the top of each stocking where her too-short, too-tight dress didn't quite cover the backs of her thighs.

"Hope your servers in the restaurant won't be dressed like that," Rickey said.

Lamotte shook his head. "No, no. We want this to be a classy joint. A whattayacallit, a destination restaurant." Rickey wondered which glossy food magazine he'd picked that up from. "We know locals are spoiled when it comes to restaurants. They won't come all the way out here to eat food that's a cut or two above your typical casino buffet. We want to do something special here, and we're willing to spend the money to make it happen and advertise it so locals know it's here. All we need is the right chef, somebody who can do something New Orleans has never seen before. Somebody like you."

Rickey was intrigued by the promise of money and willingness to spend it. Too many would-be restaurateurs wanted to spend the bare minimum and end up with a cash cow. People didn't realize the sheer expense of opening a restaurant: the remodeling, the supplies, the staff you had to start paying long before you ever saw a penny in sales, the ten thousand little expenses you never thought of. He and G-man could only have dreamed about doing it without Lenny's help, and of course Lenny had taken a major gamble on them. The gamble had turned out successful, but a great many restaurants failed in their first year, and even more failed to stay open for five. Liquor certainly looked as if it would hit that mark, but even when you'd won a Beard award and had a following, you never knew.

As diplomatically as he could, he said some of these things to Lamotte and Fairbairn. He felt like an ass lecturing these men about restaurant economics, but by now the waitress had brought their drinks (along with a tray of miniature quiches and taquitos Rickey supposed qualified as "snacky things"), and it helped to have a drink in his hand: the feel of the highball glass, the soft clink of the ice cubes, and the high-octane vanilla smell of the Wild Turkey were as comforting to Rickey as a blanket to a baby. He hadn't been drinking as much as usual lately, and now he felt an almost nostalgic wave of affection for liquor. Vicodin might ease his back and soothe his mind, but there was no ritual attached to it, nothing that oiled awkward social situations like this one. He finished his drink and waved to the waitress for another, giving her what he hoped was a conspiratorial, I'm-with-these-assholes-but-I'm-not-like-them smile as he pointed at his empty glass.

When Rickey was done speaking, Lamotte and Fairbairn glanced at each other and shared a little grin that made Rickey realize they either hadn't heard a word he'd said or simply didn't care. "We're quite aware of the expenses involved," Fairbairn said. "They are . . . how can I put it? . . . not an issue."

"So you wanna take a look at the space?" said Lamotte.

"I should get going," said Fairbairn. "Planned to squeeze in a workout before I went home."

That was one thing Rickey had noticed about the rich: they worked out. Their jobs didn't require any physical exertion, for the most part, so they paid good money to run and sweat and lift weights. He'd be willing to bet Fairbairn worked out at the New Orleans Athletic Club, a snooty downtown gym in an old Rampart Street mansion that still retained its hardwood floors and hand-carved fixtures. Politicians and judges exercised side by side with doctors and literary types. Former DA Jim Garrison was said to have groped teenage boys in the steam room. It was a whole different world, and an incomprehensible one to cooks whose exercise routine consisted of lifting heavy boxes, slinging sauté pans, and spending long nights on the hot line.

Rickey grinned—let 'em think it was the Wild Turkey—and said, "Sure, let's check out your restaurant."

•   •   •

Forty-five minutes later Rickey was back in the bar, sitting across from Dr. Lamotte again, sipping another drink and feeling somewhat chastened. He'd seen beautiful kitchens before. All of Lenny's kitchens were designed by world-renowned experts. He'd been in the kitchen at Commander's Palace, with its gleaming copper pots and giant kegs of housemade Worcestershire sauce. The kitchen at Liquor was no slouch either; they'd adapted it from the kitchen already in the building, but he thought they had done a pretty good job. The kitchen he'd just seen, though, topped them all. Brand-new, top-of-the-line fixtures, a special shock-absorbent rubber floor to protect cooks' aching feet, a hot line arranged in an innovative circular fashion so that everybody could see each other: everything was not just perfect, but perfect in ways Rickey had never seen before. Lamotte said it was the brainchild of a Swiss firm that specialized in every aspect of restaurant design. "Restaurant *environments,* they call it," he said, "but that's Eurospeak for you."

Rickey, who knew nothing of Eurospeak or Euro-anything else, didn't care if they called it a design, an environment, or a brick shithouse; it was simply a masterpiece among kitchens, and he felt its seductive pull. *Your feet would never hurt if you worked in me,* it seemed to whisper. *You could see every single one of your cooks as you expedited. Or you could work sauté if you liked—check out this twelve-burner flattop that can boil water in fifteen seconds.*

He knew it would never happen, and yet the seed of an idea had begun to unfurl a green shoot in his mind. Rickey wasn't a reader except of cookbooks and food magazines; if asked, he'd say his only real smarts were of the street and kitchen variety. But sometimes good ideas came to him—just popped into his head fully formed. That was how he'd gotten the idea for a restaurant whose menu revolved around liquor. He thought he might be having one of those ideas now.

"You want to give New Orleans something it doesn't have," he said. "You need to, otherwise locals won't come to a casino to eat."

Lamotte nodded. "Exactly."

"Well, what if you could give New Orleans *everything* it doesn't have, all rolled into one restaurant?"

"I'm listening."

"OK, one of the big foodie trends of the last couple years was comfort food. It's mostly bullshit—that's how we ended up with wasabi mashed potatoes and foie gras mac'n'cheese—but I think the root of it was people wanting not necessarily the food they ate as kids, but the food they thought *other* people ate. Everybody thinks home cooking is the best, but plenty of people had moms who couldn't cook at all, who just threw something in the microwave or took 'em to McDonald's. They're nostalgic for something they never had." The cocktail waitress approached their table, but Rickey shook his head; he was on a roll and didn't want to be distracted by one drink too many. "Now, that might not be the case in New Orleans, because most people here *do* cook and we think we've got the greatest food in the world. Maybe we do, maybe we don't. The truth is, we've got enough restaurants that serve New Orleans food and we don't need another one. But what if we served *everybody else's* home cooking?"

"Not sure I get you," Lamotte said, but he looked interested.

"I'm thinking of a restaurant that serves the soul food of all cultures. American, Asian, African, you name it. New Orleans is a wasteland when it comes to good ethnic food. There's a bunch of great little Vietnamese places, some pretty crappy Thai, some Chinese-American . . . and that's about it. Look at us. We call ourselves a multicultural city, we got roots in Spain, France, Africa, Italy, Ireland, Germany . . . but we don't take advantage of any of that, food-wise."

"We got Italian restaurants."

"Sure, and they're great, some of 'em, but they're *New Orleans* Italian. *Yat* Italian. I'm talking about real home cooking from Sicily, Tuscany, Rome . . . country cuisine from different regions of France . . . the food people grow up eating in Bangkok, Hong Kong, Bombay—hell, Addis Ababa. Every kinda soul food in the world. People love to try real, authentic shit. They'd go nuts for it. And here's the clincher: we call the restaurant *Soul Kitchen*."

"That's your concept, huh? You think it'd really work?"

"Absolutely."

"You think you could make all that food?"

"Oh no, not *me*." This was the risky part, but Rickey thought he could pull it off. "I already got a restaurant to run, and I don't have the training for all those different cuisines. But I know a chef who *can* do it. Milford Goodman."

Lamotte's eyes narrowed, just as Rickey had known they would. "The ex-con?"

"No—the awesome cook. The guy who can identify every ingredient in a dish just by tasting it—hell, maybe just by smelling it. The guy who can taste a dish once and re-create it without a hitch. Forget the ex-con shit. Milford had twenty years' cooking experience before all that went down. He's a roller, he's an amazing talent, and I don't believe he ever killed anything bigger than a cockroach."

"Hey, like I told you, I don't care if Jeffrey Dahmer cooks my food as long as it tastes good." Lamotte considered this for a moment. "Well, and as long as it's not Filet of Fag." He burst out laughing.

Rickey stood up. "Doc, I'm not one of these sensitive PC types, but I'm not gonna sit here and listen to fag jokes. If you're not interested in Milford, then I can't help you, so I guess I'll just—"

The doctor grabbed Rickey's arm and hauled him back down. "Sorry, sorry, I'm an idiot." He didn't sound particularly sorry, but at least he was right about one thing. Rickey fixed him with what the kitchen crew called his death stare, and Lamotte subsided a little. "I didn't mean anything. See, lots of people don't remember you're gay, because you don't have the homosexual personality type. It's a compliment."

"Yeah, like telling an educated black guy he doesn't seem black, I guess. Forget it—I didn't come here to discuss my personal life."

Lamotte nodded, and actually had enough sense to look a little ashamed of himself.

"Now look—if you like my Soul Kitchen concept, you can bill me as your executive chef and Milford as your chef de cuisine. I don't have time to design a whole menu for you, but I'll work with Milford on designing his. You'll have the best of both worlds: my name, if that's what you want, and a chef who'll really throw himself into the project."

"What if we called you the executive chef and hired somebody else to be chef de cuisine?"

"No way. If my name's going on this place, I want somebody I trust cooking the food. Milford's the only person I know who's good enough and available."

Lamotte appeared to consider the offer carefully. At last he said, "If Goodman's so great, how come you're willing to give him up?"

"Because he deserves better than we can give him," Rickey said truthfully. "There's not much room for advancement at Liquor. With me and G-man as co-chefs, we don't really need a sous chef, so nobody else can be more than a well-paid line cook. Milford's too good to stay a line cook. He was an up-and-comer before all that Top Spot shit went down, and if somebody gives him a chance to try again, they'll make a lot of money and have a great restaurant."

"And you don't think local diners would be offended if we hired him?"

"We got a couple complaints, but we got ten times as many supportive calls thanking us for giving him a fair shake. Remember, you're going for the fine-dining crowd. They're not rednecks. They're sophisticated, and if they remember Milford Goodman at all, they know he's a hell of a cook and he's been exonerated of any crime. Hell, you might even get some coverage from the national food press—'Bum-Rapped Chef Gets New Lease on Life,' that kinda thing."

"The Lamb Shank Redemption," said Lamotte, and for once Rickey found himself able to laugh at one of the doctor's awful jokes.

Driving home from the lakefront, he felt better than he had in weeks. His back didn't hurt; hell, maybe he wouldn't even need the nightly Vicodin he'd become accustomed to. He and Lamotte hadn't agreed on anything definite—Lamotte had to talk to his partners, and Rickey couldn't just give away their best line cook without consulting G-man, especially after losing Tanker—but he had a feeling that the project was going to happen. Even more surprising, he thought it could do well, which he would never have said about a casino restaurant prior to today. Not an ambitious one like this, at any rate. Casinos were mainly known for all-you-can-eat buffets. If they wanted to get fancy, they might open a steakhouse or an upscale Asian restaurant, but that was mainly the big Vegas and Mississippi Gulf Coast casinos, not the smaller, poorer New Orleans ones. Soul Kitchen was a brand-new concept, something no one here had done before. If he and Milford could make this succeed, Rickey thought, the American food world would never forget their names.

8

SEVENTY thousand *dollars?*" Rickey said.

Oscar De La Cerda nodded, munching the cheese straws Mo had set before him. They were sitting in the bar at Liquor, where dinner service wouldn't begin for a few hours. Rickey had just made fried chicken for staff meal, and most of the kitchen crew was sitting in the dining room eating it.

"Yeah—it actually sold for a little more than that, but you figure in repairs, agent's commission, my cut, all that crap, you'll net about seventy-five. Course you'll have to sign a chunk of that over to Uncle Sam, but you've still done pretty well off this whole deal."

"I'll say." Rickey's brain couldn't quite wrap itself around the figure. He routinely handled large amounts of money in connection with the restaurant, but most of that went right back into the business. He'd certainly never had possession of seventy-five thousand dollars all at once, or anything close to it.

De La Cerda was Lenny's longtime attorney. Rickey and G-man had sort of inherited him when they opened Liquor. Last year Lenny had financed his run for district attorney, when the

DA who'd been in office for a quarter-century retired, but he was beaten by a candidate known primarily for his taste in hats. "New Orleans will never elect another white DA or mayor," De La Cerda told TV news crews, cheerfully if somewhat offensively, in his concession speech. "The coroner's the last holdout, and he's getting old. Now that Placide Treat's gone, the city is totally controlled by the black elite, and I'm cool with that. Probably it's a sign of progress. Down with whitey and all that good [bleep]. Hey, it's healthy for us white folks to be a minority once in a while, see how it feels."

Privately, Rickey thought De La Cerda had lost the election not because of his race, but because he was such a slob. Right now there were cheese straw crumbs in his moustache and a stain of indeterminate origin on his tie. He was an excellent lawyer, but given a choice, New Orleans voters would always pick the guy with the sharp suit and snappy lid.

He was here today to discuss the proceeds of an estate he'd settled for Rickey. Last year, an old friend had died and left Rickey a house in Dallas. He didn't want to deal with the property at all, so De La Cerda found a Dallas real estate agent to handle it. Now, apparently, it had sold for far more than Rickey ever dared to expect.

De La Cerda stuffed more cheese straws in his mouth, then waved at Mo. "Yo, babe, you sure you made this martini with Stoli?"

"You sat there and watched me make it," the bartender told him.

"I was busy talking to Rickey. I wouldn't ask except it tastes kinda peppery."

"There's Tabasco in those cheese straws. Maybe if you quit cramming your face with them, you'd be able to taste your drink a little better." Mo turned on her heel and walked away. She always knew which of her male customers liked that sort of talk and which required more careful handling.

Rickey had known in an abstract way that the Dallas property was valuable, but he hadn't expected to net anywhere near that much. He was amazed to realize that the news stressed him out as much as it pleased him. Of course he and G-man could use such a huge windfall, but it bothered him that he hadn't earned it, that no work or sweat or talent had gone into the getting of it.

His gut knotted as he thought about how much his life had changed since he opened the restaurant. As a kid growing up in the Lower Ninth Ward, he'd known that very rich people lived in New Orleans, but they had seemed as distant and irrelevant to his existence as those fantastic African tribes with lip plates and neck rings he sometimes saw while looking at *National Geographic* in the school library. As a young, dirt-poor line cook, he'd been a little more aware of rich people, but only in an abstract, vaguely resentful way. They were like huge sharks and rays moving below the surface of dark water, something he didn't want to mess with or even know much about.

Since becoming one of the city's hot chefs, he had actually come into contact with New Orleans' wealthy elite, even gotten to know some of them. It had begun with Lenny, but Lenny was an outsider, born and raised in Portland, Maine; no matter how long he stayed here and how much New Orleanians liked him, he would never be considered a local. People like Clancy Fairbairn, though—not only did they have more money than God, but their families had been here for generations upon generations. Rex, Comus, and the other old-line krewes were just outward manifestations of how these people really viewed themselves: a form of royalty every bit as legitimate as the ruling families of Europe. No wonder they'd hated Huey Long; they didn't *want* every man to be a king. They considered themselves the kings and queens of New Orleans, and while they were willing to socialize to an extent with people who performed some glamorous-but-useful function—chefs, for instance—everyone else was supposed to know his place and stay in it.

Rickey was better off now than he'd ever expected to be, but he never expected to be rich. His and G-man's extravagances were small: good knives, tickets to Hornets and Saints games, a nice dinner out every once in a while. His new, secret dream—one he hadn't even mentioned to G-man yet—was a camp in Shell Beach, no fancier than Anthony's ramshackle little place. Just somewhere to get away from the restaurant and the city now and then, but close enough to get back within the hour in case of emergency. Before today, he had doubted that even this modest wish would ever be within his means. The rich took such things for granted—Rickey had the idea that wealthy men bought fishing camps and fancy boats the way he might go to Walgreen's and pick up a bottle of shampoo or a new blade for his safety razor—and while he was happy enough with his own life not to resent this, it did make them seem sort of like a different species.

Seventy-five thousand dollars was a long way from what the Clancy Fairbairns of the world considered serious money, but it was more than Rickey had ever had at one time before. He was unfamiliar with the vertiginous sense of panic that sometimes overtakes those who have just hit the jackpot or won the lottery, and he couldn't understand why he felt scared rather than elated. After he had shooed De La Cerda out, he went back to his office and dry-swallowed half a Vicodin. Though he had never taken one during a shift before, he'd started keeping a couple in the drawer of his desk just in case. He'd never asked himself "just in case" of what, but he guessed this qualified. Thirty minutes later, a little distressed to realize that half a Vicodin no longer had any effect on him, he took the other half.

G-man, who'd gone to drop off next week's ad copy at the local papers, returned about an hour before service. When Rickey gave him the news, his eyes grew large behind his shades. "Did you think it was gonna be that much?" he said.

"Nowhere near. It wasn't in a great area of the city, and it had all that fire damage, so I didn't want to get my hopes up. What you think we ought to do with the money?"

"Invest some, put some in a money market account," said G-man, who had a talent for figures. "If we don't touch it and let the interest build up, I bet we could buy Lenny out in another couple years."

"Good deal."

As Rickey was turning away to continue the prep work he'd been doing, G-man put a hand on his shoulder and gave him a long, searching look. Rickey bore it a little uncomfortably. At last he said, "What?"

"Are you on those pills right now?"

"Dude, I took *one*. I was freaked out about this money thing, and you know they help calm me down. I didn't—"

"Go home."

"Huh?"

"Go home. We can't have you taking that shit at work—it's too dangerous. You could cut yourself, burn yourself, God knows what. At the very least, you'd probably fuck up somebody's order."

"G, cut it out. I'm fine. I'm not going home."

"I'm sure you think you're fine, but we can't take the risk. Put your shit up and go. I'll tell the others you got a virus or something. We'll cover."

"Since when are you Mr. Clean? Seems like I remember us snorting coke off the bar at the Peychaud Grill—"

"Yeah, *after hours.* You know we didn't do that kinda stuff while we were working. Look, if you don't go home, I will. You can explain why I'm not here. I got no desire to screw you over, but I thought we had standards and I'm not gonna stand here and watch you violate them."

"Don't talk to me about standards, motherfucker. I *set* the standards around here. I decide who's fit to work and who isn't."

"Would you listen to yourself? You're the big asshole now, huh? Well, too bad, Mr. Asshole. One of us is going home, and if it's gotta be me, I hope you enjoy working shorthanded *and* fucked up."

"*I need the goddamn pills!*" Rickey shouted. "In case you forgot, I hurt my back! Besides, you liked 'em OK when I first got the prescription, when I felt better and we were having all that sex—"

"You never even want to have sex anymore! Now you can't wait to get home, take your pill, and pass out. Most times you don't even shower first—"

"Is that what this is about? You're not getting laid enough?"

Dizzy with frustration, G-man slammed the heel of his hand against the countertop. "Course that's not what it's about!"

All at once they were fighting in earnest, standing nose to nose and really screaming at each other, as they had only done a few times in all the years they'd been together. For a few terrible moments Rickey was so angry that he forgot where they were. Then he remembered and forced himself to back off, grateful that no one was nearby to hear them. "I'm not doing this here," he said.

"Fine," said G-man. "Good call, actually. We can fight all

you want later on. Right now you need to get the hell out of here and let me do my work."

"You're really serious, huh?"

"You're goddamn right I'm serious. We gotta talk about this, but I'm not trying to punish you, Rickey. I'm just not willing to let you fuck up like this. Go home."

"Nice way to celebrate us getting rich."

G-man took off his shades and looked Rickey right in the eyes. "I'll say it is."

Rickey kept standing there for a minute, but he couldn't think of anything to say to that. He wiped off the knife he'd been using, put it away, went out to the parking lot, and got in his car.

So I'm too fucked up to work, but not to drive? he thought with a sudden, gut-twisting surge of spite. *If I'm so fucked up, how come he didn't offer to drive me home? Serve him right if I had a wreck on the way!* But he knew that was useless thinking. Whether or not G-man wanted him driving, they couldn't both leave the restaurant this close to service. Anyway, he was fine; the whole thing was stupid. He'd only left because he was too angry to remain in the same room with G-man.

Viciously, Rickey jammed his key into the ignition and started the car. He was halfway home before he admitted to himself that most of his anger was due to shame. The times he'd disappointed G-man were few and far between. Crazy as it might be, G-man had always seemed to look up to him. To have G-man throw him out of the restaurant—to declare him unfit for work, as if he were some raw pantry cook who'd shown up drunk—was almost too much to bear.

·   ·   ·

G-man leaned back against the counter and ran a hand over his face, waiting for his heart to stop racing, wondering if he'd done the right thing. He'd never liked people who tried to assume the moral high ground, had left the Catholic Church because of such people, not because of a lack of belief in its basic teachings. *Judge not, lest ye be judged.* It seemed to him that most of the Church hierarchy had forgotten this directive. Now was he disregarding it too?

No, he decided, he was not. What he'd said about only doing drugs after work wasn't strictly true; there had been a few occasions when they'd smoked a joint behind the Dumpsters before service or downed a shot of Wild Turkey during a particularly hairy rush. But surely that wasn't the same as working under the influence of an actual narcotic, something that said DO NOT OPERATE HEAVY MACHINERY right on the label. Was it?

G-man realized he didn't really know all that much about the drug Rickey was taking. Until he knew more, he wouldn't be able to tell whether he'd made the right decision or was simply walking around with a giant stick up his ass. If it was the latter, then Rickey would just have to accept his apology. If the former . . . well, he didn't know what he would do next.

Tonight, at any rate, he could do nothing at all: by sending Rickey home, he had condemned the restaurant to spend the evening shorthanded and possibly in the weeds. He could only prep like a madman, ride herd on the rest of the crew, and hope for a slow night.

Thirty minutes later, as G-man was zesting lemons for his truffled arancini with citrus vodka, Karl walked into the kitchen. "Hey, G, where's Rickey?"

"He had to leave. Caught a virus—the twenty-four-hour kind, I hope."

"Aw, no, and we got all those doctors coming in."

"Doctors?"

"Yeah, some kinda retirement dinner for this old guy who used to be an Army surgeon. It's a twenty-top."

"FUCK!" yelled G-man, and just barely managed to keep from hurling the zester across the kitchen. That was the sort of thing Rickey did when he lost his temper. Of course, Rickey also kept track of the reservations, especially big parties and VIPs. G-man had always been perfectly happy to let him handle such things. Tonight, of course, he couldn't—and didn't it just have to be goddamn *doctors*?

"Are we supposed to do a special menu?"

"No, they just want to order off the regular menu."

"Great." That made things even more difficult. If a large party ordered a special, preset menu, it was easier to coordinate the dishes and get them all out at the same time. Having parties order à la carte created all sorts of problems: for instance, if some wanted fish and some wanted well-done steak, the entrées were almost certain not to be ready at the same time. This was the sort of problem any busy kitchen faced all night, every night, but large parties made it infinitely worse.

For a moment he was tempted to call Rickey, grovel a little, and ask him to come back in. Rickey would do it: even if he was really mad at G-man, he wouldn't let their personal issues jeopardize the restaurant. But he'd sent Rickey home for a reason, and he knew he had to stand by it. The increased stress of a twenty-top would only make Rickey more likely to injure himself or screw something up.

Instead of calling Rickey, G-man checked his steaks and redfish filets (the two most popular entrées; a big party was just about guaranteed to order several of each), alerted the rest of the crew to the situation, and put Milford on sauté. G-man would take Rickey's place at the expediting station by the pass, where he could control everything that went on in the kitchen. Or at least that was the idea. G-man knew how to expedite, but it wasn't one of his great strengths: he preferred the sauté station. A good sauté cook was not just a cog in a machine but the actual fulcrum of the kitchen, the supporting point without which no other part of the machine could move. He was lucky to have a rock-solid cook like Milford to provide that fulcrum, but he was going to miss providing it himself.

For the first time, G-man became aware that he was not just worried about Rickey or irritated at him, but really angry. Taking pills for the back pain was understandable. Even getting hooked on them was understandable, if the things were as addictive as G-man feared. But taking them on the job, not even for pain, but because he'd been stressed out over inheriting a lot of money? That was totally, inexcusably weak. Using a trick Rickey had taught him—or at least explained to him, since G-man wasn't usually subject to free-floating rage—G-man stepped on the anger and forced it down, compressed it into a flat layer at the bottom of his mind, something that could be dealt with later. Right now the first dinner tickets were coming in, and anger wouldn't help him.

As it turned out, nothing much would help him.

If anything, Milford was faster and steadier on sauté than G-man. If Milford really did leave to head this new casino restaurant Rickey had been talking about, G-man would hate to lose him. He stood with his feet planted solidly in front of the stove and his hands moving so fast they were almost a blur, never missing a beat or needing an order repeated. The others picked up his rhythm and worked faster than usual. It was a good showing, but it just wasn't enough. No matter how good Milford was, they needed two guys on sauté when it was this busy, and with Tanker not yet replaced there was no leeway in the crew, nobody they could call if someone got sick (or found out about an inheritance, got his panties in a wad, and took a pill that rendered him unfit to work).

Orders came in thick and fast, and all at once they were in the weeds, the state of flailing chaos that was the worst thing that could happen to a kitchen crew. Waiters came in yelling for orders that should have been ready twenty minutes ago. Dishes already promised to diners had to be 86'd. Terrance started hollering at Marquis to go get him some more motherfucking peeled garlic cloves, he didn't care if Marquis had thirty salad orders lined up, he couldn't make these here steaks until he had his motherfucking peeled garlic cloves. When Marquis went running off toward the walk-in, G-man saw that the kid was close to tears.

G-man left the expediting station and joined Milford on sauté. Every couple of minutes he would leave what he was doing to dash up to the pass, rip the new tickets out of the machine, and call out the orders to the various stations. At one point, Karl came in and said, "We got people walking out because I can't seat 'em fast enough."

"Fuck 'em," said G-man, and he meant it: if they were too tight-assed to have a drink and wait twenty minutes for a table when the place was obviously slammed, they could keep walking. "That twenty-top here yet?"

"I just seated them."

"Good." He meant that, too: at this point, the twenty-top was a known quantity, and therefore more desirable than any surprises that might trickle in. "Their food's gonna take awhile to come out no matter what they order, so buy 'em a round of drinks at some point, huh?"

"You got it."

As it happened, the arrival of the big party was the evening's turning point, the point at which things started to calm down and smooth out. When you were in the weeds, you couldn't believe that it would ever end, but it always did. It helped that the doctors ordered as predictably as G-man had expected: steak, redfish, shrimp. Only one ordered G-man's dinner special, a pan-fried softshell crab with asparagus risotto and cognac-scented morels. Hardly adventurous, but compared to what the rest of the party had eaten, it was in the stratosphere. G-man wondered if the guest of honor had ordered it. Since things were winding down and the kitchen was finally under control, he decided to go find out.

He wiped his hands, checked his jacket for stains, and grabbed a tall paper toque off a shelf—the kind of chef's hat sometimes known as a coffee filter. When Liquor opened, Rickey had intended for the cooks to wear these all the time, but they slid down, fell off, and tore when they got sweaty, and everyone had quickly grown sick of them and replaced them with bandannas or baseball caps. Now they only wore the things when going up front. Rickey didn't even wear one then, most of the time, but Rickey was comfortable making dining-room rounds. Swanning around the tables collecting compliments always made G-man feel like a huge asshole; he figured he'd be more convincing if he at least looked the part. He crammed the toque over his unruly hair, stowed his dark glasses on a shelf above the expediting station, and left the safety of the kitchen for the foreign, possibly hostile territory of the dining room.

He thought he caught a few glares as he crossed the room, but that was probably just paranoia. Diners who didn't understand the inner workings of a restaurant tended to blame their waiters when their food took forever to come out, as if maybe the

finished plates were sitting around in the kitchen while the waiters played pinochle, diddled themselves, or smoked cigarettes out
back. G-man figured this was pure instinct: when you had a problem, you wanted to blame someone you could actually see, a vis-
ible object for your frustration. A great many diners seemed to
think their food just magically appeared from behind those
swinging doors, and even the ones who understood that there
were people back there would have to be pretty foolhardy to barge
into a kitchen, with its slippery floors, open flames, and knives
close at hand.

The diners at the twenty-top had finished their desserts
(mostly banana cream pie sent over from Lenny's, since Liquor
still didn't have a pastry chef) and were sipping coffee and after-
dinner drinks. All were men, and all seemed to be talking at once
with no regard to what anyone else was saying. Only the skinny,
white-haired old guy at the head of the table was silent, listening
to everyone else with what looked like deep amusement. G-man
approached him, introduced himself, and shook his hand. "Hope
you enjoyed your meal."

"Terrific," said the man. "Best softshell crab I ever had. I'm
Benjamin Stone, by the way. Used to be *Dr.* Benjamin Stone, but
they're putting me out to pasture. This your place?"

"Mine and my partner's. More his than mine, really." G-man
felt a stab of guilt and stepped on it as he had his anger earlier.
That was turning out to be a pretty useful trick. "So I hear you
used to be an Army doctor."

"Yeah, I was a sawbones in Vietnam. Patched up kids who'd
gotten holes blown in them so they could go blow holes in other
kids."

Stone's gaunt face darkened, and G-man wondered if he'd

said the wrong thing. He attempted to save the moment by asking one of Rickey's favorite questions any time he found out somebody had visited an exotic locale: "What'd you eat there?"

The doctor grinned. "Depends on where I was. One day it might be a gourmet French meal, the next day roasted frogs in gravy—no, I'm serious, it's a specialty of the Central Highlands. And then there was the *ruou can*. Your basic rice liquor, except it also contained an extract from a grass that was a nerve toxin. Done right, it gave your lips a nice little tingle. Done wrong . . . well, I'm sitting here talking to you, so obviously I never had it done wrong."

"We could make an interesting dish with that. Come to think of it, the roasted frogs in gravy might go over pretty good too—Louisianans love us some frog legs."

"That's true, isn't it? You can probably tell I'm not from here. I've been practicing in New Orleans for twenty years, but I'm originally from Vermont."

"What's it like there?"

"Green." Stone waved a hand, dismissing Vermont. "New Orleans is my home now. This place gets in your blood."

"I guess so. It's always been in mine."

"A native son, right, I could tell by your accent. You sound like you're from Brooklyn, so I knew you must have been born and raised in New Orleans."

They laughed together, and G-man shook Stone's hand again. He seemed like a good guy. Why couldn't Rickey have found a doctor like this one rather than that oily creep Lamotte?

Back in the kitchen, a sense of gloom and foreboding came over G-man as he broke down his station. The only good thing about being in the weeds was the way it wiped all your other troubles right out of your head. Calmer now, he began to brood about the fight with Rickey. Had he overreacted? Even if he hadn't, was it worth humiliating Rickey and screwing up the entire dinner service? Half of him wanted to rush home and apologize; the other half wanted to stay here as late as possible, maybe doing the books or making next week's schedule, anything to avoid going home and dealing with whatever lay ahead. The problem was solved for him when Terrance, who'd known Rickey and G-man long enough to sense discord between them, came over and patted him on the back. "G, why'nt you go on? We can finish cleaning up."

Due to Liquor's popularity and the boozy nature of the menu, there were almost always a few taxis lined up outside the entrance. G-man climbed into one, reflecting that it would have made more sense for Rickey to take a cab and leave him the car, but nothing about today seemed to make sense. "Marengo Street just past Magazine," he told the driver.

"You the chef?" the cabbie asked. From his long nose and large, beautiful eyes, G-man thought he might be Ethiopian.

"One of 'em."

"Man, how you think of so many ways to put liquor in your recipes?"

This was a question Rickey and G-man had long since gotten sick of. There was no good answer for it, but there were plenty of flippant ones. G-man offered one now, hoping the cabbie had a sense of humor: "It's easy when you're a drunk."

The cabbie laughed. Gratefully, G-man closed his eyes and leaned back against the seat. He usually enjoyed the company of cabdrivers, deliverymen, and other working joes, but tonight he didn't feel like talking.

Marengo Street was dark and still, fragrant with the scents of sweet olive and night jasmine. He let himself into the house quietly, figuring Rickey would be asleep, drugged, or both. Sure enough, G-man could hear him snoring thickly in the bedroom. He stripped out of his sweaty work clothes, stepped into the shower, and stood for a long time with his forehead against the cool tiles, food odors rising and dissipating in the steam. Eventually he killed the water and toweled himself off. A deep, persistent ache had wrapped itself around his skull several hours ago and refused to go away. He opened the medicine cabinet to look for aspirin, and instead his eye fell upon Rickey's prescription bottle of Vicodin.

G-man took it out and turned it in his hand, reading the various warning labels: DO NOT TAKE WITH ALCOHOL. IF YOU EXPERIENCE NAUSEA, TAKE WITH FOOD OR MILK. MAY CAUSE DROWSINESS. DO NOT OPERATE MACHINERY UNTIL YOU KNOW HOW THIS MEDICATION AFFECTS YOU. Surely he'd been right not to let Rickey work under the influence of this shit. It occurred to him that now would be a good time to find out. Back in their Peychaud Grill days, they'd done just about every other drug known to man, but they'd never been into pills. He really ought to know exactly what Rickey was doing. Before he could change his mind, he popped the childproof cap, shook a big white caplet into his hand, and swallowed it with a glug of water from the toothbrush glass.

Still a little damp from his shower, G-man entered the dark bedroom and slid into the slightly stale but familiar warmth of the bed. He wrapped his arms around Rickey, molded his chest to Rickey's back and spooned with him. Whatever ugliness might pass between them, this was his man, the center of his life, and G-man would not go to sleep angry with him. Rickey stirred and made a sleepy sound in his throat. G-man half-hoped he wouldn't wake up; if he did, they might argue some more, and this was better than arguing.

"How'd it go?" Rickey asked.

"OK," said G-man. He didn't want to get into the particulars of the night, not now.

"For real?"

"Well . . . " He wasn't actually going to lie to Rickey.

"Y'all got weeded, huh?"

"A little bit," G-man admitted.

Rickey rolled over, hooked an arm around G-man's neck. "I'm sorry," he said. "It was my fault."

"Aw, I probably shouldn't have sent you home. You're a big boy. You should decide for yourself whether you're fit to work."

"Yeah, but you're right, G—I got a problem. I need to stop taking this shit."

"What about your back?"

Rickey hesitated. Even in the dark, G-man recognized the expression on his face: he was about to say something he didn't really want to say. "I don't know if I still need it for my back," he whispered, "or if I just like it."

G-man felt a surge of pride for him. It couldn't be easy to admit a thing like that. "I know it makes you feel . . . what? Calmer?"

"Calmer, quieter in my head, less pissed off. I get so tired of being pissed off all the time, G. I've always wished I could be more like you—nothing ever seems to get to you. Me, I eat my liver out every goddamn day. Or at least I used to."

"But isn't it good for you to be pissed off sometimes?"

"How do you mean?"

"Well, if you hadn't gotten pissed off at those Tequilatown chuckleheads, we probably wouldn't have a restaurant now. You get some good ideas when you're pissed off."

"Yeah, but what if I end up with an ulcer or something?"

"I don't know, dude. These pills can't be good for you either."

"They sure feel good."

They did. A deep, subtle warmth had begun to spread out from G-man's midsection and seep into his limbs. The tribulations of the evening seemed very far away. He could see how somebody would want to feel like this all the time, especially somebody like Rickey whose normal personality should bear the label WARNING: CONTENTS UNDER PRESSURE.

"The only other time I felt that good was when we went fishing down in Shell Beach. It was like I didn't have a care in the world. That's how the Vicodin makes me feel."

"We'll go back there soon," G-man promised. He put a hand on the side of Rickey's face and tilted it up, kissed him lingeringly. Rickey's arm tightened around his neck. They were so good together, always had been. "I'll help you any way I can," G-man said. "You know I'd do anything for you, Rickey."

"I know it," Rickey said a little huskily. "You must think I'm a prime asshole, though."

"Course I don't think you're an asshole. You hurt yourself and you thought those pills would make you better. Anybody's an asshole, it's Lamotte."

"Aw, no, he was just trying to help—"

"He's an asshole. I know you gotta work with him, I know it's a great opportunity for Milford, but I don't trust the guy. If your back keeps hurting, I wish you'd go see somebody else."

"I will," Rickey promised. "On one condition."

"What?"

"Gimme another kiss like that one you gave me a minute ago."

G-man did. Then he gave him another, and then another after that.

Later, as they were falling asleep, Rickey said something that G-man didn't quite catch. "Huh?"

"What are we gonna do with all that money?"

Incredibly, G-man had almost forgotten about Rickey's inheritance, the fuel that had started today's fire. "Save it, I guess," he said. "Let the interest build up so we can buy Lenny out."

"I guess."

"Why, you got some other idea?"

"Nah." Rickey was silent for a few minutes, and G-man thought he had fallen asleep. Then he said, "Hey, listen, thanks for kicking me out today. I would've been fine to work, but I needed the wake-up call."

"No problem," said G-man. He wondered, though, whether it would be the only wake-up call Rickey needed. He had enormous respect—awe, almost—for Rickey's sheer force of will, but he could tell just from taking one pill that this drug could really get its hooks in a person. Safe in bed, sated with sex and comfort, Rickey might have every intention of quitting. But what would happen the next time his back really started aching, or a purveyor didn't deliver the seafood order until half an hour before dinner started, or . . . ?

That was pointless thinking. When those things happened, Rickey would deal with them, and G-man would help him. For now, with Rickey's arms around him and Rickey's breath warm on the back of his neck—not to mention the last traces of the Vicodin high still caressing his tired muscles—he simply let himself sleep.

9

MILFORD wondered later whether the conversation and the events it prompted would have happened at all if his sister hadn't just come from church. She wasn't usually one to get all up in other people's business, but that day she was full of hellfire and shalt-nots and sundry other words of the Lord. She'd dragged Milford to the First Zion Holy Sword Baptist Church a couple of times right after he got out of prison. Despite its grand name, it was just a little bitty storefront off Claiborne Avenue, set at one end of a litter-strewn parking lot, always stuffy because the two ancient window units were no match for seventy or eighty people hollering and praising Jesus and occasionally falling on the floor. The preacher was a firebrand, though, a former Freedom Rider who had his eye on a city council seat. Milford guessed the man's message had gotten to Eleonora today.

He was getting ready for work when she came home, standing in the kitchen in his check pants and a T-shirt, ironing his white jacket on the card table where Eleonora's family ate their meals, wrote out their homework, sewed, folded laundry, and did just about everything else that required a flat surface. The apartment was small and narrow, half of a Section 8 shotgun double that had been badly renovated sometime in the sixties: cheap cracked linoleum that never looked clean no matter how much you scrubbed it, window frames pulling away from the wall, an endless supply of that mysterious gray-brown dust that got all over everything in New Orleans—the dust of old buildings and vacant lots, of falling plaster, of age. Between Eleonora, her four kids, and her sometime boyfriend, there wasn't much room in the apartment, and even less with Milford here.

Rickey had told him three or four times that he didn't have to iron his jackets. Rickey didn't, G-man didn't, nobody else in the kitchen did as far as he could tell. Milford still couldn't break the habit. He'd always ironed his jackets before Angola, and he supposed he'd keep doing it as long as he had access to an iron. He just didn't like wrinkles.

"You goin to work?" she said—unnecessarily, it seemed to Milford.

"In a little while. Soon's I get this here jacket pressed."

"You really gonna keep workin for them people?"

Milford's hands stopped moving. He set the iron aside carefully, making sure that no part of it touched the clean white fabric of his jacket. "What you mean?"

"Reverend Charles told me somethin about them people."

"Told you what, Elly?"

"I think you know what I mean." Now he could see that she was working herself up to throw a fit. She'd been like this since they were kids, she the elder by two years: she'd start out soft and end up howling. "Don't know how you could work around such a thing all this time and not even mention it."

"You talkin about Rickey and G-man?"

"Whatever their names are. Them two men. If you want to call them men."

"Aw, dammit, Elly, that ain't none of your business or mine. You know they's old friends of mine and they give me work when nobody else wanted to hear about me. Now Rickey got this idea to make me head chef of a big casino restaurant. You mean to tell me I should walk away from that cause of what they do in the privacy of they own home?"

In truth, Milford hadn't been crazy about homosexuals himself when he met Rickey and G-man all those years ago. It wasn't a religious thing with him, just a matter of distaste: he didn't like to think about two men getting it on together. His time in prison had softened his stance somewhat—though he'd avoided both the punks and the bull queens, he had seen less rape than he'd expected, and more genuine love relationships—but he still didn't care to imagine such matters. The thing was, though, by the time he realized they weren't just roommates, he couldn't think of them in the abstract, as "homosexuals"—they were just Rickey and G-man, guys he worked with every day, strong cooks who could keep their shit together during a rush, talented cooks with a curiosity about food Milford had seen too seldom in his career.

He tried to say as much to Eleonora, but she was having none of it; she only set her mouth in the stubborn line he knew so well and said, "It's dirty. You could even catch somethin, bring it home to the kids."

Milford looked at her: a forty-six-year-old woman with a kind face, tired from her job supervising the housekeeping team at a downtown hotel, not fat but well-padded, dressed in a gold-trimmed white skirt suit with matching hat and shoes. Her church clothes. He had known her all his life, knew she wasn't a bad person, but he could hardly believe what had just come out of her mouth. "Now that's a silly-assed damn thing to say. What you think, they down in the clubs on Bourbon Street? They ain't no different from a married couple—"

"*That's a lie!*" she hollered. "I know they tryin to change the law to say that, but that don't make it so. A married couple can't be nothin but a man and a woman."

"Yeah, and not so long ago it couldn't be nothin but a white man and a white woman, or a black man and a black woman."

"Ain't the same thing. They ain't been through the same things we did. Two men callin theyselves married, you might as well let somebody marry a dog or a horse if they got a mind to do so."

"Elly, that's just nasty."

"Well, so's this!" She approached him, took his hand. Milford was tempted to pull it away, but she was still his sister and she'd taken him in when no one else would. "Honey, I know you workin hard and trying to do right. But I can't let you stay here if you gonna keep workin with them people."

Simple loyalty to Rickey and G-man wouldn't have been enough to push Milford to a decision, but the Soul Kitchen gig was simply too good to pass up. If he didn't do it, he might never get another chance to be a head chef in New Orleans. "What we still conversatin for?" he said. "You want me to move out, I'll move out."

It was a decision Eleonora clearly hadn't expected. In her eyes he could see her totting up the meals he cooked, the money he paid toward the rent, the reassurance of having a man around when her boyfriend made himself scarce. She'd never been one to back down, though. "Well," she said, "I guess you will."

"When you want me gone, Elly?"

"I ain't gonna put you on the street. You can let me know when you find a place."

"I'll be out by the end of this week."

"I wish you'd reconsider."

The only thing I might reconsider is how I feel about my sister, he thought, but didn't say it. If he'd ever been in a position to judge anybody, he surely wasn't now. The world had slapped him down plenty of times, and someday it would probably slap Eleonora down. For now, he could only keep on making the best food he was capable of, and Rickey was the only person interested in giving him a chance to do that.

"My mind's made up," he said, quietly and without rancor. "We done here? I gotta get to work."

"I guess we are."

He turned off the iron and picked up his jacket. As he headed for the door, Eleonora said, "Milford?"

He turned and looked at her.

"They *ain't* been through the same things we have," she said. It seemed she was speaking with an effort now, as if the words hurt her but she had to say them. "Nobody siccin dogs on 'em. Nobody tryin to hang they daddies from a oak tree cause they wanted to go to a good school. It ain't the same thing, and it cheapens our struggle when folks say it is."

"That how we measure people now?" Milford said. "Only treat 'em right if they suffered as much as we done?"

Her mouth thinned to nothing at all, and he knew she was done talking to him. He buttoned up his jacket and went to catch the bus to work.

●   ●   ●

Rickey was making groceries in the big Sav-A-Center on Tchoupi-toulas. He was halfway through his second week off Vicodin and sore as hell. G-man had offered to do the shopping, but Rickey thought it would do him good to get out of the house. Now that he was actually here, he wasn't so sure. All the new products seemed to be getting on his nerves. He hadn't been to the store for months and had nearly forgotten how much stupid food was out there. Precooked pasta slithering around in a vacuum pack for people too lazy to boil water. "No-carb" versions of products that had never contained carbohydrates. Frozen hamburgers, bun and all. Going to the store reminded him how badly most people ate, and he was in no mood for that.

In his line of work, Rickey occasionally encountered people who liked to tell him "I don't care what I eat!" as if that were something to be proud of. He regarded these people with a sort of puzzled contempt—how could you not care about something that kept you alive and had the potential to provide so much pleasure?—but he had always comforted himself by assuming they weren't from New Orleans, where *everyone* cared about food. Scanning the stores of a big supermarket made him think maybe such people existed here after all. Otherwise, who was buying all this garbage?

"Cute," he muttered, fingering a jar of concentrated soup stock with a plastic top fashioned to look like a chef's toque. "Use this shit, you're automatically a chef, I guess."

"Hey, everybody's a chef these days," said a familiar voice. "Not like it's hard or anything, right? Just stack some crap on a plate, garnish it with a sprig of herbs, bam, you're a chef."

Rickey turned and saw Tanker pushing a cart full of TV dinners, instant macaroni and cheese, and Tater Tots. Registering the horror on Rickey's face, Tanker said, "Aw, you know how it is. I don't have time to cook at home."

"I heard you was working at the Polonius Room. What, they're too cheap to give you staff meal at that fancy joint?"

"We get staff meal, but it's usually not too good. Chef lets the pantry bitches make it most of the time. Job's great otherwise, though. I'm really learning a lot."

"Yeah? Like what?"

"Well, gelees and . . . " Tanker appeared to stop and think. "Lots of gelees. Oh, and yesterday I made an aspic."

"Tanker, an aspic is the same thing as a gelee."

"Not in Jaap Noteboom's kitchen it isn't. There's a world of difference—he could tell you about it for hours. An aspic's firmer, for one thing. Anyway, it's a great place to work. I'm real happy there."

"Well, that's good."

"How's things at Liquor?"

"Oh, great, great. We just hired a new line cook." The kid was twenty-two and almost completely clueless, but Rickey had been ready to hire anyone who knew how to sauté. Milford would start testing recipes for Soul Kitchen in another couple of weeks, and they'd be up a creek if they hadn't trained a new cook by then. "I'm opening another place too, you heard?"

"Nuh-uh."

Rickey explained about Soul Kitchen, making sure to stress the gorgeous kitchen and the amount of money Clancy Fairbairn, Dr. Lamotte, and company were pouring into the place. Tanker just raised an eyebrow—a talent Rickey had always found annoying—and said, "You really think people will come to a casino for fine dining?"

"Maybe not for classic fine dining, but this concept is different. People like the idea of international soul food. Besides, we plan to turn it into a destination restaurant."

"What's that really mean, though, Rickey? A destination is just a place people go. If people don't go to your restaurant, you're out of business. By definition, almost any restaurant that stays open longer than a couple months is a destination restaurant."

"No it's not! It's not, Tanker." In his zeal to defend Soul Kitchen, Rickey forgot how much the term "destination restaurant" had irked him the first time Dr. Lamotte used it. "See, in *professional* terms, a destination restaurant is someplace people will go out of their way to eat at, someplace they might not normally go if the restaurant wasn't something special."

Tanker raised the other eyebrow.

"Well, anyway," Rickey said, shoving his fists into his pockets in an effort to curb his impulses, "I think it's a good idea and it's gonna be a great chance for Milford. Bring him back into the New Orleans dining scene, make people start thinking of him as a top chef again, not that guy who got sent up the river for killing his boss."

"Yeah, well, I hope it works out. So . . . uh . . . what kinda desserts y'all doing now? You still using my recipes, or is your new chef doing other stuff?"

"Oh, you know. A little of this, a little of that." They still hadn't found a candidate for the job who could make anything other than bread pudding, cheesecake, crème brûlée, pecan pie, and flourless chocolate cake.

"Y'all *do* have a new pastry chef, don't you?"

"Well," Rickey said. "I mean, sure, we're all right."

"You don't need anybody, huh?"

Was Tanker hinting that he wanted to come back? Rickey would rehire him in a second, but he wasn't going to be the one to suggest it. "What's the matter? They don't let you make desserts at the Polonius Room?"

"Oh, sure, I get to make desserts. I'm garde-manger, so I don't get to do them a whole lot, but I've done some. It's just that the pastry chef's kinda temperamental, and she doesn't really like anybody stepping on her toes."

"That's tough."

"Yeah."

For a long moment they both stood scanning the shelves as if the thread of their conversation might have been lost among the soup cans and gravy packets. Finally Rickey said, "You working tonight?" .

"Yeah," Tanker sighed, and surely the haunted look that came into his eyes must be Rickey's imagination. The job couldn't be *that* bad.

"Well . . . have a good one, man. Glad I ran into you."

"Yeah, it was great to see you, Rickey."

"Yeah, great."

Tanker disappeared around the end of the aisle. Rickey stood there for a minute thinking about the conversation. He wondered if he could question Mo, find out if Tanker really hated the job. If he did, maybe there would be a way to lure him back without losing too much face. Rickey had his pride—maybe a little too much of it sometimes—but he cared more about his restaurant than he did for any stupid pissing contest, and customers had been complaining about the disappearance of Tanker's excellent desserts.

Desserts! What a stupid thing to have to worry about when there were far more important matters afoot. The meeting tomorrow morning, for instance; he and Milford were meeting Dr. Lamotte to talk about advertising. Lamotte would probably ask him how his back was doing, maybe offer a refill of his prescription, and Rickey would have to find it in himself to say no. He snarled, half in pain and half in disgust, and moved on down the aisle in the opposite direction from the way Tanker had gone.

• • •

Tanker hurried through the rest of his shopping and managed to leave the store without seeing Rickey again, which felt like a minor miracle. No matter how vast a modern New Orleans supermarket might be, it always seemed that if you ran into somebody you didn't want to see, you were just about guaranteed to cross paths with them two or three more times before you got out of the place. Probably end up behind them in the checkout lane too.

He was especially chagrined that Rickey had seen his junk-food stash. Tanker had a deep, passionate interest in fine food and enjoyed eating it as well as cooking it, but at the end of a long night, he often wanted nothing more than a Hungry Man Salisbury Steak dinner. He knew it was crap, but there was something comforting about its crappiness.

Had Rickey intuited that things weren't going well at the Polonius Room? Tanker hoped not. Jaap had recently released a Chef's Mission Statement, which he handed out to all the cooks and had printed on the backs of the menus:

This menu is lighter than a soap bubble
and heavier than lead.

It is crunchy liquid, frozen heat,
deep analysis, and blind faith.

It is the product of a lifetime and it is
being born at this very moment.

It is unlike any other food you will eat in New Orleans,
yet it captures the essence of New Orleans
as perfectly as any menu you will find.

"It captures the essence of New Orleans as perfectly as my black ass," one of the line cooks had commented.

"I dunno, man," Tanker told him. "I think your black ass probably has a lot more New Orleans essence than this menu."

A couple of weeks ago, buoyed by having a strong cook like Tanker around, Jaap had really begun branching out. He bought a laser printer that could transfer soy-ink images onto edible rice paper, which could then be applied to the food. This resulted in "edible menus" featuring pictures of dishes on crackers that were served before the actual dishes. He had created a battery-powered, multichambered atomizer that sat in the middle of the table, periodically puffing out aromas that he claimed would enhance the diners' enjoyment of their meals, and was now experimenting with injectable helium to make certain dishes float right off the plate. Tanker wasn't necessarily opposed to avant-garde cuisine, even when it got as goofy as this; the problem was that Jaap took it—and himself—so damn seriously. He found himself missing the camaraderie of Liquor, the foul-mouthed, good-natured banter, the sense that every cook in the kitchen was contributing to a better menu. At the Polonius Room, everything was about executing Jaap's ideas, building Jaap's reputation, tasting Jaap's genius. For all its craziness, the Polonius Room wasn't much fun.

He drove to his and Mo's house on Telemachus Street near Canal. As he was unloading the groceries, a bum he sometimes saw around the neighborhood walked by, spied him, and started pawing at his sleeve. "Hey man. Hey man. Lemme talktya a second. I's in the war, see, and—"

"I got no money. Get the fuck outta here."

The bum drew himself up with an air of injured dignity. "Well, ya don't gotta be *mean* about it!"

As the man walked off toward Canal, leaving only a faint aroma of sour beer behind him, Tanker recognized the truth of those words. He *was* getting mean. He'd snapped at Mo yesterday, something he never did, and yelled at one of the pantry cooks for forgetting to put up the aioli. The goddamn job was getting to him. And, joy of joys, he had to be there in just under two hours.

Tanker fixed himself some instant Kraft macaroni and ate it in a hurry, changed into his whites, and trudged up toward Canal to catch the streetcar. The hotel charged employees to park in their lot, so it was easier to just leave early and take the slow-assed rattletrap that passed for public transportation. He could scarcely believe how much joy had gone out of his life since he'd left Liquor. Damn Rickey anyway.

· · ·

The week after the argument with his sister, Milford found a residential hotel room in one of Uptown's shabbier neighborhoods. It wasn't clean or comfortable, but it would do for now. He'd upgrade later, when the big casino cheeses put him on salary. Just now he had to prioritize his expenses. Without his sister driving him to work, he needed a car, and he'd bought a 1984 Oldsmobile Cutlass Supreme. Its tires were bald, its air-conditioning was balky, and its dashboard was such a horror of cigarette burns that it appeared to be sculpted out of soft chocolate, but it was the first car he had owned in a dozen years and he named it Irma.

He lugged his few possessions up two flights of uriniferous stairs and set them on the scarred table, on the rickety shelf, and on the floor around the narrow bed. There wasn't a shortage of room. His family had sold or given away most of his things when he'd gone to prison. He missed his cookbooks, but didn't really need them. As usual, he had only to think a little while about a dish to make it take complete shape in his head.

The lack of space and possessions didn't matter: in a place like this you ran a constant risk of getting ripped off anyway, and he would be spending most of his time at the restaurant. The only thing that really bothered him was not being able to press his jackets. He'd have to pick up a cheap iron somewhere.

Despite his willingness to leave his sister's house in order to keep working with Rickey, Milford did have his qualms about the job. He'd defended Rickey and G-man to Eleonora because he believed in their right to live as they pleased; ten years under lock and key had taught him the importance of that right. The trouble was that he had begun to realize he didn't really *like* Rickey all that much. A couple of times in his life he'd accidentally bitten into a piece of tinfoil while eating a sandwich, and being around Rickey gave him that same shuddery, nerve-ridden feeling. Something had happened to Rickey since his days as a line cook at Reilly's; he'd come a long way and learned a great deal, but he had also turned into a kind of human flame that threatened to sear the people who spent too much time around him. It wasn't anything he did so much as just an atmosphere he gave off, a jangling, teeth-gritting intensity. Milford didn't know how G-man stood it.

This realization made him feel deeply ungrateful, because he knew he mightn't even be working right now if not for Rickey. Certainly he wouldn't have been hired for a head chef job. Then he got mad at himself for feeling ungrateful. Rickey hadn't hired him out of charity, but because he was a damn good cook. Why should he feel grateful?

But Rickey had kept him on after the parking lot fire. Not everybody would have done that, even for a damn good cook.

But it wasn't Milford's fault what race-baiting idiots did, so why should he be held responsible?

He couldn't shake this confusing jumble of feelings, so he tried to ignore them. Over the years he'd learned to ignore much worse. He liked working with G-man and the others, and he could deal with Rickey.

Altogether, the Soul Kitchen deal was so good for him that Milford decided to continue with the project even when he found out about Clancy Fairbairn's involvement. He feared this would end up being a terrible mistake, but he wasn't sure what choice he had.

Besides, Fairbairn went where he liked and did what he wanted. He had done so at the Top Spot, and he had been doing so ever since.

10

LENNY Duveteaux had an idea that things were going wrong at Liquor, but he knew he couldn't ask the boys directly: Rickey would get mad and deny it, and G-man would just deny it. Instead he invented an excuse to drop by on a Saturday afternoon, not long before service. On Saturday, any restaurant should have its strongest crew working, its best specials running, and its general shit together.

As he walked into the foyer, Karl was just inserting freshly printed menus into their leather folders. "Rickey around?" Lenny said, picking one up and scanning it. Tonight's entrée specials were vermouth shrimp gratin, veal with crawfish-cognac sauce, and trout amaretto, Rickey's boozed-up version of trout amandine. Lenny couldn't remember seeing a less inspired menu in the three years Liquor had been open. When you worked with another chef or even just paid close attention to his food, you learned his patterns, his strengths and weaknesses. This easy-ass old-school splooge was the kind of food Rickey resorted to when he was feeling insecure or otherwise put-upon. Usually G-man balanced it out with a more adventurous dish or two. These didn't always work, but they were an antidote to Rickey's relentlessly rich Creole fare. Tonight, though, G-man seemed to have made no additions to the menu.

"He's back there somewhere," said Karl. "Just listen for the cussing."

"Something wrong?"

"Business as usual lately."

Lenny walked through the dining room, along the pass, and pushed through the swinging doors into the kitchen. He saw Terrance trimming fat off pork chops and a kid he didn't know sautéing something. Catching sight of Lenny, the kid lifted the pan off the heat and attempted the circular wrist movement hotshot cooks use to stir their ingredients without a utensil. Ideally, the ingredients fly up and fall back into the pan. In this case, the ingredients—it looked like potatoes and kale—rained down all over the stovetop.

Lenny gave the kid a hard stare as he walked on through the kitchen. The walk-in cooler was open, and Lenny glanced in to see if Rickey was in there. He wasn't, but G-man was, rummaging through boxes and looking harried.

"How's it going?" Lenny asked.

G-man shrugged. "Great, if you like having half your produce order not show up. Course, the way things been going, I can't actually be sure anybody called the shit in."

"That bad, huh?"

"Aw, Christ . . . " G-man rubbed a hand over his eyes, then lowered himself onto an upturned crate. His shoulders sagged. "You ever went through a stage where you just wanted to dump it all and go sit on a beach somewhere?"

"About once a year."

"Seriously?"

"Yeah, of course I have. It's a natural part of the business.

You've got to realize, G, you guys have had it easy in a lot of ways. I know you've worked your asses off, but you've also had me smoothing the way. You got great reviews and a lot of pub right off the bat. And then there was the Beard award. You didn't have the rough times early on like a lot of restaurant owners do. Could be you're just due for some."

"Maybe." G-man shook his head slowly. "Sure doesn't make it any easier to take, though."

"What's the problem? Is something going on with Rickey?"

"Nah, nah, nothing like that. Rickey's fine. We just lost some key people and haven't really replaced 'em yet. It's not Rickey's fault."

Lenny had known he would say that, no matter what the truth was. "You don't have a problem with him opening this new place when you guys are so understaffed?"

"Not at all." G-man raised his head and tried to smile. The effect was a little ghastly. "I think Soul Kitchen's a great idea and a great opportunity for Milford. We're gonna be fine."

"Well," Lenny said carefully. He'd never seen G-man in a mood quite like this. "Anyway, uh, is Rickey around?"

"Go look in the dessert nook."

"The—"

"I don't want to talk about it. That's where he is."

Lenny left looking puzzled, and G-man went back to searching through the boxes, hoping against hope that his fresh chervil and mixed microgreens would turn up. If not, they were going to be sending out a lot of naked-looking appetizer plates tonight.

· · ·

Sure enough, Rickey was in the dessert nook at the far end of the kitchen. Lenny had missed him when he'd walked through earlier, probably because he'd never seen Rickey there before. He didn't look as if he belonged there now. He was surrounded by cookbooks, his jacket was covered with sticky stains, there was a smear of chocolate across his cheekbone, and his eyes had a thousand-yard stare.

"What are you doing?" said Lenny.

"What the fuck does it look like?" Rickey indicated a row of lopsided chocolate orbs on a sheet pan. "I'm learning how to make desserts. We can't find a decent pastry chef, so I'm gonna train Marquis to do it. First I gotta figure it out myself."

"I thought you didn't care about desserts."

"I never did, but diners been complaining that ours aren't as good as they used to be, and I remembered something Tanker said to me one time when I was ragging on pastry puffs: 'Either the whole meal matters or none of it matters.' And you know what, the asshole was right. We can't keep serving people great apps and entrées and following them up with crappy desserts. Looks like nobody's gonna come along and fix the problem for me, so I gotta do it. As usual."

"Welcome to the restaurant business."

"Yeah."

Lenny pointed at the chocolate orbs. "What are those?"

"Rum truffles. It says to freeze 'em, then bake 'em inside a chocolate soufflé. They won't melt all the way, but they'll get soft and runny. Then you pour caramel sauce over the goddamn shit." Rickey shook his head. "It's nothing I'd want to eat, but I figure people order all those fucking molten chocolate cakes, this'll be a nice twist."

Karl had been right, Lenny reflected. Rickey was always pretty foul-mouthed, but today he was really over the top. Lenny could sympathize; a head chef being forced to do desserts was something like a star quarterback suddenly being demoted to free safety.

"Wanna try one?"

Lenny plucked an orb from the sheet pan and put it in his mouth. The rum flavor was strong enough to make his eyes water. "Man," he said, "you really liquored them up, didn't you?"

"Yeah, the amount of rum in the recipe seemed kinda low, so I tripled it. Think that'll keep 'em from freezing?"

"Hell if I know. I'm no pastry puff."

"Me either." Rickey stepped away from the dessert counter, put his fists in the small of his back, and stretched. "Aw, goddammit. God fucking dammit!"

"What now?"

"Nothing."

"Did you hurt yourself?"

"Yeah, a couple months ago, but it's fine now. I just had a twinge."

"You don't want to fool with back problems, Rickey. You should see a doctor."

Rickey gave Lenny such a black look that Lenny almost took a step backward. He hadn't gotten where he was today by backing down from little punks in bad moods, though, so he stood his ground and attempted to change the subject. "What's up with this new place? Soul Kitchen, is it?"

"Yeah." Rickey appeared to perk up a little. "I think it's gonna be a blast. Milford's real excited and the backers are throwing stupid money at it. Looks like we might be able to open by early fall."

"Not spreading yourself too thin, are you?"

He figured that would piss Rickey off, but Rickey appeared

to give the question serious thought. "I don't think so. We got the slow summer season to get through. By the time Soul Kitchen opens, we'll have our new cooks trained here, and Milford will have things under control there—he won't need me around much. I think it's gonna be fine."

"What does G-man think?"

"He's cool with it." Rickey glanced at Lenny. "Why? He told you something different?"

"No, of course not. You know he wouldn't talk to me behind your back. Hell, G-man's never really trusted me anyway."

"I don't mean that. It's just . . . " Rickey pushed the bandanna up on his forehead and added a smear of chocolate there to the one gracing his cheekbone. "I don't know. He keeps telling me, yeah, go for it, consulting's a great gig, I can handle things here, you gotta make us some extra money and help out Milford. Most of the time I even believe him. But once in a while I feel like there's something he's not telling me, and that's never happened to us before."

"Something he's not telling you? Like he's keeping a secret?"

"No, nothing like that. Just . . . it's like he wishes I wouldn't do this casino thing, but he won't admit it."

Lenny shrugged. He had never been in a long-term relationship; he enjoyed the company of strippers and was uninterested in answering to anyone about his late hours or single-minded commitment to his restaurants. This kind of talk was foreign to him. "Business is business," he told Rickey. "If he's got something to say, he'll eventually come out and say it. Until then, you need to go full speed ahead with your plans and not let anyone or anything get in your way."

"That's what you always did, huh?"

"Precisely, and I've never regretted it."

"You ever have times when the pressure built up, you found yourself maybe drinking a little too much or something?"

"Rickey, you know what I admire most about you? You're tough, you're stubborn, and you've got a self-preservation instinct ten miles wide. Those are the reasons I was willing to invest in you, and those are the reasons I know you'll beat whatever problems you run into. You're not going to turn into a drunk or a cokehead, because it would interfere with your ability to do your job right. And I know you're going to do your job right, if for no other reason than you wouldn't be able to stand the things people would say about you if you fucked up."

Rickey looked alarmed. "What people?"

"Come on, Rickey, don't be naïve. You must know how many people in this town would love to see you go belly-up. It's not even that they have anything personal against you—although I guess they might; you can be kind of an asshole—it's just that you're young, you're good-looking, you've gotten an incredible amount of hype. People are jealous. That's their nature. The same people who suck up to you today, if you went out of business tomorrow, they'd say, 'Oh, I saw it coming, he wasn't as good as he used to be.' I've been there. I know what I'm talking about."

"Well, I don't think like that, OK, Lenny? I don't give a fuck what people say. I mean, I don't love it when people talk shit about me, but I don't run my life around it either. The reason I don't fuck up is because I'm *not a fuckup*. The reason I keep making great food is because great food is worth making. You got that?"

"I got it," Lenny said. "It's what I like to hear."

"Well, good."

"So maybe you should make some of that great food instead of fucking shrimp gratin and trout amandine."

"*Not you too!*" Rickey yelled. "I knew you been talking to G! Listen, goddammit, there's nothing wrong with that food, it's classic, it tastes good—"

"Yeah, and you could make it in your sleep."

"What are you talking about? You serve the same kinda shit at Lenny's!"

"Yeah, I do, but that's what people come to Lenny's for. It's not why they come to Liquor. Your diners expect something a little wild, a little adventurous. They don't want—what do you always call it?—Creole splooge."

"They been ordering it," Rickey said sullenly.

"Yeah, sure, you can always sell that stuff in New Orleans, plus you're putting a twist on it with the liquor. You keep it up, though, you're going to lose your reputation as an interesting restaurant, a place people can go when they want something different. Word will get out that you've been Creolized."

"Lenny, we signed a contract, remember? I can show you a copy. It says you don't have any creative control over Liquor's menu. None. Zip. G and I make the decisions."

"I know that." Lenny raised his hands in a placatory gesture. "I'm not talking to you as Mr. Big Shit Investor, Rickey. I'm talking to you as a friend. A friend who's been in the local restaurant business for a long time and maybe knows a little something about how it works."

Rickey glared at him for a moment longer, then sighed and looked away. "OK, OK, I hear you. Things haven't been easy lately. Maybe I'm in a little bit of a rut. But pretty soon I'll be spending more time over at the casino with Milford, and G will have to take over the specials. I'm sure he'll do some wild shit. I mean, not outer-space wild like the stuff Tanker did when we went out of town, but wilder than what we got on now."

"And that's another thing. What if I were to talk to Tanker, find out if he's happy at the Polonius Room, see if maybe he wants to come back? He was always such a key part of this kitchen."

Rickey pointed a chocolate-smudged finger at Lenny. "Don't you dare. If I decide I want to talk to him, I'll talk to him. I told you, I don't need you handling my business for me."

"I understand," Lenny said, making a mental note to call Tanker.

"Look, I gotta get back to work on these stupid-ass desserts. Don't you have some Creole splooge to cook? Or do you just hang around bothering people these days?"

"Boy, you're in a lovely mood."

"You would be too if you had to demote yourself to pastry puff."

"You're probably right," Lenny said. "In fact, I'm sure you're right."

·   ·   ·

Late that night, long after the restaurant was closed and G-man was asleep, Rickey stepped out onto the front porch. He had tossed and thrashed for what felt like hours, then finally extricated himself from the sweat-soaked bedclothes. He turned on the TV, but nothing caught his interest. He tried the radio, but turned it off when he realized he'd just spent ten minutes listening to the religious guy on WWL enumerate all the reasons he was going to hell. When he found himself in the bathroom staring at the mirrored door of the medicine cabinet—willing himself not to open it—he knew he had to leave the house entirely, if just for a few minutes.

Marengo Street was dark and still. Rickey remembered how,

in childhood, the hush of a late-night city street had made him feel as if all the world was waiting for something to happen. Now the idea seemed as foreign as the memory of a time without physical pain. Nothing was going to happen. The pain wasn't going to go away. He wondered what he had been waiting for.

Christ, this wasn't him, this weak, whining crybaby. He didn't know himself these days. He remembered Lenny telling him, *You're tough, you're stubborn, and you've got a self-preservation instinct ten miles wide . . . you're not going to turn into a drunk or a cokehead, because it would interfere with your ability to do your job right.* When they'd started working with Lenny, they had considered him kind of a joke, a soft-handed celebrity chef who hardly knew his way around a kitchen anymore. "Hell," Rickey remembered saying, "the hair on his arms isn't even burnt off." That was a long way from reality, Rickey knew now. He wanted to be independent of Lenny someday, but he'd learned more from Lenny than from anyone else he'd ever known. Lenny had no idea how much Rickey admired him, and Rickey wouldn't want him to know.

Those words tonight, though, made Rickey feel as if Lenny didn't know him at all. How tough was he these days, and how self-preserving? The damn drug had gotten on top of him. Even now, when he hadn't taken any for two weeks, it was all he could think about.

His back hurt most of the time. When faced with the low, constant throb, a wide array of over-the-counter painkillers had laughed weakly, laid down, and died. Even more than an end to that, though, he craved the slow spreading warmth in his belly and his mind, the feeling that was like being cradled in the hand of God, though he had never believed in God. The pills had given him a vacation from his own constant, grinding rage. In his heart he knew he needed the rage, but it had been nice not to be at its mercy all the time.

He walked out into the middle of the street and craned his neck, looking for stars. The lacework of the summer trees and the ambient pale purple glow of the city hid most of them, but a few glittered directly overhead, farther away than he could imagine. Though he knew they were made of gas and fire, it seemed to him that they must be cold. How many miles? How many years of pain and gnawing at his own heart stretched out before him?

"Fuck it," Rickey whispered. He turned and walked back into the house, locked the door behind him, went straight to the medicine cabinet, and shook two pills into his hand. They sat there white and blameless on his roughened palm, promising only good things: what was wrong with not wanting to feel pain and rage? Rickey ran water into the toothbrush glass, washed them down. Almost immediately the warmth came over him, long before the drug could have had any true physical effect. He felt his way into the dark bedroom and crawled into bed. G-man turned over and laid an arm across his chest, but Rickey squirmed out from under it. He was a failure now, and didn't deserve the comfort.

11

G-MAN had told Rickey he was driving out to Chalmette to buy some late-season Creole tomatoes at a farm stand he knew. He actually did go get the tomatoes, just so he wouldn't have lied to Rickey. The stand also had some nice little seedless watermelons, so he grabbed a few of those too; a watermelon and lump crabmeat salad would jazz up the menu. Maybe some sort of vodka dressing.

He loaded the produce into his car and cranked up the air conditioner, but didn't pull out of the parking lot. Instead he dialed information, got the number for Benjamin Stone, M.D., and let the automatic operator connect him.

The phone rang many times, and G-man was about to end the call, figuring maybe the doctor had celebrated his retirement with a vacation or something. Then the receiver on the other end was lifted and a woman with a heavy black New Orleans accent said, "Hello, this Dr. Stone's residence."

"Hi, uh, listen, I don't know if the doctor remembers me. I'm one of the chefs at Liquor. I talked to him at his retirement dinner a few weeks ago."

"If you met him one time, he gonna remember you. Hang

on." The woman went away, and a few moments later Dr. Stone came on. "Hello there, Chef Stubbs! Or is it Chef Gary?"

"Uh, everybody calls me G-man."

"G-man it is. Good to hear from you. How's the restaurant?"

"It's OK. Summer's the slow season, you know."

"Sure, sure. It was always the opposite for me—but I'm afraid they're all slow seasons now. This retirement nonsense is taking some getting used to. I'm driving Devida here crazy, rattling around the house talking to her while she tries to get work done."

Dr. Stone laughed. G-man sensed that the man would talk half the afternoon without ever asking what the call was about, so he said, "Well, then maybe you won't mind if I bother you about something."

"By all means! Bother away."

"I was hoping to ask you about a drug."

"I know a little something about those. I've spent the past few years working with a rehab program—in fact, that's where I hired Devida from. She's been clean for two years and insists I tell everyone about it."

G-man heard the woman say something in the background. He wasn't sure, but he thought it might have been "Bullshit."

"Um," he said. "It's not exactly an illegal drug I wanted to ask about. It's something another doctor prescribed for me." He felt pretty sure the old doctor was trustworthy, but he wasn't going to discuss Rickey's business with a virtual stranger based on gut instinct.

"Prescription drugs can get ahold of you just as bad as the street stuff. Worse, sometimes."

"That's kinda what I wanted to talk about."

"Chef—excuse me—G-man—would you like to come out here? I hate talking about serious stuff on the phone, and if you don't mind my saying so, you don't exactly sound comfortable with it either."

"Well, sure," said G-man. In truth, he had been hoping the doctor would suggest this. He didn't particularly mind talking on the phone, but he wanted to be able to look into the man's face when he asked him about the pills.

•　　•　　•

Metairie Heights was a quiet neighborhood near Lake Pontchartrain, and Dr. Stone's house was the last one before the levee, a one-story brick ranch with a mailbox made to resemble a large-mouth bass. As G-man got out of the car, the heat and the smell of the lake wrapped around him like a moist, dirty blanket. He thought longingly of the watermelons in the backseat, picturing the cool frosted-pink flesh inside—he thought he might set one aside to cut up and puree in the blender with ice and vodka—but that could come later. What he had to do now might not be pleasant, but it was more important than a cold drink, and that was some important in the heat of a New Orleans summer.

Devida let him in. She looked a lot like any number of girls he'd grown up with in the Lower Ninth Ward: elaborate hairstyle, long fake fingernails painted with fanciful blue and gold designs, her own name tattooed in cursive script just above the swell of her cleavage. Ghetto-fabulous, except that her eyes were sad and sober and a small silver cross hung above the tattoo. As she ushered him through the living room, he saw a shelf full of oddly shaped candles: some of them looked like stacks of pancakes or ice cream sundaes, some like pieces of sushi. One was the very image of a McKenzie's king cake, the kind topped with colored sugar, sprinkles, and candied cherries that always looked (and tasted) petrified. G-man hadn't seen one of those since the McKenzie's bakeries closed years ago, and he had never seen a wax version.

"I like things that look like other things," the doctor explained, appearing from an arched doorway. "Come on into my office."

G-man entered the cool, dim room and took a seat on a chair shaped like a giant cupped hand. On Dr. Stone's desk he noticed a rubber fried egg and a cotton ball dispenser in the form of a rabbit: the cotton ball formed the rabbit's fluffy tail, and when you pulled it off, another one popped out. Rather than being put off by the small indications of weirdness, G-man found them comforting, another sign that he might be able to talk to the doctor. When you spent your life in the windowless world of a kitchen, working when most people were having fun and going to sleep around the time everybody else was getting up, another person's weirdness tended to be a sign of kinship rather than something off-putting.

"I enjoy visitors, but I won't waste your time with small talk," Dr. Stone said. "You wouldn't be here unless you felt there was a problem. So talk to me."

"Well," G-man began, "it's like this, Doc. I hurt my back on Mardi Gras lifting a sack of oysters . . ."

He told the entire story as if it had happened to him instead of Rickey: the prolonged pain, the visits to Dr. Lamotte where no X-rays had been taken and no diagnosis made, the increasing dependence on the prescription. He'd never been a very good liar and felt bad about being dishonest with Dr. Stone, but he told himself it wasn't *really* lying; he'd just changed a few details to protect Rickey's privacy. "I quit taking the pills about a month ago," he concluded. "Stayed off 'em a couple weeks, but then it got to be too much and I started again."

"The back pain?"

"That and . . . " What had Rickey called it? "The gnawing. I got a tendency to eat my liver out all the time over things I can't change. And I got a pretty bad temper. The pills help with that stuff too."

Dr. Stone rested his elbows on the desk and gave G-man a searching look. G-man tried not to squirm under the scrutiny of those deep-set, intelligent eyes. At last the doctor said, "You strike me as a rather easygoing fellow. Not someone with a temper or . . . what was that excellent phrase? . . . a tendency to eat his liver out."

"I guess I hide it well," G-man said uncomfortably.

"You certainly do. Either that, or you're compassionate enough to pretend you have a drug habit yourself rather than violate the privacy of someone you care for."

G-man started to speak, and the doctor held up a hand. "No need to tell me one way or the other. Not yet, anyway. Whatever the case may be, there's a problem and you want my advice. Is that about right?"

"Yeah."

"How much Vicodin are you taking now?"

G-man gave up the ruse then. What was Stone going to do, call *Gourmet*? "It's not me, it's my partner and I don't know how much he's taking. At least a couple pills a night—I don't think he can get to sleep without it. Maybe more than that sometimes. I feel like I don't know anything for sure anymore."

"You two are more than business partners."

"Yeah, we're partners in everything, have been for sixteen

years now. I don't know if you got a problem with that but I don't see what—"

"Calm down, calm down. I don't have a problem with anything. I just like to know the situation. If you're the person he's closest to, it stands to reason you know as much about his habits as anybody. Therefore, nobody really knows how much Vicodin he's taking except him and his doctor."

"Can you talk to the doctor?"

"Possibly later, but it's not my place to tell him how to prescribe for his patients. And if he's ethical—"

"He's not."

"—he won't talk to me anyway. For now . . . " Dr. Stone had ignored G-man's interruption and seemed to be thinking. "Two doses a day isn't a great deal. He may be experiencing rebound pain—that can happen when the body gets used to regular doses of any painkiller, even aspirin—but at this point I'd guess the addiction is still more psychological than physical."

"The stuff I told you about—the gnawing and all that—it's Rickey. He's just like that. He says the pills make him feel calm. Oh, God, I shouldn't be telling you all this. We never talk to anybody else about this kinda shit."

"Maybe that's part of the problem."

"How do you mean?"

"Do you two have a lot of friends?"

"Well, sure. I mean, the crew at work, we see those guys every day, we get along great with them. And there's our partner, Lenny—Rickey likes him better than I do, but he's OK. And we know people in restaurants all over town. Sure we got friends."

"But do you socialize? See people outside of work? Outside the relationship, even?"

G-man thought about it. "Well . . . I guess maybe not. We

pretty much do everything together. But, I mean, we like it that way. That's why we started the restaurant, so we could work for each other instead of working for other people."

"And that's fine. But think about this: what if Rickey finds it difficult to rely on you all the time? His stress levels must have increased a hundredfold in the past few years. What if he likes having something else he can lean on, something that won't ask questions or reproach him for making mistakes?"

"I don't—"

"I'm not saying you do. But it's hard for any person to be as comforting as the right drug."

G-man clasped his hands between his knees, stared down at them. "I thought you said you were a surgeon. You sound more like a psychiatrist or something."

"My rehab folks taught me a great deal. I see what these people are giving up when they give up these drugs. It's not just a high. It becomes their best friend, their lover, their family."

"I don't think Rickey would go into a rehab thing. He's not really into that you're-OK, I'm-fucked-up kinda talk."

Dr. Stone smiled. "If he's only been taking the Vicodin for a couple of months, I doubt he'll need rehab. I don't suppose he *would* consider seeing a psychiatrist?" One look at G-man's face provided the answer to that. "Well, in that case, he'll need to address the pain. He really should have a set of X-rays done. An MRI, too, if your health insurance will cover it."

"We don't exactly have health insurance."

"Don't *exactly*?"

"We been looking into group plans for the restaurant, but they're so damn expensive, and we figured there's always Charity Hospital—"

"All right, all right. I won't give you a lecture on how foolish it is not to have health insurance, or what you'd face in the event of a catastrophic illness. He can probably do without the MRI. If his X-rays come up clean, I'd suggest trying acupuncture."

"Acupuncture!" G-man yelped. "You mean get needles stuck in him?"

"Well, yes, but it's not as bad as all that. The needles only go in a fraction of an inch, and there's no pain involved. Of course I'm most familiar with the Vietnamese methods. In addition to the needles, they employ electricity, heat, cupping—that's where they spread alcohol on the skin, set it very briefly afire, and cover it with a glass cup, creating a seal and a welt—"

"Uh, look, Dr. Stone, I can't tell you how much I appreciate you talking to me and all, but I gotta get back to the restaurant. I'll think about the acupuncture, I really will, but I should get going."

"Oh, hell, I didn't explain this very well, did I? We surgeons tend to get ahead of ourselves and misplace our bedside manner."

"No, no, it's nothing like that, I just lost track of the time, I gotta go. Thanks a lot. I'll call you."

"At least look into it!" Dr. Stone shouted as G-man backed out of the office.

G-man smiled too widely and nodded. "I sure will!"

Devida let him out. In the car, he cranked the air back up and leaned his head against the seat, appalled at what he had almost gotten Rickey into. Needles! Electricity! And setting people's skin on fire! Dr. Stone had seemed so sane and nice until all that came up. G-man wondered if there could be something to the needles, but what good could it possibly do to set somebody on fire? Rickey would never go for it. The doctor must have spent too much time in the jungle.

He just hoped Dr. Stone would keep his mouth shut, because there would be no end to the strife if Rickey knew G-man had been discussing his problems with a third party. Weren't there laws about doctor-patient confidentiality? He thought so, but did they apply if the doctor was retired, or if you weren't really the doctor's patient?

Great, G-man thought, *something else to worry about.* He wasn't accustomed to worrying a lot—even as a restaurant owner, he had always been relatively carefree. Now worry seemed to be turning into a way of life.

12

LENNY Duveteaux was on the phone with his attorney. "Oscar. You know anybody in the INS?"

"The what?"

"The INS. Immigration and Naturalization Service."

"You mean the Department of Homeland Security?"

"Yeah, yeah, whatever spook shit they're calling it now. I'm trying to find out about the status of a non-American living in the States."

He figured the easiest way to deal with the whole Rickey/Tanker situation would be to get Jaap Noteboom deported. A little rustling through the leaves of his restaurant grapevine had told him that if Jaap were to leave, the hotel manager would probably promote the pastry chef, Martina Jesus-Vasquez, to executive chef. He knew Tanker and Martina couldn't stand each other, so Tanker would surely quit and return to Liquor. This would bypass the entire problem of dealing with the various chefs' fragile egos.

But Oscar De La Cerda just groaned. "Lenny, no. I don't know anybody in Homeland Security, and if I did, I wouldn't use them to help you get somebody deported."

"What makes you think I want to get anybody deported?"

"I know how your mind works. Hey, you're not taping this shit, are you?"

"You know I don't do that anymore, Oscar. Thanks for nothing."

A few more inquiries provided him with the information that Jaap Noteboom was married to an American woman, which allowed him to live in the United States indefinitely. Lenny decided the plan had been too convoluted anyway. He was a great admirer of G. Gordon Liddy, but sometimes he wondered if he had read *Will* once too often. His first instinct when someone got in his way was to have the poor bastard neutralized. Sooner or later, Lenny knew, this was going to get him in trouble.

Instead of pursuing the Noteboom plan, Lenny called Tanker's home number, but he got Mo. This was actually preferable; she had been the bartender at one of his restaurants before Rickey hired her, and Lenny found her levelheaded and easy to deal with. "What's going on with Tanker?" he said, feigning ignorance for the moment. "How's he liking that Polonius Room gig?"

"Oh, Lenny, I've never heard him bitch and moan so much in my life. If he'd been like this when we met, I wouldn't have started dating him. His whole personality has changed—he doesn't even *look* like himself anymore."

Lenny had seen this phenomenon in people with hellish restaurant jobs. The work was so physically tiring that there wasn't much room for huge psychic stress on top of that, and when it came anyway, it shaped its victims in a brutal fashion. Their shoulders drew up, their features became pinched, and they took on an entirely different physical appearance. It could be frightening for those around them, but when the situation improved, they usually went right back to their old selves. "What exactly is the problem?" he asked, wanting to draw out the conversation a little before he got to the point.

Mo filled him in on the horror of the gig: Chef Jaap's hysteria, the silly food, Tanker's failure to make any desserts. Lenny smiled when he heard that last: the desserts, he knew, were the key to bringing Tanker back where he belonged. "I hear Liquor still doesn't have a pastry chef," he said cautiously.

"Is that what this call is about? Are you cooking up some scheme to bring Tanker back to Liquor?"

He didn't say anything, knowing his silence would confirm it and waiting to see if Mo would blow up at him.

"Lenny, if you could do that, I'd love you for the rest of my life. I'd promise you my firstborn except I know you'd probably put him to work in the pantry."

"He'd have to wash dishes first. I start all the new meat right at the bottom. Listen, Mo, if you think Tanker wants to go back to Liquor, I know Rickey would love to have him. The problem is, neither one of them will admit it."

"I know—they're still pissed off about that stupid fight they had after the cross-burning. But if you could somehow make each of them think it was his idea . . ."

"I like the way your mind works."

"How would you do it, though?"

"Let me give it some thought," Lenny said. "I'll get back to you if I need your help." Privately, he hoped he wouldn't. If Tanker ever found out that Mo had plotted with Lenny, he might resent it, and on matters like this, Lenny preferred to work alone.

•   •   •

Rickey was sitting in his office opening the mail and, in the back of his mind, counting the hours until he could go home and have a pill. He took Excedrin all through the days now, but it left him with the unpleasantly wired/drained feeling of coming down off a cocaine high, and it only reduced the back pain a little.

The mail wasn't very exciting: invoices, restaurant supply catalogs, a sample issue of a glossy new trade magazine called *Sauté* that would probably last about two issues. Rickey sneered at the blandly handsome, grinning young chef on the cover, somebody's Flavor of the Month. He was getting as bad as his mentor, Paco Valdeon, who hadn't wanted to hire Rickey at first because he thought Rickey was too good-looking. Rickey sometimes thought the best years of his life had been when he and G-man worked under Paco at the Peychaud Grill. It was an intense place with a hard-drinking, hard-drugging crew, and eventually it had imploded under the weight of its own craziness, but he'd learned more about food at that job than at any before or since. He wondered where Paco was now: still on a beach somewhere in Mexico, selling lobster ceviche out of a little straw hut? Or had some less happy fate befallen him? Paco had never seemed long for this world, somehow.

Rickey also wondered what Paco would think of *him* now, popping pills and making gimmicky food. Rickey seldom felt constrained by the liquor gimmick, which had set him and G-man free to cook pretty much as they wished. He suspected Paco might feel otherwise, and he'd always sort of hoped Paco wouldn't see his glamour-boy coverage in *Bon Appétit* and the other glossy food rags.

He pulled himself away from that train of thought and opened the last piece of mail, an envelope hand-addressed to him, with a New Orleans postmark and no return address. Out dropped a glossy brochure with an odd-looking diagram of the human body on the front. The body seemed to be divided into segments and was marked by dozens of red dots with numbered lines running to them. Examining the thing more closely, Rickey saw that it was an advertisement for an acupuncture clinic out East, where the local Vietnamese community was.

Well, that was weird. Had somebody gotten wind of his back problems, maybe even his drug problem, and sent this in an attempt to make him paranoid? Rickey knew he wasn't the most popular guy in the New Orleans restaurant world—you couldn't be, if you snagged a lot of media hype and a Beard award before you hit thirty—but he was pretty sure nobody knew about his problems except G-man and Dr. Lamotte. He refused to complain in front of the crew in case they thought it gave them a license to whine about their own aches and pains. He didn't believe G-man would tell anybody, and Lamotte wouldn't want him to try acupuncture; he had a vested interest in keeping Rickey on the pills. Rickey realized this and had begun to resent it, but that didn't make it any easier to stop filling the prescriptions.

As Rickey paged through the brochure, G-man came in to get a pen. "Whatcha looking at?" he asked.

"Some crap about acupuncture." Rickey fanned the pages. "They say it's real good for back pain."

He thought he saw the faintest shadow of Catholic-boy guilt cross G-man's face, but he dismissed it as more paranoia; he was really jumping at shadows today. "Looks pretty painful itself," G-man said, glancing away from a photo of somebody's shoulder bristling with long, thin needles.

"I don't know. Says here you only feel a little prick."

G-man snorted. "It does not."

"Well, OK, but it says it doesn't hurt. Even if it did, I don't see how it could hurt as much as my fucking back does sometimes."

"No shit? You'd try that?"

"I'm not rushing right out to make an appointment, but dude, I'd try almost anything at this point. I'd go to one of those goddamn faith-healing churches down in the old hood if I really thought it'd help."

"Rickey . . ."

G-man stopped, and Rickey looked up at him. "Yeah?"

"I don't know if I should even mention this, but isn't your dad a chiropractor?"

Rickey was pretty sure his jaw didn't actually drop, but he felt just as stupid as if it had. In all the time since he'd hurt his back, that stark and simple fact had never occurred to him; it was as if he'd blocked it out completely. In fact, he probably had. Rickey didn't really know his father. His parents had divorced when he was just six, and Oskar Rickey moved to California soon after. Since then, Rickey had seen him just twice. They'd last met when Rickey was seventeen and spending too much time with G-man for Brenda's taste. She'd gotten together with Elmer and Mary Rose Stubbs, who hadn't been as accepting of their youngest son's sexuality back then, and worked up a plan whereby she would convince Oskar to send Rickey to cooking school in New York. The parents seemed to think the two-year separation would nip the relationship in the bud, and maybe it would have. Rickey never found out, since he was expelled four months into his stay for beating up his homophobic roommate.

He called Oskar soon afterward to thank him for paying the tuition and offer to repay what he hadn't spent. Oskar declined the refund, but bawled him out for being a quitter. "What the hell you think you did to our family?" Rickey shot back, and the conversation went downhill from there. Since then they had only spoken a handful of times, always in stilted language that avoided more than it addressed and left Rickey feeling bad for days.

They'd last talked not too long after Liquor won the Beard award. With a couple of drinks in him, Rickey had called Oskar, ostensibly to share the good news, but with a strong vein of *Look, Dad, I did just fine without you* running along the bottom of the conversation. Never having heard of James Beard or his awards, Oskar wasn't as impressed as Rickey thought he should be, and it hadn't ended particularly well. The thing Rickey envied most about G-man was not his even temper or his ability to shake off life's petty annoyances, but his close and comfortable relationship with Elmer Stubbs.

"I never thought of that," he said. "You know, I'm not so sure I *could* call him to ask for help."

"You don't have to ask him for help. Just see if he knows a good chiropractor in New Orleans. He worked here for a long time, huh? He must know some people."

"Yeah, he used to treat a couple Saints players," Rickey said absently. Truth was, he didn't remember all that much about what life had been like when his father still lived with him and Brenda. "I guess he might could give me a referral."

"You still got his number?"

"Unless he moved and didn't bother to give me the new one." *Which is always a possibility,* Rickey thought, but didn't say it; he'd been gloomy enough lately.

"Well, it's worth a try anyway."

"I guess. My mom spent all those years after they split up saying how chiropractors aren't real doctors."

"Your mom says a lot of stuff."

"That's true."

"And what have real doctors done for you lately, huh?"

"Yeah."

Rickey took a deep breath. It caught in his throat, and he was appalled to realize that he was close to tears. G-man came to his side of the desk and put an arm around his shoulders. "Dude. Dude, it's gonna be OK."

"No it's not. It's just gonna keep hurting, and I don't even want to quit taking the pills, and you know my dad could give a fuck about any of it."

"I'm sorry. I shouldn't have brought him up."

"It's not your fault." Rickey swiped at his eyes impatiently. He wasn't really crying, just leaking a little. G-man knelt beside his chair and rubbed the back of his neck. Rickey bowed his head, trying to take comfort in the touch.

"Um, Chef?"

They both looked up. The new line cook, Devonte, stood shifting from foot to foot in the office doorway.

"What's up, Devonte?" said G-man.

"Uh, uh . . . " He glanced nervously at Rickey, who looked away. "I was just wondering how we gonna do the sauce on the halibut."

G-man sighed. "I told you twice, it's a Creole tomato butter with lemon vodka. Just like it was yesterday and the day before."

"Oh, OK."

"You remember how to make it?"

"Yeah . . ."

"You sure? You want me to come show you again?"

"Naw, naw. I got it. No problem."

"You want something else, then?"

"Naw." The young cook cast another anxious glance at Rickey. "You awright, Chef?"

"I'm fine, Devonte. I'm absolutely fucking peachy. Now you think maybe you could get back to work?"

"Yeah, sure. Sure. Sorry."

Devonte disappeared down the hall. Rickey raked his hands through his hair. "Great. Just great."

"Don't worry about it."

"He doesn't know how to make that fucking butter, either."

"I know it. I better go stand over him." G-man pushed himself up, groaning a little as his knees popped.

"See? You got aches and pains. We all do. I had 'em since I was a fifteen-year-old dishwasher. I don't know why this back thing's gotten to me so bad."

"Rickey . . ."

"What? Quit saying my name and waiting for me to say *what,* would you? If you got stuff to say to me, just say it."

"OK, I will. I'm not saying your back problem is, like, in your head or anything. I know it's not. I know you hurt yourself on Mardi Gras. But you take things so hard, and you never give yourself a break, and I think that's part of it."

Rickey started to argue, but realized he couldn't disagree with anything G-man had said. A great weariness came over him. "Maybe so," he said.

"When was the last time you felt totally good? Totally relaxed?"

Rickey didn't hesitate. "Shell Beach."

"Well, why don't we go back out there for a couple days?"

"G, you know I can't. We got this lame-ass crew here, I'm already behind at Soul Kitchen, I gotta figure out these fucking desserts and teach 'em to Marquis—"

"All that'll keep for two days. We drive down Sunday night after service, come back late Tuesday."

"I just can't."

"That's why we have a restaurant, huh? So it can keep us prisoner all the time, even in the middle of the summer when we're doing forty, fifty covers a night?"

"Things will go to shit."

"We'll come back and fix 'em. Or, hell, we could even *close* for a few days like we did our first summer. Two days, Rickey. Isn't your sanity worth it? You got this thousand-yard stare lately— you're scaring me."

Rickey closed his eyes and thought about it. In his mind he could smell the saltwater and boat fuel, hear the gulls calling, see the sunlight sparkling on the wide expanse of water at the road's end, so close to New Orleans and yet so far it might as well be the end of the world. Three years on, he truly loved his restaurant; it was what he had been born to do and he knew he was very good at it. But how wonderful it was, just for a little while, to be in a place where the restaurant could not touch him.

"Well," he said. "I guess maybe Terrance could hold down the fort for a day or two."

"Course he could."

Rickey leveled a pointing finger at G-man. "I want you to know I don't feel good about leaving my kitchen in the hands of a guy who was a dishwasher just three years ago."

"See, that's part of the problem right there. You're too much of a control freak. I know you gotta be one to a point, but c'mon— you know Terrance can do it, and if you don't think he can, then close for a couple days. We need to do this."

"I guess," Rickey said grudgingly, but in his heart he believed G-man was right.

· · ·

G-man stood over Devonte and walked him yet again through the steps of making the Creole tomato butter, but he didn't particularly mind having to waste part of his last prep hour going over something a competent cook would have gotten the first time, because he was so pleased that Rickey had agreed to take another brief vacation. The back problem was troublesome but presumably not life-threatening. He sometimes worried, though, that Rickey would eventually gnaw himself into high blood pressure or even a heart attack if he didn't learn to let go of things a little.

After leaving Dr. Stone's house but before returning home, G-man had stopped by a little church on Louisiana Avenue, Our Lady of Good Counsel, to catch the afternoon Mass. He supposed he had begun to think of this as "his" church; he didn't attend every week, but when he did go, this was where he always seemed to end up. It was a comfortable place with a congregation that seemed to encompass all ages, races, and possibly even orientations; at any rate there was never any sermonizing about the homosexual agenda or any of the other things that had driven him from the Church at sixteen.

One of the hymns that day was "Make Me a Channel of Thy Peace," whose lyrics were based on the Prayer of St. Francis. G-man knew this prayer well since Francis was his middle name: *O Divine Master, grant that I may not so much seek to be consoled as to console; to be understood as to understand; to be loved as to love.*

He had always realized that this was all he could do for Rickey: make a channel of his own peaceful soul and hope Rickey would use it. He wasn't sure what had happened to him over the past year or so, all this churchgoing. He didn't talk about it with Rickey, not because he wanted to hide it so much as because Rickey didn't want to hear about it. It wasn't a big deal, since he didn't have much to say about it anyway. He no longer believed all the doctrine of the Church, but going to Mass was something he did to locate a quiet place deep within himself, a place he felt he had lost touch with in recent years.

After the Mass, G-man had lit a candle beneath the statue of St. Joseph and said a quick, private prayer for the relief of Rickey's pain. He only hoped that candle and that prayer were working now.

13

SO they returned to Shell Beach for a couple of days, and fished and fucked and lay around doing absolutely nothing, which is a cook's dream vacation: people who spend their days destroying their feet, breaking their backs, and frying their brains on the hot line are unlikely to climb mountains or run marathons in their leisure time. Nothing horrible happened at home, and they allowed themselves an extra night at Anthony's camp. Driving back to New Orleans on Wednesday morning, they saw a pair of hawks tumbling out of the sky, wings spread and talons linked in the world's most dramatic mating dance. Rickey felt his soul lift a little. His gloom and his back pain had receded during the days on the water, and despite the crew problems at Liquor and the upcoming responsibility of Soul Kitchen, he actually looked forward to getting back to work.

"You know," G-man said, "I think I really like fishing."

"You been doing it all your life."

"Yeah, but just around New Orleans. Wetting a line in Bayou St. John or even dropping it off the Lake Pontchartrain seawall, that's not the same as going out on the water. There's something about being out there . . ."

"I know what you mean. It feels like the world can't touch you."

"Exactly." G-man took one hand off the wheel, reached over and gently knuckled Rickey's shoulder. "You ever think . . ."

"What?"

"Well, we got all that money from your property in Dallas. You ever think maybe we should buy our own camp down here? I noticed they got a bunch of 'em for sale."

Rickey looked out the window, though they were now on the boring part of the drive and he saw nothing but flat green fields and an occasional small house. It had always seemed to him that G-man could read his mind at certain moments, but he hadn't thought he was so obvious about his fantasy of a little place in Shell Beach. "I don't know," he said. "Seems like we should put that money into the restaurant somehow. You know how long we been talking about buying Lenny out."

"I know, but remember one thing we promised ourselves when we opened Liquor? We said we weren't gonna let it eat our lives completely. We knew it mostly would, but we swore we'd keep a few things just for us. This could be one of those things, and who knows when we'll ever get the chance to do it again." G-man shrugged. "Course it's up to you—the money's yours really."

"There's no *mine* or *yours,* dude. You know it's never been like that. The money's ours—we both decide what to do with it."

They rode along in silence for a while. G-man glanced over at Rickey, saw that he was still gazing out the window, knew he must be thinking and decided to leave him alone. Eventually Rickey said, "You wanna know the truth, Lenny owning twenty-five percent doesn't really bother me much anymore. I guess in some ways me and Lenny have gotten pretty tight."

"I've noticed."

"I thought you still had problems with him, though."

"Well . . ." G-man tapped the edge of the steering wheel, trying to gather his thoughts on Lenny. "It's hard not to like Lenny on a personal level. He's one charming motherfucker when he wants to be. I'm not crazy about some of the things he's done. But, you know, if you're gonna be in the restaurant business in New Orleans, you're gonna deal with some sleazy characters. Maybe it's good we got a few on our side."

"That's pretty much what I've always thought."

"I just don't want to turn into sleazy characters ourselves."

"Yeah, by all means, we gotta stay alcoholic, pothead, Vicodin-popping pillars of the community."

"You know what I mean," G-man said. "That stuff, that's our own business. It doesn't interfere with anybody else. Lenny, somebody gets in his way, he thinks nothing of interfering with them. Sometimes interfering them right out of existence. I'm not into that."

"Me neither, but there's been a couple times I was real glad Lenny had our backs." Rickey picked at a peeling sunburn on his leg, just below the frayed hem of a pair of check pants he'd cut off at the knees. "Well," he said. "Well, I don't know. Jeez."

G-man laughed. "You sound like Anthony B."

"I know, but c'mon, G, we never spent that much money on anything in our lives. Seventy-five thousand dollars? You think that'd buy one of those camps?"

"Be a hell of a down payment, anyway. And don't forget—you'll have the money from the Soul Kitchen consulting job, too."

"Yeah . . ."

Rickey leaned back in his seat and tried to imagine what it would be like. He and G-man were the primary leaseholders on the Liquor building, but they'd never actually owned any property other than the place in Dallas, which Rickey felt no connection with and had been eager to get rid of. He supposed he would inherit his mother's house on Tricou Street when she passed, unless she'd written him out of her will and left it all to the Chihuahua Rescue Network or something, but despite the uneasiness of their relationship, he hoped that wouldn't happen for a long time. The truth was that he couldn't quite realize how it would be to have a place that was just his and G-man's, a place they could go any time they wanted to, a refuge from the restaurant and the city that was still close enough to get back quickly if need be. Maybe they would close the restaurant for two weeks next summer, as they'd done the first year they were open. That year they had gone out to Cajun country, their first real vacation ever. This time, maybe they'd spend the whole two weeks down here, just fishing and getting sunburned and enjoying each other's company with no restaurant business to get in the way.

"Wow," he said.

"It'd be nice, huh?"

"I'll say."

Before they could really take the idea seriously, they would have to back away from it, reapproach with caution, nibble at its edges and reconfigure its ingredients a few times. They didn't have the kind of background that would allow them to spend a large sum of money without some agonizing. Maybe a camp in Shell Beach was exactly what he needed, though. If so, it was no surprise that G-man had come up with the idea.

•   •   •

"I don't think it's s'posed to be this spicy," Milford said, sampling the Korean tofu and oyster soup. "It's a comfort dish, like your momma serves you when you're sick in bed."

"Yeah, but how do you know for sure?" Rickey asked him. "It's not like either of us ever ate real Korean food before."

Milford turned and gave him a stare. It wasn't quite a baleful stare, but it wasn't all that friendly either. Rickey had been seeing a great deal of that expression lately, and he wondered if the jurors had ever seen it during Milford's murder trial; it could explain a lot. "If you ain't gonna trust my palate," Milford said, "what are we even doin here?"

"You're right," Rickey admitted, not for the first time. "It's just that you make me feel . . . kinda redundant, I guess. I'm not used to feeling redundant in the kitchen."

Milford shrugged. "You a real good cook, Rickey, but I'd be fine here on my own. We both know the suits want you here more than you want to be here or I need you here."

Rickey nodded. They'd been testing recipes at Soul Kitchen for a week now. The counters and shelves were lined with unfamiliar ingredients bought at the city's various ethnic markets or ordered off the Internet, many of which neither Rickey nor Milford had ever cooked with before: Ethiopian berbere powder, pomegranate molasses, dried red dates, and the like. It was fun learning about these exotics, but Rickey was a little taken aback by how dramatically Milford's personality had changed once he'd spent a couple of days in his own kitchen. He wasn't rude—Milford had never been rude—but there was an arrogance to him that hadn't been present at Liquor, or even when Rickey had worked under him at Reilly's. It reminded Rickey that Milford had been a head chef in his own right once, and would very likely be as well known as Rickey now if events hadn't intervened.

That hadn't stopped Lamotte from calling Rickey on the third day of testing in something of a lather: "I stopped by the

boat today and you weren't in the kitchen! You know we're counting on your involvement in this restaurant."

"I *am* involved," Rickey had told him. "That doesn't mean I
can be there every single day. I still got my own place to run, and
Milford doesn't need me standing over him the whole time."

"Well, will you be there tomorrow?"

"Yeah, Doc, yeah. First thing tomorrow."

So Rickey was splitting most of his days, spending mornings
and early afternoons out at the lakefront, then heading back to
Liquor to work dinner. G-man was holding down the fort together with Terrance. Marquis was doing a credible job with the
few desserts Rickey had been able to teach him, though customers
were still begging for the return of the old dessert list Tanker had
created. Even Devonte had improved a little; he was no longer the
freshest meat in the kitchen since they'd hired another sauté cook,
and his precarious seniority seemed to give him confidence.
Things were going all right at Liquor, but it drove Rickey crazy
being there only half the time. He had promised himself that after
this he would never do another consulting job, but when he mentioned his decision to Lenny, the older chef just smiled his de-
mented smile and said, "You know, Rickey, God loves to make us
break our promises."

So far he and Milford had made low-country shrimp and
grits with red-eye gravy, Brazilian fish stew, Greek moussaka, Al-
satian choucroute garni, Russian borscht, and a host of other
international dishes. Like most chefs, Rickey didn't eat a lot of
his own food. Most of the dishes at Liquor were so familiar that
he knew their flavors by heart and could re-create those flavors
without tasting. Even his specials tended to follow certain taste-
patterns that were deeply familiar to him. Some of these were
the patterns of New Orleans; some were his own creations. The

dishes at Soul Kitchen didn't fall into either category, so he had to do more tasting than usual, and sometimes even full-fledged eating in order to follow the flavor arc of a dish from start to finish. The soups—the cool, creamy borscht, the fiery Brazilian coconut-fish stew known as *moqueca*—went down easy. It was harder to eat a whole plate of Thai red-curried catfish or Polish stuffed cabbage with sweet and sour tomato sauce. The weather wasn't conducive to big plates of food, and the pills cut his appetite. Even so, it was fun trying all these new dishes. The best thing he'd made so far was *doro wat,* the national dish of Ethiopia, a buttery, spicy brick-colored stew of chicken drumsticks and hard-boiled eggs. Unfortunately his attempt to make *injera,* the traditional Ethiopian flatbread used to scoop up the food, had been a flop. If they kept that one on the menu, they'd have to find a mail-order source.

The innovative kitchen design put everything within reach; the shock-absorbent floor meant their feet were hardly tired at the end of a shift. There were also interesting little touches and quirks, such as a wood-fired tandoori oven, a wholly computerized ordering system, and a baking station that doubled as a spyhole: it was an alcove walled off from the rest of the kitchen so that you couldn't see who was in there, but some trick of the air vents made it possible to hear everything that was happening on the line. Rickey caught himself wishing he had such a thing at Liquor before he realized what a bad idea it would be; there wasn't anyone he actually mistrusted, and he didn't really want to hear the random trash his cooks probably talked about him when they thought he couldn't hear them.

Overall, the casino kitchen was a joy to cook in. Occasionally, though, Rickey found himself doubting the concept as he had never done with either of his previous two restaurant ideas. It was great food, all of it, but would it hang together; would the menu have any kind of coherence? And would New Orleanians order this stuff? He knew it was too late for such doubts and did not voice them. Anyway, Milford seemed to have enough confidence for the both of them. When Rickey brought in Mary Rose Stubbs' family recipe for spaghetti with sardines, fennel, raisins, and pine nuts, Milford vetoed it: "They got enough Italian food in this town."

"No they don't. They got Yat Italian—red gravy and breadcrumb stuffing. This is a real recipe from G's great-grammaw."

"Well, I don't care. I don't want to do Italian stuff."

"It's your kitchen, dude," Rickey said, but he was a little stung. If his name was going to be on the place, he thought he should have more input than Milford seemed inclined to give him. He couldn't find the strength to argue much, though. Personally and professionally, Rickey was at a low ebb. The Vicodin had taken a lot of the fight out of him, and while he'd liked that at first—the unfamiliar calmness, the not always having to gnaw— he was beginning to wonder if it was a good thing after all. Far too often, he felt tired and queasy by the middle of the day. Sometimes he took out the acupuncture pamphlet and flipped through it, or looked at the telephone and thought about calling his father, but he couldn't commit to either thing. It was easier to just keep taking the pills. When he let himself think about it, Rickey had to admit that he didn't respect himself very much these days, and that was a totally new experience for him: he had always respected himself, sometimes maybe a bit too much.

They finished up the Korean soup. It was delicious, but Rickey wasn't sure anybody in New Orleans would order something called tofu soup even if it had oysters in it, and for once Milford agreed with him. They decided to go with the oyster-scallion pancakes they'd tested earlier in the week instead. Then Milford busied himself with a new cornbread recipe—his two-hundredth-and-first, Rickey guessed—while Rickey broke for lunch. After eating a bowl of soup, he decided to take a stroll around the boat.

Though it was only a little past noon, the place was already full of gamblers, mostly old ladies of various races. Again those doubts touched Rickey. These people certainly weren't going to eat at Soul Kitchen. Would anybody? Well, past a certain point, it wasn't his problem; he had accepted a flat fee for the consulting, which was being paid to him in biweekly installments, and he wouldn't see any of the profits or lack thereof. He worried a little that being involved with a casino restaurant, especially an unsuc-cessful one, would hurt his reputation. He knew there had already been chatter on the local Internet dining boards—*Is Chef John Rickey selling out?* and so forth—but he refused to look at those boards; they raised his blood pressure and he was half-convinced that most of the participants never ate out anyway. Besides, Lenny had consulted at the Gulfport branch of the Pot O'Gold a few years ago and it hadn't hurt him any.

Soon the clanging bells and sirens and cigarette smoke got to be too much, and Rickey retreated to the kitchen. As he pushed through the swinging doors, he saw the silver mane of Clancy Fairbairn and the bald dome of Dr. Frank Lamotte; they were standing in the middle of the hot line, right in Milford's way. Mil-ford continued to work as he talked to them, explaining what he was doing but not looking very happy about it.

"Rickey!" said Lamotte. "Good to see you here for a change."

"I'm here all the time, Doc."

"I know, I know—I'm just messing with you. So how's things going?"

"Real good. Milford's coming up with some great stuff. I mean, I'm helping out, but he doesn't really need me."

Rickey waited to see if Milford would contradict him, but Milford did not.

"We come asking favors, I'm afraid," said Fairbairn.

Milford still didn't seem inclined to say anything, so Rickey said, "Oh yeah? What can we do for you?"

"We'd like you to make dinner for us next weekend," said Lamotte. "Just us two and our wives. So we can, y'know, get a feel for what you've come up with so far."

Rickey glanced over his shoulder at Milford, who shrugged. Rickey couldn't figure out what was up with him. When they were in the kitchen alone, he'd been very much in charge. Now that the suits were here he'd clammed up, almost as if he were deferring to Rickey. Rickey wasn't going to let him off that easy, though. If he was the head chef, he needed to make the decisions here. "What you think, Milford? We set up enough to do that yet?"

"Fine with me."

Christ, it was like pulling teeth. Rickey gave up. "Sure," he told Lamotte and Fairbairn. "We haven't hired any of our crew yet, but if you can arrange for a food runner from the buffet, I'll bring in one of my cooks from Liquor to help us out. Just so you know it's a work in progress."

"Absolutely," said Fairbairn. "We won't expect much."

"I don't know about that. Everything we've come up with is pretty goddamn good." Rickey remembered Fairbairn's aggressively unadventurous eating habits. "Course, we got no steak or gumbo on the menu."

Fairbairn inclined his head almost graciously, as if ceding a point to Rickey. "I'm sure I'll survive somehow."

"Say!" said Lamotte. "I remember I lured you in by giving you a tour of this kitchen. Now that you've got things all set up, how about you give me a tour?"

"Well, I don't know if I'd call it all set up yet, but sure, I'll give you a tour. You wanna come too, Mr. F?"

"No thanks. I believe I'll just stay here and chat with Milford."

Rickey was glad, though he couldn't say why Fairbairn creeped him out so much. It wasn't the withered hand; hell, he'd known cooks with burn scars that looked worse. Probably, he figured, it was just the whole Comus thing: the idea of a dark Carnival god was bad enough, but actually knowing the god's identity was far worse. He hoped Lamotte hadn't let on to Fairbairn that Rickey had recognized him during the Meeting of the Courts.

But Milford looked alarmed. "Hey, Rickey," he began, then couldn't seem to think what to say next.

"Yeah?"

"Uh . . . I thought you was in a big hurry to make that sauce."

Rickey hadn't mentioned making any sauce, and Milford knew he hadn't. As far as he could tell, this was a transparent ploy to get Rickey to stay here. *Well, fuck that,* he thought. If Milford couldn't handle talking to the bigwigs alone, he was going to be in a world of shit when this place was his own. Besides, Lamotte had asked for a tour of the kitchen, and Rickey didn't see how he could blow him off. "I'll make the sauce later," he said, meeting Milford's eyes and frowning a little.

Milford's shoulders sagged. "Awright, then," he said, turning away as if Rickey could never help him again.

Rickey led Lamotte around the kitchen and back to the

walk-in pointing out the changes he and Milford had made. "Once we're actually open for business, I'm gonna get a dehydrator, an ice cream maker, some gadgets like that. I'm not into the super-innovative stuff myself, but I thought it'd be cool to see what Milford does with them."

"You really think he's that good, huh?"

"You just wait till we cook you dinner next weekend," Rickey promised. "You're gonna see he's even better than I make him out to be."

They stepped into the baking alcove. "Now this is interesting," Rickey said. "Doesn't seem like we're close enough to the line to hear what they're saying, right? But listen—check it out."

They both stood listening, but soon realized the voices coming through the vent system were angry. Not wanting to eavesdrop on anything private, Rickey was about to back out of the alcove when he heard Milford say very clearly, "*Course* I knew you killed her. You thought somethin different?"

He tried not to glance at Lamotte, but couldn't help it. Lamotte's eyes met his, wide and startled. They both looked away quickly, but each knew that the other had heard the words.

"If you try to do anything about it now," Fairbairn said, "things won't be any more pleasant for your family than they would have been back then."

"Got no family left to speak of. My momma and her brother both died while I was locked up. Just got one sister left, and me and her done had a fallin-out. But don't worry, Clancy Fairbairn, I ain't interested in goin up against you. I figure I'd have the life expectancy of a snowball in July if I tried it."

The loathing in Milford's voice was one of the worst things Rickey had ever heard. He took a step backward, trying to get out of the alcove, but bumped into Lamotte. Lamotte stumbled a little and gripped Rickey's arm, steadying them both. "Can they hear us too?" he hissed in Rickey's ear.

"No, it only works the one way."

The awful disembodied voices were still coming through loud and clear. "I'm not threatening you, Milford."

"Bullshit, you just did."

"Not at all. I like having you here at the casino. I like being able to keep an eye on you, and I always did love your cooking."

"Fucker!" Rickey whispered.

"I thought you said they couldn't hear us!"

"They can't."

"Then why are you whispering?"

"I don't know. Shut up."

Milford had just said something Rickey didn't catch, but he felt fairly sure it wasn't "Happy Birthday," because when Fairbairn spoke again, he sounded the tiniest bit peeved. "Well, Milford, it seems like you don't care so much about your sister, but what about those four kids of hers? Think she could spare one? I hear life's cheap in the ghetto."

"You motherfuckin cracker-ass—"

"Now, now, I didn't mean anything by it. As long as you and I stay friends, I'm sure those kids will be just fine."

"We ain't friends."

"Associates, then. Any problem with that?"

If Milford replied, Rickey didn't hear it, but Fairbairn must have been satisfied, because he gave a little sigh and said, "Well, hell, I better see what's happened to Frank. Our tee time's coming up, and if we miss it, Lord knows how many hackers may get ahead of us."

Lamotte turned almost blindly, as if he meant to run right out of the kitchen. If Fairbairn knew the doctor had overheard the conversation, he would know Rickey had heard it too. Rickey grabbed Lamotte's shoulder and squeezed it hard. "Be cool, Doc. You gotta act like you heard nothing. He doesn't know about the vents in here. Far as he's concerned, we were on the other side of two walls. Now go on out there before he comes looking for you."

"But they were talking about murder! Goodman said Clancy murdered that woman, and Clancy didn't even deny it!"

"Well, he didn't admit it either." Rickey thought Fairbairn's words had been as good as an admission, but he needed to calm Lamotte down so he could think how to handle himself.

"That's true . . ."

"So why don't you just go find him and act like you're impatient to get going? Say I had to take a call in the office or something."

"Christ! What are we gonna do? Do we move ahead with the restaurant? Do we go to the police? I don't know what to think anymore!"

Rickey stared hard at Lamotte, wondering if this could be an act. The rabbity look in Lamotte's eyes and the oily beads of sweat popping out all over his scalp didn't seem like an act, though.

"Go on," he said, and gave Lamotte a little push. "You don't have to think anything at all, least not right now. Just deal with him the same way you always did. I mean, it's not like you ever thought he was a nice guy, right?"

This last seemed to give Lamotte some sort of bizarre comfort. "I guess you're right," he said. "I already knew about a bunch of crooked shit he's done. But murder . . ."

"Shut up about it. You're just gonna get yourself worked up again. Forget it for now and go play golf with him."

Now it was Lamotte's turn to stare at Rickey. "You know what, Chef? You're kinda cold-blooded."

"Yeah, well, I gotta be sometimes. Go on now."

Lamotte went. Rickey let his knees buckle, sank down onto an upturned milk crate, and rubbed his hands over his face. Restaurants. Goddamn them. Was there any business in New Orleans more likely to put you in the pockets of thieves, lowlifes, and killers? If so, he couldn't imagine what it might be. He wondered if he really was cold-blooded. Maybe so. Hell, Lenny had probably had a guy killed so they could open Liquor, and now Lenny was just about his best friend after G-man.

After a while, Rickey went back out to the main part of the kitchen. Milford was still in a mood, but more understandably so now. For fifteen minutes or so they worked side by side without saying much of anything. Finally Rickey couldn't stand it. "Look, man," he said. "I couldn't help hearing some of that shit you and Fairbairn said to each other. Are you into something bad? Do you need help?"

"Y'all was in the bread nook, huh?"

"Yeah."

"I hoped you was. That's why I tried to get him on the subject. I was scared to bring it up, but I was more scared not to. I wanted you to hear."

"How come?"

Milford laughed, though there was no humor in it. "Just in case anything should happen to me, I guess."

"Milford . . . " Rickey couldn't find the right words for what he wanted to know. He wasn't entirely sure he wanted to know anything, but he already knew too much. "What happened at the Top Spot?"

"Oh boy. Ain't that the million-dollar question."

Milford took a swig from his water bottle and palmed sweat off his forehead. "Listen, I don't think we gonna get much more done today anyway. I don't wanna talk here. You got time to go get a drink before you head over to Liquor?"

"Sure, man." Rickey really didn't, but he needed to hear what this was all about.

They cleaned up the kitchen, left the casino, and drove their separate cars to a ramshackle little tavern on Hayne Boulevard, right across from the levee. Inside, the bar was dark and cool, smelling somehow pleasantly of cigarettes and mildew and old yeast, empty except for a couple of drinkers on barstools and a crapulous-looking man lackadaisically feeding dollars into the video poker machine in the corner. Rickey reflected how comforting he had always found bars, and how little time he had been spending in them lately.

"I'll get the drinks," he told Milford, and ordered them each a Dixie beer; it seemed too early for Wild Turkey, though he feared he might need one after he'd heard this story. He brought the frosty bottles back to the table and set one in front of Milford.

"Thanks," Milford said. "Hope you told that bartender to keep 'em comin."

He picked up his bottle and drained half of it in one swallow. Then he began to talk.

14

ONE of Eileen's big secrets—and she had plenty—was that she came from a real blue-blood Uptown family. Mansion on Audubon Place, went to school at Sacred Heart, the whole deal. They weren't Carnival royalty, though, and I think she always found that kinda exotic about Clancy Fairbairn. His family goes way back with that shit.

"Well, the Trefethen money had pretty much went to hell in the oil bust by the time she opened the Top Spot, so she had to find investors, and Fairbairn was one of her big fish. Course that had to be kept secret, being as she was the damn civil rights queen, least to hear her tell it—marched in Selma, sat at the Woolsworth lunch counter with them black kids, I don't know what all else. Fairbairn wasn't no Klansman or nothin, but his daddy was a state senator who won three terms on a segregation ticket, and Clancy himself sure fought to keep blacks out the old-line Carnival krewes back in '92. You remember that council-woman who pushed the nondiscrimination ordinance through? I heard somebody sent her a buncha pictures of her grandbabies at their schools, at friends' houses and everything else—the kinda stuff you'd take with a long-range camera—and they had hang-man's nooses and things drawn on 'em, and she always thought that shit came from Fairbairn. But I can't say for sure."

Rickey remembered Fairbairn's soft, cultured voice asking Milford if he thought his sister could spare one of her kids. *I hear life's cheap in the ghetto.* Then he pictured Fairbairn in the grinning Comus mask, a god's silver cup in his withered hand. He shuddered a little, but kept quiet.

"When Eileen hired me as her head chef, I didn't know shit. I started at Reilly's washin dishes when I was nineteen, stayed there more'n ten years. When I got to be lead cook, I thought that was as high as I'd ever go in the restaurant business. Yeah, I put in some applications for chef jobs, but I never expected nothin to come of it. High school dropout who'd cooked at one restaurant, and that was a crappy hotel joint—they weren't exactly linin up to hire me. I could hardly believe it when Eileen axed me to come in and cook for her. When she offered me the job, I figured I might as well benefit from whitey's guilt complex. Now I kinda think she just wanted somebody she could control.

"Don't get me wrong. I know she liked my cookin. Eileen was no fool, and she wouldn't have hired a bad cook just to look good in front of her civil rights friends. I cooked her a damn good tryout meal and I cooked damn good food at the Top Spot. But she knew I was ignorant and not real sure of myself, and I think she figured I wouldn't give her much trouble. I didn't mean to, neither." Milford chuckled. "But me and Eileen, we just set off each other's temper. Everybody at the restaurant knew it. Hell, they could hardly miss it the way we hollered at each other sometimes. That was one of the things looked real bad for me at the trial.

"I don't know when she and Fairbairn started sleepin together. Maybe it was before she opened the restaurant, maybe it was after. I don't think he was mainly interested in Eileen that way—he knew she had the hots for him, and he figured he could use her better if he had that kinda power over her, was the way I figured it."

"Use her how?" Rickey asked.

"Cleanin up his dirty money by way of the Top Spot."

"Laundering?"

"Yeah, far as I could figure. It wasn't like they let me in on their business schemes, but I saw a lot of weird invoices, had city inspectors call up and ask about renovations that never happened, that kinda thing. Sometimes I think Eileen woulda fired me way before she got killed, except she thought I knew a lot more'n I did. Hell, I *wish* she woulda fired me. I'd a been pissed off at the time, but maybe I wouldn't have lost ten years of my life."

"Was Fairbairn into something? I mean, did the money come from anywhere in particular?"

Milford shrugged. "You know how it is. Guy like Fairbairn, place like Louisiana, the money rolls in from everywhere. Kickbacks for contracts. Kickbacks to keep him from givin out contracts. Sweetheart deals. Payoffs. Just plain bribes. Far as I'm concerned, it all adds up to about the same thing."

"Yeah, you right," Rickey said.

"I tell you one thing, I wasn't surprised when I heard he was on this here casino board. Casinos gotta be one of the best ways to clean up some dirty money."

"How do you know all this?"

"Ain't much to do in Angola unless you wanna fight, fuck, or maybe go to church. I spent a lot of time readin, and whenever I could, I read about Clancy Fairbairn. Had an idea maybe I could get some kinda revenge one day. Man, was that ever stupid. I'm gonna feel lucky if he just lets me and what's left of my family live out our natural spans."

"Jesus."

"I'm gettin ahead of myself, though. I never did put it all together, but far as I could tell, Eileen figured out that Fairbairn didn't give a fart in hell about her, and she dumped him, told him to take his dirty money and stick it somewhere dirtier. Fairbairn didn't take real kindly to that, I guess. He came back to the Top Spot one night after hours, maybe tryin to change her mind or just get one more throw, and things went bad."

"He killed her?"

"He killed her. Don't know if he meant to, but he did. Beat her fuckin head in with some of the art lyin around. And then good ole Milford walks into the middle of it, just tryin to get the paycheck I forgot."

"I didn't know you walked into the middle of it."

"Well, not the middle exactly. Fairbairn was on his way out, and I only saw his back. Didn't matter—even if he'd a been halfway home by the time I got there, I woulda known he done it."

"But didn't you tell the cops . . ."

Rickey saw the look Milford was giving him and trailed off.

"Didn't I tell 'em what? That King Shit of Blue-Blood New Orleans Clancy Fairbairn was the one who really killed my boss, even though they found me standin over her body? Sure, I told 'em. Told 'em a bunch of times. They was so impressed they left me in a room handcuffed to a table for eight hours, told me maybe I could get a cold drink and a phone call if I stopped lyin about citizens who had somethin to contribute to this city. Maybe they'd even let me have that lawyer I kep on axin for. Well,

I finally got the lawyer, and he never did believe a word I said, and then one day he come in whiter than usual and told me I'd never say another word about Fairbairn if I wanted to see my sister's kids grow up or my momma die of old age. Fairbairn got to him."

By now they were almost finished with their second round of beers. Milford signaled the bartender for two more. Rickey didn't need another, not before work. If there was ever a good time to refuse to drink with a friend, though, this wasn't it.

"Well, but," Rickey said, and didn't know how to continue. "But, jeez, Milford." Christ, he sounded like an asshole. "What are we gonna do?"

"Do? Thanks, baby." This last was addressed to the bartender; apparently Milford had loosened up around women since that first night at Liquor. "What you mean, *do*?"

"I mean what are we gonna do about the restaurant? How can we keep working with Fairbairn?"

"Rickey," Milford said patiently, "ain't nothin changed for me. I'm sorry I dragged you into this. Yeah, I'm scared of Fairbairn, and I guess I wanted somebody else to know how things was. I got nobody else to tell, so you're elected."

"And I'm just supposed to live with that? I don't get a vote on how we deal with it?"

"What you mean, *vote*? You can walk if you want to. You got somewhere else to go. Me, I got nowhere else, and I knew I was gonna be workin under Fairbairn's thumb when I found out he was involved with this place. I'm under his thumb no matter what, know what I'm sayin? Long as we're both alive, that motherfucker gonna be keepin an eye on me, and I'll be lucky if that's all he does. Least this way I got a job doin what I love."

"But that means he gets away with it."

"You startin to see how things are."

"I didn't think they were like that anymore. I thought . . ."

"You thought there was justice for the black man in New Orleans, huh? Well, sure, sometimes there is. If he got money, or connections, or maybe just light skin. I ain't got none of that— shit, I ain't never even ate at Pampy's. Far as I'm concerned, I'm lucky to be sittin here drinkin beer instead of sittin in a cell drinkin white lightning."

"White lightning?"

"Yeah, you'd save some rice and maybe a piece of fruit, mash it all up and let it ferment in your locker box, stick a bottle of bleach in there to kill the smell. White lightning. Think you could choke that shit down? Nah, I didn't neither, but you might be surprised what you'd do to get a little bit fucked up in that place. To try and forget it for a little while."

Rickey lifted his beer, took a long swig. It bathed his throat and tasted wonderful going down, maybe the best Dixie he'd ever had.

He remembered the thought he'd had the day he learned about his Dallas inheritance, the idea that the wealthy elite of New Orleans were like great dark sea creatures circling below the water's surface, things not to be messed with or even much thought of. Now he felt as if, swimming, he had accidentally brushed one with his foot and was waiting to see if it would ignore him or chomp him down. He could actually feel his skin contracting into goosebumps and his balls trying to climb into his body. *Nope, no balls here, nothing for you sharks to grab onto*—and that was about the size of it, wasn't it, if he let this get on top of him? Fairbairn was an evil bastard, sure, but Rickey had mixed it up with worse people and come out on top. Besides, if he backed out of the project now, he doubted Milford would get to keep his job. Lamotte and Fairbairn wanted Rickey's name on the thing.

Rickey would be happy to take Milford back at Liquor, but now that Milford had been reminded what it was like to run his own kitchen, Rickey doubted he'd be happy in someone else's. As well, there was something appropriate about Milford getting his big chance from the man who'd put him away for a decade.

"OK," he told Milford. "I think it's fucked all to hell, but if you can keep working with the guy, I'm not gonna tell you otherwise, and I'm not gonna mess up this gig for you. You deserve a good gig—better than this one, maybe. Listen, I gotta think about getting to work."

"Sure thing," said Milford. "Believe I'm just gonna sit here awhile longer."

As Rickey stepped out into the dazzle of the summer afternoon, he paused for a moment and looked back into the darkness of the bar. Milford was slumped in the booth picking at the label of his current beer; there was already a fresh bottle in front of him. Rickey imagined how he must look to Milford right now, a flat black cutout silhouetted by the brilliance of sunlight bouncing off the lake and back into the sky, a simple shape among other simple shapes. But he couldn't tell if Milford was looking at him or just staring into the round eye of the bottle.

·   ·   ·

G-man had spent the early part of the afternoon learning something from his new cook, a novel and encouraging experience after the confederacy of dunces that had passed through Liquor's kitchen in recent weeks. Alain was a handsome young Cajun from Cut Off, a little bayou town near the Louisiana coast. For the dinner special G-man had assigned him, he asked if he could make the stuffed pig's stomach known as chaudin. "Sure, if you'll show me how," G-man said. "Dunno where you're gonna get a pig's stomach on short notice, though."

Alain grinned. "I live right near here, and I got one in the freezer. Bring you some deer jerky too. Gimme fifteen minutes."

He was back in ten. The stomach looked awful, grayish-pink, wrinkled, and slimy, but G-man was happy nonetheless. It had been way too long since he and Rickey cooked anything new together, and he missed it. Alain put the thing to soak in a bowl of water spiked with baking soda and vinegar—he said that would kill any residual smell—and they stood munching the deer jerky, which was smoky and salty and faintly gamy. "You made this yourself?" G-man asked.

"Sure did. Bagged the deer myself too. You hunt?"

"No, I never killed nothing bigger than a fish. I don't think I could shoot anything."

"My papa always told me you gonna eat it, you better be able to kill it." Alain pronounced the word *papa* with the accent on the second syllable. His accent was very faint, just a soft musical undertone running through his speech, nothing like the hokey "Cajun" accents Hollywood assigned to anyone from Louisiana.

"Oh, I agree in theory. But in practice I guess I'm kind of a wuss."

"You got a gentle soul."

G-man raised his eyebrows. In seventeen years of kitchen work, no cook had ever said anything to him like, "You got a gentle soul." Even Rickey had never said such a thing, though G-man was pretty sure he thought it. Kitchen culture was all about being macho and ragging on the other guy, and though G-man played the game as well as anybody, he got tired of it sometimes.

While the chaudin was soaking, they chopped their Holy

Trinity—onions, celery, and bell pepper—and sautéed it with garlic, mushrooms, andouille sausage, ground beef, and ground pork. A savory smell filled the kitchen. "What liquor you think we should hit it with?" G-man said.

"Aw shit, I forgot about the liquor. We gotta do it?"

"We gotta do it."

"Tell you what, give it a little whiskey now. When we oven-poach it later, we can add a little more."

G-man selected a bottle of Irish whiskey from his mise-en-place of the standard liquors. He upended it over the sauté pan, and the pour spout dispensed a shot.

"Don't really think it's gonna add much," said Alain. "This dish got so much flavor, nobody gonna notice a little whiskey."

"Fuck, man, it's not like anybody's gonna order the thing anyway. We'll be lucky if we sell one. You know that, right?"

"Yeah, I know." Alain sighed. "Probably they wouldn't even order it in Cajun country. This here is old folks' food, but I love it."

"That's cool. It's slow enough we can afford to have some fun. Anyway, it doesn't matter too much if nobody can taste the whiskey—it's the idea of the thing. We gotta carry out the concept."

"It's a good concept," Alain said, and G-man was surprised again. Most new cooks eventually made some veiled crack about the liquor gimmick, or at least asked if he didn't get tired of it sometimes. They didn't dare pull that shit with Rickey, but they tried it with G-man. Of course he *did* get tired of the gimmick sometimes, but he wasn't going to tell that to a line cook who'd been working here for two weeks. Yet he didn't get the idea that Alain was trying to kiss his ass; he just seemed genuine. In a business full of posturing thug-wannabes ready to brag about their burns and knife wounds, this was kind of refreshing.

When the meat was browned, Alain added Italian bread-crumbs and a double handful of chopped scallions. "Some cooks put egg in it now, but I don't like to."

"It holds together pretty good?"

"Good as any Cajun food, I guess. We not really about the presentation."

"Yeah, but dude, remember we gotta plate this up. We can't just have a big brown pile of meat laying there in front of the customer."

Alain laughed. "Thought you said nobody was gonna order it."

"If you make a dinner special, you gotta at least pretend somebody's gonna order it."

"OK, OK, I'll put a couple eggs in. But I do it under duress."

"Yeah, I'm such a whip-cracker."

"I bet."

Suddenly there was a weird, not entirely unpleasant tension in the kitchen. G-man didn't quite understand where it had come from and thought he might be imagining it. He looked around for help, but the rest of the crew was elsewhere. "Um," he said. "Well. Yeah. Put a couple eggs in, why don't you?"

"Yeah, I will."

They avoided each other's eyes as Alain took the pig's stomach out of its soda-vinegar bath and rinsed it carefully, making sure not to tear it as he worked the slippery flesh between his fingertips. G-man realized he was holding his breath, made himself quit it. What was going on, anyway? Maybe it was just the banter that had sprung up between them, so easy and comfortable. He hadn't had enough of that with Rickey lately, and he realized he missed it.

Rickey arrived a few minutes later as Alain was stuffing the chaudin. When he came over to see what they were doing, G-man smelled beer on him. Ordinarily he might've busted Rickey's chops a little for that, but right now he felt so guilty that he let it slide.

"What the hell *is* that thing?" Rickey said.

Alain explained the recipe.

"Huh. Cool. When we first opened, I wanted to put veal kidneys à la liégeoise on the menu, but G said nobody would order them."

"Yeah, he said the same about this."

"He's probably right."

Alain tied up the open ends of the chaudin with heavy-gauge kitchen string, laid it in a Dutch oven, and began to sauté it in olive oil with more Holy Trinity. "What do you do?" Rickey said. "Brown it off, then hit it with some stock and poach it?"

"You got it. I do my poaching in the oven, though—it frees up a burner and I think the flavor's better that way."

"Awesome." Rickey turned and walked away toward the office, and G-man followed him without a backward glance.

"I think he's working out real good," Rickey said.

"Who, Alain?"

"Yeah, Alain. Who the hell you thought I was talking about?"

"Nobody. I mean . . . Anything happen today?"

"We made Korean tofu soup," Rickey said. "I don't think anybody'll order that either. And I stopped off for a beer with Milford. Hope you don't mind—I figured y'all could handle things."

"Course I don't mind." Looking into Rickey's eyes, G-man thought it might have been more like two or three beers. That wasn't enough to make Rickey drunk, but G-man knew the look. When you'd been with someone for sixteen years, you knew every look there was. He hung on to that thought and tried to put the last hour or so out of his mind. Besides, with twenty-two diners on the books, it would hardly matter if the entire crew had drunk a six-pack each.

"Oh yeah," Rickey said, "there was one other thing."

"What's that?"

"Me and Milford gotta cook a dinner for the suits next weekend. Saturday night. Seems like you and Alain work pretty good together—you wanna schedule him on sauté?"

It would be fine. Rickey wouldn't have suggested such a thing if he thought there was any tension of the kind G-man must have imagined. He was glad of it; he liked Alain.

"Sure. Schedule Terrance too, and we'll knock it out, just the three of us."

"I was kinda hoping to borrow Terrance for the night. Get him to do some prep and maybe wash a few dishes. I mean, since we haven't hired our crew over there. You think you could get by with Devonte?"

"Hell, we could probably get by without him. Gonna be slow the whole rest of the summer."

"Yeah." Rickey scowled. "Well, just you and Alain then. And Marquis on desserts, I guess."

They were silent for a moment, contemplating Marquis' misfortune. Then Rickey laughed. "Alain sounds just like Bobby Hebert, huh?"

In G-man's mind, that settled any possible problem. Bobby Hebert had a radio sports show on WWL now, but he was dear to Louisiana hearts because he had been the Saints' first Cajun quarterback. The "Cajun Cannon" had helmed the team at the first Saints game Rickey ever attended, when he and G-man were thirteen. For Rickey to compare Alain to Bobby Hebert in any fashion meant Rickey was pretty impressed with their new-est cook.

"Yeah, he does," G-man said inadequately.

"Well . . . " Rickey stepped into the tiny employee bathroom next to the office. "Lemme offload some of this brew. I'll see you in a minute."

"Hang on." G-man put his hand on the door as Rickey was about to shut it.

"What?"

G-man leaned in and gave him a quick kiss. For an instant, as he pulled away, he thought Rickey looked guilty too. But of course Rickey hadn't; there was no reason he should. G-man's imagination was really getting the best of him today.

15

G-MAN sat on a bench in Audubon Park staring out over the lagoon and the golf course beyond. It was just past dawn, the temperature not yet set to broil, the sky full of pink and gold light. The lagoon was a separate, upside-down world of wavering trees and reflected sky. At the water's edge, ducks paddled among cypress knees and clumps of Louisiana iris, ignoring G-man because he had already fed them the crumbled bread heels he'd brought. Other, more graceful birds swooped around the island in the middle of the lagoon, egrets and herons and ones whose names he didn't know. There was a raw, wet freshness to the air, somewhere between jasmine and sperm. He believed this might be the most beautiful place in New Orleans, but its beauty didn't stop him from feeling miserable.

Late last night in the bar, after everybody else went home, Rickey had told him about overhearing Milford and Clancy Fairbairn in the casino kitchen. Very rationally, Rickey laid out his revulsion at Fairbairn and his conviction that he had to go ahead with the project anyway. G-man couldn't argue with any of it, not really. At first he'd had wild ideas about bringing justice down upon Fairbairn's head—"What if Milford had a tape recorder running in his pocket? Fairbairn admitted it once, he'll admit it again!" More gently than G-man had expected, Rickey shot him down: "Dude, he never *admitted* shit. Nothing he said would hold up in a court of law. He's too smart for that. Besides, I don't think Milford would do it—he just wants to get on with his life."

G-man could see that. Three years ago, when he and Rickey were on the verge of opening Liquor, things had been much more black and white for him. An old man named Rondo Johnson had tried to block Liquor from opening in his neighborhood, then died of a sudden, convenient heart attack. Rickey and G-man were about ninety-five percent sure that Lenny had engineered it, but they'd never been able to figure out how. G-man had *known* beyond the shadow of a doubt that it was wrong to forge ahead with the restaurant if Lenny had harmed that old man to protect it, even though he saw the restaurant as a force of good (a very small one, but still) and the old man as an evil crank devoted to spreading misery wherever possible. G-man had always counted this incident as one of his private moral failures, an instance of what he wanted (and, perhaps more importantly, what Rickey wanted) overcoming what he knew was right. The fact that Rickey characterized this as his "goddamn altar-boy ethics" changed his feelings not a whit.

Things didn't seem nearly as clear-cut now. When you were trying to run a restaurant in a place like New Orleans, you had to develop a certain ruthlessness or the business would just rumble roughshod over you. He wondered if restaurant ownership had made him a worse person.

The main difference between this and the incident with the old man, though, was that this was Milford's deal, not theirs. If what Rickey said was true, Clancy Fairbairn had already stolen ten years of Milford's life. For whatever reason, Milford didn't

need revenge for those years, was even willing to work for Fairbairn if that was what it took to regain control of his own kitchen
and rebuild his reputation. Surely that was Milford's decision to
make. "Who am I to screw it up for him?" Rickey had asked
rhetorically.

"Well, the guy with his name on the place, for one thing."

"I know it. Believe me, I'm not too crazy about that. If it was
just me, I'd be happy to give 'em the concept and cut my losses.
But I got Milford into this—seems like I oughta help him stay in
it if that's what he wants."

G-man saw his point. Besides, he knew Rickey had been
scared to tell him about all this, and he appreciated the fact that
Rickey had come clean even if it had taken him a day or so. But
the truth, which terrified and appalled him, was that he felt just
the tiniest bit sick of Rickey. He had never felt that way before,
not once in all the twenty-three years they'd known each other or
the sixteen they had been lovers. Now, though, the pills, the temper, the constant drama, and most of all Rickey's absence from the
restaurant weighed on G-man's heart. He knew perfectly well that
none of this was Rickey's fault. They'd agreed on the consulting
job, he had urged Rickey to go to the doctor about his back, and
the temper and drama were part of the person he had fallen in
love with. And anyway, Rickey needed him now.

He remembered sitting in this same park with Rickey almost
four years ago, both of them just fired from crappy line jobs,
drinking vodka and orange juice out of a thermos and wondering
how they were going to make the rent. Self-righteous indignation
had united them; in the face of dire misfortune they knew that
whatever happened, they were in it together. That was the day
Rickey came up with the idea of a restaurant with a menu based
entirely on liquor, an idea that changed their lives. They had more

money and freedom now, but G-man wondered whether they were as united as they had been that day.

He had thought he might attend morning Mass, but he was impatient with himself for running off to church every time something worried him; if he was truly coming back to some kind of faith, he shouldn't use it as a crutch. Besides, the new pope's pronouncements about the sanctity of marriage made him feel unwelcome. In his experience, the kindness and tolerance of lay Catholics—even most local priests—stood in direct contrast to the hostile positions of Church hierarchy. G-man wasn't very political, but it would always be a sore spot that the Church officially considered the best thing in his life worthless and sinful.

And the relationship *was* the best thing in his life, no question. He couldn't even begin to imagine his life without Rickey. Trying, he felt all the things that had distracted him over the past couple of days—Soul Kitchen, Clancy Fairbairn, that weird moment with Alain—recede into unimportance.

Just as the intensifying sun cleared the treetops, G-man's cell phone rang. He fished it out of his pocket and flipped the cover open. The Marengo Street number flashed on the caller ID. He didn't think "Rickey"; he thought "home." There was no way home could mean anything else, no way they could ever extricate themselves from each other. Realizing this, G-man felt a little better.

Rickey's voice was thick with recent sleep, but edged with worry. "Dude, where are you?"

"I couldn't sleep, so I drove over to the park."

"You coulda let me know."

"I left you a note on the coffeepot."

"I didn't see it. I just woke up to pee, and . . . you weren't anywhere."

Imagining Rickey wandering from room to room, bleary-eyed and pillow-snarled, G-man felt awful. "Sorry, sweetheart," he said, meaning it. "I got restless and wanted some fresh air. I'm coming home right now."

·   ·   ·

Rickey hung up the phone and crawled back into bed. He knew he should start the coffee, but even that small effort seemed beyond him at present. Except for the few days he'd spent in Dallas last year, he couldn't remember the last time he had woken up and G-man hadn't been there. It gave him a horrible empty feeling, a foretaste of what life would be like if he ever went far enough sideways to drive G-man away permanently. These days, he sometimes wondered if he wasn't on the verge of it.

Milford didn't need him, one of his current employers was a murderer, the other one had him hooked on pills, and G-man would rather get some fresh air than wake up with him. If his work ethic were a hair less deeply embedded, Rickey would have thrown it all aside and driven out to Shell Beach for the day. Maybe Captain Alan would be available to take him fishing. If not, he could just wet a line from the rocks at the end of the road. A slideshow of tantalizing images flickered behind his eyelids: the comical pelicans on pilings, the comfortable clutter of the marina, the boat slips and lanky sun-baked men unloading oyster sacks, a gorgeous speckled trout flashing on his hook . . .

It all brought a lump to his throat. A lifelong, die-hard city boy, Rickey realized with amazement that somehow Shell Beach had become possibly his favorite place in the world.

But it would be hotter than hell out on that water today, and he had two kitchens to run. Or one to run and one to show up in, anyway. Rickey forced himself to get up, go to the kitchen, and start spooning coffee into a filter. A few minutes later, intangible relief flooded him as he heard G-man's key in the front door.

•   •   •

Dr. Lamotte fretted as he went over patients' charts, occasionally making a desultory note but not really paying much attention to the details of X-rays, medications, surgeries, or the endless litany of *It hurts, Doctor.* There had been a time when he was meticulous about all these things, a time when he saw himself as a healer, someone who could cure the pain they spoke of rather than masking it with pills. One problem was that most of them preferred the pills. Another was that he had become distracted by a multitude of things, most recently the Pot O'Gold, Soul Kitchen, and Clancy Fairbairn.

The golf game hadn't gone well. They were starting too late in the day—Fairbairn didn't like getting up early—and the sun was murderous. Fairbairn seemed oblivious, but Lamotte sweated and suffered and finally said, "Clancy, how do you do it?"

Fairbairn straightened up from his swing—Lamotte had always been surprised at how good his game was, given the diminished strength in his hand—and squinted behind his expensive sunglasses. "How do I do it?" he repeated. "I don't really know, Frank. I guess I just lead a charmed life. My father before me and my grandfather before him did worse things than I've done, and we won't even *talk* about my great-grandfather and those poor Sicilians they lynched at the old Parish Prison. And yet not a single Fairbairn has ever been required to answer for his sins." He squinted at Lamotte again, then smiled. "If you want to call them sins."

He leaned on his iron carelessly, carving a divot in the turf. A passing foursome glared at him. Lamotte felt panic welling in his throat; was Fairbairn still talking about keeping cool on a hot summer's day, or was there deeper meaning in his words? Rickey had seemed certain that Fairbairn didn't know his conversation with Milford Goodman was being overheard. Even if Fairbairn did know somehow—who had paid for all that fancy kitchen equipment? You'd expect him to be familiar with the place— Lamotte didn't dare acknowledge that he'd heard. The doctor wasn't above shady dealings, not by a long shot . . . but for some time he'd been feeling he was in over his head, and the truth was that even before today he'd been scared of Fairbairn.

Frank Lamotte had never known Eileen Trefethen. The Top Spot wasn't his kind of joint; he hadn't liked the art, and the clientele was always a little too well-dressed for his taste. Lamotte didn't like dressing up and didn't do it well; outside the office he favored sports shirts and Sansabelt slacks. So it wasn't any personal anguish over the woman's death that bothered him now; it was just the shock of knowing his associate had deliberately, brutally taken a life. *It's not like you ever thought he was a nice guy,* Rickey had said, and that was true. But should a doctor—sworn to the Hippocratic oath, bearer of the caduceus—knowingly associate with a cold-blooded murderer?

He skimmed the chart of a seventy-five-year-old woman with osteoporosis, barely seeing his own notes on the thinning of bone and curvature of the spine that caused her such pain. She was on a heavy dose of Darvon. Everybody had a pill, it seemed, something to stave off the world's grinding. Rickey liked his Vicodin, just as Lamotte had hoped he would. He'd offered the young chef that first appointment in hopes of getting a free meal or two out of it, but had soon realized that Rickey was more likely to take the consulting job if Lamotte held the strings of his . . .

well, surely you couldn't call it an addiction. A predilection, maybe. There was nothing wrong with taking away people's pain. Rickey would have the medication he wanted and Lamotte would have a talented chef to oversee the opening of his restaurant. As ever in New Orleans, one hand washed the other. But now the withered hand of Clancy Fairbairn was stirring the mix in a way Lamotte hadn't foreseen.

Well, he couldn't do anything about Fairbairn, and he was into the casino and the restaurant project far too deep to pull out now. Besides, there was also the dirt Fairbairn had on him, that business with the painkillers planted in the car of a judge's enemy; Lamotte had provided the pills. In a process Rickey might have understood all too well, Lamotte abruptly decided to put the knowledge of Fairbairn's long-ago deed behind a high, thick wall in his mind. He wouldn't be able to forget it, but he wouldn't have to see it very often either.

• • •

Lenny had known Tanker for a long time and considered him a straight-up guy, so he figured the direct approach would be best. Getting hold of him proved to be harder than Lenny had expected, but he finally caught Tanker at home one morning.

"I've been trying to call your cell phone," Lenny said. "No luck."

"Yeah, I left the goddamn thing on the streetcar and still haven't got it back. Went to RTA Lost & Found, looked through five boxes of 'em, some so old they looked like TV remotes. Mine wasn't there. I tell you, Lenny, I hate taking public transportation."

"I can imagine," said Lenny, who couldn't. "Can't a nice hotel like the d'Hemecourt give you a parking space?"

Tanker just laughed shortly. "You been out of the hotel business awhile, huh?"

"I was never really in it."

"Lucky you."

Lenny was surprised and encouraged by the bitterness in Tanker's voice. "But what about the food, Tank? I heard they were doing some interesting food over there. It's gotta be a far cry from Liquor. Hell, Rickey's doing shrimp gratin and trout amandine now."

"He is?"

"Yep." Lenny allowed his tone to become sepulchral. "But what's worse is the dessert list."

"Not . . . the usual suspects?"

"Crème brûlée, bread pudding, pecan pie, chocolate soufflé . . ."

"Wow."

Tanker sounded gratified by the boringness of Rickey's menu, and Lenny reflected silently on the power of schadenfreude. Then Tanker slid back into despair. "Anyway, interesting isn't the word for the food we're doing. Jaap's gone completely around the bend. He's in outer space. He's popped his top. He's a fucking loon. He—"

"I get the idea," Lenny said hastily. "What do you mean? He treats you bad?"

"Nah, no worse than ever. He's always been a screamer, but I don't give a damn about that as long as he doesn't get personal. No, it's the food. It's just . . ." Now Tanker's voice was quiet, almost awed. "Tell you the truth, I'm not even sure it *is* food anymore."

"Well, if it's not food, then what is it?"

"It's air. Vapors. Structures. Little pieces of paper. Fuck, man, I don't know. I thought I wanted to get experimental, but not like this." The whisper rose to a wail. "I want to *feed* people, not *mystify* them!"

"Yeah, be careful what you wish for, huh?"

"You got that right." Nobody said anything for a moment. Lenny let the silence spin out, giving Tanker time to contemplate whatever was going through his mind. "Listen, Lenny, why you called? I gotta get to work pretty soon."

"Just wanted to see how you were doing, buddy."

"Rickey didn't ask you to call, huh?"

Lenny thought Tanker sounded a little hopeful, but he didn't take the bait. "You kidding? You must've forgotten how stubborn Rickey is. He wouldn't ask me to do any such thing."

"I guess not."

"No—he'd rather just let his dessert list go to hell, lose a few sweet-toothed customers. Well, it was good talking to you, Tank. I'll try to stop by and see what you're up to sometime."

"You do that. Be sure and order the—what the fuck is he calling it now? He changes the name of the tasting menu every other day or so—oh yeah, the Grand Narrative. He says it tells the culinary story of his life."

Christ on a crutch, Lenny thought, but he only said, "I wouldn't miss it for the world."

They hung up. Lenny nodded to himself, satisfied at a seed well planted. Tanker had created that dessert list, had helped make Liquor the success it was. The thought of its ruination would gnaw at him, especially given his unhappiness with the Polonius Room gig. If he could be made to believe he was being the bigger man by returning to Liquor, rising above Rickey's stubbornness for the greater good of the restaurant . . . and if Rickey could be led to a similar belief . . .

But Lenny was getting ahead of himself. This was just seed-ing the fertile earth, and a good job of it too. A trifle compared to some of the social engineering he'd had to do in his day, but a pleasing one because no one would be hurt and everyone concerned would benefit.

His only real regret was that he didn't have the whole thing on tape.

16

RICKEY was out East, driving along Chef Menteur Highway, when he saw the storefront clinic advertising Acupuncture & Traditional Medicine in three languages. At least, he assumed the Vietnamese and Spanish words advertised it; he could only read the English. He didn't know if the place would be open yet— he'd come out to the weekly Vietnamese farmers' market, which mostly took place between 5:00 and 8:00 A.M., and was now headed back into town with a cooler of shrimp and a crate full of beautiful herbs and salad greens—but on impulse he swung into the parking lot anyway. His back had given him holy hell all through dinner service last night, and for the first time ever, two Vicodins when he got home had scarcely touched the pain.

There were no lights on inside, but the glass door swung open at his touch. The place seemed to be deserted, or at least the waiting room did, if that was what this was; it didn't look like any doctor's waiting room Rickey had ever been in. Didn't smell like one, either. The scent was part antiseptic, part herbal, part smoky. Some memory receptor lit up deep in his brain, and he realized it reminded him very faintly of Chinatown in New York City, that strange and deeply exciting neighborhood he'd first encountered as an eighteen-year-old in culinary school.

He glanced around nervously. There was the chart of the human body he'd seen on the acupuncture brochure, now hanging life-sized on a wall. There was a wall of shelving stocked with apothecary jars of what looked like dried herbs, and in front of it, a glass case as in a jewelry store. Rickey bent over and peered into the case. It was hard to see anything in the dim light, but he began to make out shapes and colors . . . a row of boxes with Chinese lettering . . . a packet of roots . . . a bundle of dried . . . no, it couldn't be . . . yes, it was; dried centipedes, and next to that, small mummified snakes. He could see the eyes, and the tiny forked tongues sticking out of their mouths.

Rickey was halfway to the door when he heard footsteps coming up the hall. A woman's voice with a heavy Vietnamese accent said, "Sorry, not open yet, nine o'clock."

"That's OK," Rickey assured her, shoving the door open and practically throwing himself into the parking lot. He stood beside his car taking deep breaths of the fresh morning air. Snakes! Centipedes! He considered himself pretty open-minded as far as consumables of any type went, but if creepy-crawlies like that were involved, these folks could keep their traditional medicine.

The glass door opened and the woman's glossy head poked out. "Sir? You need some help?"

"Nah . . . no, I was just . . . " He could think of nothing to say that wouldn't sound incredibly lame. "Uh, I just wanted a brochure."

"I get you one."

She ducked back into the clinic and returned a minute later with what looked to be essentially the same brochure he already had in his desk drawer. As she handed it to him, Rickey missed his grip and it fluttered to the asphalt.

"Oops, sorry," she said, bending.

"No, don't worry about it." Rickey beat her to it, but as he straightened up, his lower back muscles twanged like a series of violin strings snapping. He must have winced, because the woman said, "You got back trouble, huh?"

"Yeah, you could say that."

"For how long?"

"About six months now."

"You had X-ray?"

"Yeah." At G-man's insistence, he'd finally gotten Dr. Lamotte to do a series of them. "It didn't show anything."

"Acupuncture maybe help. You want to try? I open few minutes early."

"The doctor's already here?"

"You looking at doctor." The woman smiled and stuck out her hand, then rattled off a series of syllables that Rickey couldn't even begin to translate. "But everyone calls me Chau," she added helpfully.

As they shook hands, Rickey looked at her more carefully and saw that she was in early middle age; only her shiny black bob and diminutive size had made her seem younger. A breath of hope touched him; then he remembered the snakes and centipedes. "Thanks, Dr. Chau," he said, "but I guess I better get to work."

"Well, you come back sometime. First treatment free. I don't want sell you no B.S. I want help you."

"No B.S., huh?" Rickey grinned. Something about this lady rubbed him the right way. "This stuff really works?"

"No promises. Help some people, don't help others. Often

very good for back pain. Seriously, you want to try, I take you now. You want to wait, I give you appointment when you call."

Maybe this would be a good time to try it after all. If he made an appointment, he would just stay awake all night dreading it. Besides, the needles pictured in the brochure weren't very big; it couldn't hurt any worse than a tattoo, and he had a couple of those. "OK," he said. "I'll try it now. But just acupuncture, huh? I don't want any herbal medicine."

"No medicine," she promised. "Maybe whiskey."

This definitely sounded like his kind of doctor. Rickey grabbed his cooler of shrimp from the backseat—they were on ice, but in this weather they'd be floating within an hour if he left them out here—and followed her back into the clinic.

• • •

Ninety minutes later, Rickey was back on Chef Menteur heading for the city. His back didn't hurt. He was more aware of it than he wanted to be—almost as if it were *waiting* to hurt again—but, for the moment, it felt better. Perhaps even more important, that little Vietnamese woman had given more attention to his problem in an hour plus change than Dr. Lamotte had given it in six months. She had taken his complete medical and work history, examined the sclera of his eyes, weighed and measured him, asked him dozens of questions about things that didn't seem relevant at all, like how much coffee he drank and whether he remembered his dreams. Then she made him strip naked, sent a nurse in to drape a businesslike towel over his butt, and inserted a quantity of needles into the skin over the lower half of his spine, so shallowly that he couldn't feel them at all. When she attached some sort of wires to the needles and zapped them with electrical currents, he damn sure felt that; it caused his muscles to twitch slightly but unpleasantly, making him feel like a half-dead fish flopping in a cooler. At the end of the session, though, he got up from the table—clutching the towel with a death grip as he realized both women were standing just outside the open door—and was surprised to realize he felt better than he had in days.

Maybe there was something to this traditional medicine. He wasn't so sure about the "whiskey," though. It was an opaque jet-black liquid in a screwtop jar that looked as if it had once held strawberry preserves, and dedicated drinker though he was, Rickey had no confidence that he'd be able to choke it down.

At any rate, it would make a good story to tell G-man. Also, he had a second appointment next week. It was a long way to drive, but Rickey thought he would probably drive to Alaska on a weekly basis if someone there could help him get his strength and his life back.

As he crested the drawbridge over the Industrial Canal, he suddenly pounded the steering wheel. "Aw, shit!" He'd been so relaxed when he left the clinic that he had forgotten his cooler of shrimp. He could picture it sitting in the corner of the treatment room. Well, he wasn't driving all the way back out there now. He'd call when he got to the restaurant, make sure Dr. Chau found it and tell her she could have them. So the first treatment hadn't been free after all, but a cooler of shrimp, even huge gorgeous ones, was a small price to pay for a day free of pain. Half a day, even, if that was all he ended up getting.

•   •   •

It was time for Lenny to set his second hook. He already had Tanker flopping at the end of a nice long line; now he needed to spend some time with Rickey. In order to implement his plan for bringing Tanker back to Liquor, he had to ensure Rickey's complete trust, and one of the best ways to gain the trust of a New Orleanian was to get staggering, stinking drunk with him. Lenny didn't know if they would go all the way to stinking, but he definitely planned to stagger a little.

"Whenever you guys have time," he said into the phone. He knew no one in New Orleans said *you guys,* but after two decades here he still could not quite fit his mouth around *y'all.* "It's nothing major. I just got to thinking how we haven't sat down and talked together for a while. You ever been to the Sazerac Bar?"

"Course I been to the Sazerac Bar. I used to work on Canal Street, you know. Haven't been there in years, though." Rickey sounded a little nostalgic. "It's a real nice bar, but somehow we always used to get in trouble when we went there."

They arranged to meet at the Sazerac on Rickey and G-man's next night off. When Rickey got there, though, he was alone. "G's watching the NBA draft," he said, rolling his eyes. "I like basketball, but staying home to watch the draft's kinda extreme by my standards."

Well, that was actually better, Lenny thought. It was Rickey he needed to work on. G-man was already amenable to bringing Tanker back, and he could be annoyingly suspicious of Lenny's motives.

Rickey got a drink and sank into an armchair. "Goddamn pain in the ass to park down here, too. They got a convention going on or something? Thank God I don't have to keep up with the conventions anymore . . . we get some business from them, but not enough so I gotta worry, 'OK, there's 15,000 kidney surgeons in town this week, 7,500 widget makers here next week . . .'"

Despite his complaining words, Rickey was gazing around the bar with obvious affection. The Sazerac was just the sort of place that would appeal to him, Lenny knew: wood-paneled, vaguely old-farty, untouched by the trends and innovations of the last half-century or so. It was in the lobby of a grand old downtown hotel that for forty years had been named the Fairmont, but which plenty of New Orleanians still called the Roosevelt. Until his deposal last year, District Attorney Placide Treat had kept a suite here. Treat had turned out to be a great enemy of Lenny's, and it gave Lenny an extra little frisson of pleasure to come to the Fairmont now that the nutty old coot had lost everything.

Lenny drank vodka tonics to Rickey's bourbon and sodas. For the first couple of rounds they talked about their various restaurants, other restaurants, and the restaurant world in general. When Lenny went to get the third round, it became evident that the bartender had overheard their conversation and subsequently recognized him. "Hey, Chef, you wanna try my new invention? I call it a Blaze Starr. You take a skewer of cherries soaked in brandy, flame it, and plunge it into a flute of ice-cold champagne."

"Thanks." Lenny tried to smile, though the thought of dumping brandied cherries and champagne on top of vodka nauseated him. A snippet of doggerel from one of Rickey's cocktail books ran through his head: *Perhaps you like it garnished with what thinking men avoid / The little blushing cherry that is made of celluloid* . . . "I think we'll just stick with what we've been having."

"Soocher self," said the bartender, sulking a little. "Listen, though, I'm an expert mixologist. Last week I invented the Raspberry Dreamsicle—framboise and Godiva white chocolate liqueur."

"Tell you what," said Lenny, trying not to gag. "Why don't you give me your card, and I'll call you if I ever need a bartender?"

"Really? That'd be awesome!" Now all was forgiven, and round four was on the house. Lenny returned to his table wondering when "mixologist" had come to mean "one who creates sticky random fruit concoctions" instead of "one who can mix the perfect highball and knows that serving a drink in a martini glass doesn't make it a martini." Even the Sazerac Bar, apparently, was no longer free from innovation.

He said as much to Rickey, who turned to glare at the bartender. "*Raspberry Dreamsicle?* I'd like to tell him where to stick his fucking Dreamsicle."

"Now, now. He's young, he wants to make his mark on the world just like you did."

"Just like I did, hell. I got my gimmick, sure, but I don't pervert my food in order to incorporate it. I just don't think Bourbon Street crap like that has any place at the Sazerac. If that's what they want, let 'em go drink a Hand Grenade or one of those glow-in-the-dark daiquiris."

"Calm down. I don't see people lining up here to order Raspberry Dreamsicles, do you?"

After a grudging glance around the bar, Rickey shook his head. "Nah, you mostly get the better class of tourist in here."

Lenny laughed; he couldn't help it. "You're turning into an old man! Listen to yourself—*the better class of tourist, not those young whippersnappers you see on Bourbon Street.* What are you, all of thirty-one?"

"I'll be thirty-two in September. I'm entitled."

"Well, pardon me then. I didn't realize I was speaking to a genuine Golden Ager."

Rickey hoisted his drink with one hand and made a half-hearted obscene gesture at Lenny with the other. Lenny laughed again. It really had been too long; he'd almost forgotten how much he enjoyed drinking with Rickey. Then he let the smile die off his face, gazed into his drink, and sighed a little.

"You OK, Lenny?"

"Aw, I guess so. I go through drinking phases and not-drinking phases. Lately I've been a little overworked, maybe a little lonely." He glanced at Rickey from the corner of his eye, wondering if he'd spilled too far over into the realm of the maudlin.

But Rickey looked sympathetic. "Fuck, man, I don't know how you're not lonely *all* the time. Dating strippers and shit. Why don't you find somebody nice and settle down?"

"Yeah, well, it's not that easy for everybody. Most of us don't meet the one love of our lives when we're sixteen."

"We actually met when we were nine. The hormones just didn't kick in until we were sixteen." Rickey considered this. "OK, maybe they kicked in a little earlier, but sixteen was when we finally figured out what to do about it."

"But what's your secret?" Lenny felt that he was laying it on a little thick here, and he gulped at his drink to make the pathos more convincing. "I mean, I've dated a bunch of women, but I can't imagine staying with anybody for sixteen years. Most of them drive me crazy after sixteen *days.*"

"I don't know, man. I can't speak for women, but I don't see why they'd be a whole lot different. Me and G, we just really like each other. I mean, we love each other too, sure, but I think maybe liking each other's even more important."

"Huh." Lenny wondered for a moment if he might actually learn something, then dismissed the thought; he wasn't here to get dating advice. "So what are you saying? In order to have a long-term relationship, you have to find somebody you don't just want to screw—you want to live with them too?"

"Not just want to live with them, I guess. It's more like you can't imagine living *without* them. I mean, some people might get sick of each other, living the way me and G do—we go to sleep together, we wake up together, we work together. But I'm happiest when I'm around him 24/7. If you never felt that way about anybody, then maybe you never been in love."

"I thought I was once." Lenny hadn't meant to say that; it had just slipped out, maybe because something about Rickey's declaration had touched his heart.

"Yeah?"

"Yeah. It didn't work out, though."

"How come?"

"Well . . ." Oh, what the hell; once in a great while, the best way to cement someone's trust was to just be honest with him. "She was the wife of a friend who died, and I met her at his funeral."

"Aw, shit. Jeez, Lenny, that's . . . wait. It wasn't Devlin Lemon, was it?"

"Yeah. I forgot you knew Dev."

"Not real well. I didn't go to the funeral or anything."

Devlin Lemon was a talented young chef who had been badly injured in a robbery as he left his Garden District restaurant, the Lemon Tree. Rumor went around that he had actually been killed, but somehow he made a miraculous recovery from being shot in the head at point-blank range and was soon back in his kitchen. A year later he was diagnosed with a voracious cancer; a year after that he was gone. It was as if the community had lost him twice over, and it hit everyone who knew him doubly hard.

"Well, I did, and that's where I met Theresa."

"You asked her out at her husband's funeral?"

"No, Rickey, even I'm not that crass, but . . . there was something there. I gave her my card, told her to call me if she needed anything at all. She called a couple of weeks later to see if I was interested in buying any of Dev's kitchen equipment. He had some really top-end stuff, and I got the idea he didn't leave her much else. I bought the whole kit and caboodle—cookware, appliances, everything. Didn't really need it, but I wanted to see Theresa again."

"And you did."

"Yeah, I did. I took her out that night. We drank two bottles of Dom Perignon." For a few minutes Lenny didn't say anything else. He was remembering the faint cinnamon scent of her hair, the way her eyes crinkled when she smiled. Theresa had been a good deal older and rougher around the edges than most of the women Lenny dated, but somehow she had also been more beautiful than any of the ones whose job it was to be beautiful.

Rickey didn't say anything either. Probably he thought he was maintaining a respectful silence, but Lenny wanted to keep talking and wished he would ask questions. When he didn't, Lenny finally said, "We really loved each other, I think, but there was just too much of Devlin between us. Maybe if we'd met a year or two later . . . it was too fresh for her, you know? For me too, I guess. We didn't last six months."

"You still keep in touch?"

"No, she left New Orleans sometime last year. Last I heard, she'd moved back to Lafayette. Her hometown."

"Cajun girl, huh?"

"Half Cajun. Her mother's side."

"Lafayette's not that far."

"I know, but . . ." Lenny gestured vaguely with his empty glass. The bartender must have taken this as a signal, for a couple of minutes later he came over with a fresh round of drinks. Not vodka tonics or bourbon and sodas, though; these cocktails were a pretty red-gold color, and Rickey stared at them with obvious alarm as the guy set them down. "These are on me. I figured since you're drinking where they were invented, you gotta have a Sazerac."

"Thanks," Lenny said hastily, hoping to distract the poor kid from Rickey's sudden snarl of loathing.

"I *hate* Sazeracs!" Rickey said when the bartender had gone. "Sickly-sweet licorice-jellybean-tasting—"

"I've heard your anti-Sazerac rant a time or two."

"Sorry. But look, we gotta get out of here. That kid's recognized you, and he's just gonna send over all kinds of nasty-ass bullshit. I can't drink this. You want mine?"

"I haven't even tasted mine yet." Lenny sipped the drink and found that it was, in fact, an exemplary Sazerac, piquant with rye and Herbsaint. "Honestly, Rickey, this is excellent."

"I don't care if it's the second coming. I hate those goddamn things. It's the taste of sitting in a goddamn restaurant listening to my parents fight."

"You know, some people who associate flavors with bad times in their life manage to get over it."

"Yeah? How much Dom Perignon you had lately?"

"Touché," Lenny said quietly.

"Aw, man, I'm sorry. I wasn't trying to score points off you. Look, let's just get out of here before that guy sends over one of his goddamn Raspberry Dreamsicles."

"He's not going to do that. Why don't you go get another Wild Turkey? I'm switching to Sazeracs. These are really tasty."

"You sure, Lenny? Those things got a pretty good kick."

"I'll be fine. I know how to drink."

"Famous last words."

"Maybe so." Lenny suddenly found that he didn't much care. His mission tonight had been to jolly Rickey around, get him drunk, make sure Rickey's trust in him wasn't fraying around the edges, all of this merely a preface to actually getting Rickey and

Tanker back together. After reminiscing about Theresa, though, he felt melancholy enough to want to tie one on. "I don't care. If you're not going to drink that Sazerac, hand it over."

•   •   •

Four hours later, Rickey pulled up in front of Lenny's house in Lakeview. They had consumed another round at the Sazerac, then moved on to the Apostle Bar, Anthony Bonvillano's much humbler joint on Tchoupitoulas, where they wound down with beer. ("Beer before liquor, never sicker," Anthony had informed them solemnly upon seeing their condition. "Liquor before beer, never fear.") Rickey didn't know where Lenny had left his Lexus, and didn't much care; Lenny could afford to taxi back downtown and pick it up tomorrow, and if it had been towed, Lenny could certainly afford to bail it out of the car pound on Claiborne. Right now Rickey was more concerned with getting Lenny out of his car and into the house.

"Lenny. Hey, Lenny. C'mon, this is where you get off."

"U bye u mye," Lenny mumbled.

"What?"

"U bye u *mye*."

"OK, whatever you say. C'mon, you just got a little ways to go." Rickey came around to the passenger side of his old Plymouth and opened the door. Lenny sort of sagged out, and Rickey caught him before he could hit the driveway.

They moved slowly up Lenny's front walk, Rickey doing his best to steer Lenny forward when he wanted to go sideways. At the front door, Lenny made a slight recovery and managed to extract his keys from his pocket. Rickey opened the door, reflecting upon how far he had come since the first time he visited this house and couldn't even figure out where the doorbell was.

"You OK now, or do I need to help you upstairs?"

"Uhhh."

"I better help you upstairs," Rickey decided. He got Lenny up the grand, curving staircase and along the ironwork-edged gallery to his bedroom. "OK, dude, you're on your own from here."

Lenny flopped down on his bed. "Rickey!" he said loudly.

"Yeah?"

"I'm prolly never gonna get married. Never gonna have kids."

"Right, you told me—"

"Shut up! Shut up! I wan' you to know this. You . . ." Lenny levered himself up on one elbow and pointed a hairy forefinger at Rickey. "You . . ."

"Yeah, Lenny, I'm right here."

"You," Lenny enunciated carefully, "are like the son I never had. I jus' wan' you to know I'm proud of you."

Rickey opened his mouth to make some smart reply, but was stopped by the absurd lump that rose in his throat. He guessed he was pretty drunk himself, and he knew Lenny probably had no idea what he was saying, but it was still nice to hear something he'd never heard from his real father. "Thanks," he said. "I'm glad."

"I jus' wan' you to know."

"Got it."

Apparently satisfied, Lenny flopped back on the bed. Within a minute he was snoring. Heartened by the exchange, Rickey took the time to remove Lenny's shoes and Rolex before descending the grand staircase and letting himself out of the house.

Headed home, the driver's-side window cranked down so that the warm rush of night air could refresh him, Rickey had to laugh at the way the evening had gone. It was obvious that Lenny had wanted to get him drunk for some reason, but after twenty years in New Orleans, you'd think Lenny would know the folly of trying to outdrink a native. Rickey must have had seven or eight drinks all told, but he felt pretty good. When he got home, maybe he'd even have some of Dr. Chau's black "whiskey." He was supposed to take a full shot twice a day, but it was indescribably foul stuff, and so far he hadn't been able to manage more than a few drops. Perhaps all the Wild Turkey would grease the skids.

A few minutes later Rickey parked on Marengo Street, glad to see a light still burning in the front room of their house. Maybe G-man was still up. He hoped so. Lenny might have all the money in the world, but it was better having somebody to come home to.

17

SO what the hell are we gonna do for the meal this weekend, anyway?" Rickey asked. "Do we really want to show off a range of world cuisine, or do we just want to impress the suits?"

"Don't worry about it," Milford told him. "I got it all figured out."

This was about the answer Rickey had expected, but it still grated on him. Since the weird scene between Milford and Clancy Fairbairn and the subsequent conversation at the bar, Milford had been increasingly dismissive of Rickey's contributions to Soul Kitchen. Rickey supposed some chefs would be fine with this arrangement—getting paid to lend your name to something while doing hardly any of the work—but for him it rankled. "OK, look," he said. "I'm not your fucking line cook. I'm not even your sous chef. I'm supposed to be the executive chef of this place, and I know it's really your menu, not mine, but don't tell me *Don't worry about it.* I'm not putting my name on something I got zero control over."

"You want control?" Milford reached into his hip pocket and pulled out a piece of paper. He unfolded it and slapped it on the counter in front of Rickey. "OK, here's the menu I had in mind. Tell me how you gonna improve on it."

Rickey flattened the menu and scanned it, feeling as stupid and superfluous as Milford always seemed to make him feel lately. Milford was one of the best cooks he'd ever known; how was he going to improve on perfection? Of course, Tanker was another of the best cooks he'd ever known, and look what had happened there. Rickey wondered if maybe he had a talent for pissing off his betters.

As he'd expected, the menu was intelligently designed, offering a good range and progression of dishes:

> Amuse-bouche: Mini spring roll with shrimp & herbs, sweet/hot dipping sauce (Vietnam)
>
> Fried chicken salad with buttermilk blue cheese dressing (America)
>
> Cold borscht with crème fraiche and caviar (Russia)
>
> Gulf shrimp and mussel sofrito with green peas (Spain)
>
> Honey-glazed cumin-roasted lamb with preserved lemons (Morocco)
>
> Palate cleanser: Lemon sorbet
>
> Sliced mangoes with black rice & coconut cream (Thailand)

"I thought you didn't want to do Italian food," Rickey couldn't resist saying.

"What Italian food?"

"The lemon sorbet."

"Hey, I figure we can get a carton of the stuff from Angelo Brocato's, that's one less thing we gotta make. I ain't about to stand on principle."

"Fairbairn's gonna freak when he sees all this foreign food."

"I'll keep a pot of gumbo on the back burner for him," Milford joked.

It was the friendliest exchange they'd had in days. Rickey decided not to point out that with a slight shift in ingredients and the addition of an extra *f,* sofrito could be Italian as well as Spanish. He could have suggested a couple of changes—given the local prejudice against cold soups, he wasn't convinced the borscht would blow them away, and with a dessert as light as mangoes and coconut rice, he didn't think they really needed a palate cleanser—but it would have felt like an attempt to leave his piss-marks on the menu. It was fine. They'd serve the dinner on Saturday night, Lamotte and Fairbairn would be impressed, Soul Kitchen would move ahead as scheduled, and pretty soon he'd be able to leave all this behind and get back to his own restaurant.

•   •   •

"You want me to make some kinda special?" Alain said.

It was the day of Rickey's casino dinner for the suits and their wives. Alain and G-man were holding down the fort at Liquor. Devonte would be in later to help with service, but it was just the two of them doing prep.

"Sure. You got some other crazy-ass Cajun dish you feel like making? Nutria brains or something?"

"Aw, you just mad cause you said my chaudin wasn't gonna sell, and it did."

"Three. We sold three."

"Yeah, but we only did thirty-nine covers that night. That means one-thirteenth of all our customers ordered my special. Not too bad for a pig's stomach, huh?"

"It was three more than I thought we'd sell," G-man admitted. He and Rickey and Alain had eaten the rest at the bar after hours, since none of the other kitchen crew or wait staff would touch it. It was delicious, spicy and porky without the whiff of bile that had been present in the sautéed pig's stomach Rickey made him taste at a Chinatown restaurant when they were in New York for the Beard awards.

"Anyway," Alain said, "down where I come from, in Cut Off, we do hunt nutria. Not for eating, though. We turn 'em in for the state bounty—four dollars a tail."

"I thought they were supposed to be pretty good eating. A few years ago, some chefs around town tried to get people interested. Had nutria jambalaya on their menus, nutria confit, sausage, you name it. I think they called 'em *ragondin* or something like that, though."

"Shit. When I was in school, my girlfriend's momma cooked a nutria one time. Said it took her weeks to get the stink out her kitchen."

"Oh yeah?" said G-man. Though he tended to assume most cooks were straight, for some reason he felt surprised that Alain was, and even obscurely disappointed. He and Rickey had never considered themselves part of the mystifying thing known as "gay culture" or even had many gay friends; in the restaurant world, your friends were the people you worked with, and most of the gay people were in the front of the house. Still, every once in a while, it was nice to encounter a fellow cook who didn't blather endlessly about pussy or use "fag" as a pejorative.

"Yeah." Alain was silent for a few minutes, topping up the

squeeze bottles in his mise-en-place. Then he said, "But I had boyfriends too."

"Oh yeah?" G-man said again, because he could think of absolutely nothing else to say.

"Yeah. But only since I moved to New Orleans. Not in Cut Off."

Something about this struck G-man as funny, and before he could help it he snorted laughter. Alain glanced over at him, frowning in a puzzled way, then laughed too.

When Devonte arrived later that afternoon, Alain and G-man were still repeating "Not in Cut Off" and snickering every now and then. He regarded them with the patient gaze of an anthropologist studying naked South Sea islanders, then turned his attention to the salad station.

●　　●　　●

The day hadn't started auspiciously. Milford kept banging around the kitchen until Rickey asked him what was wrong, but Milford just said, "Nothin." Rickey thought of pointing out that it was an awfully loud form of nothing, but decided to keep his mouth shut. The noise was actually a nice change of pace. This was shaping up to be the quietest kitchen he'd ever worked in, and it didn't feel good. Kitchens were supposed to be loud places of hissing oil, clanging pots, and trash talk.

At the last minute (which was around six-thirty, since the dinner was set for eight) Milford realized he had forgotten the caviar to be spooned atop the little islands of crème fraiche in the cold borscht. Terrance was already there helping out with prep, so Rickey volunteered to drive up to the Sav-A-Center near UNO. He grabbed a jar of black lumpfish eggs, inferior stuff, but he'd have bet money that neither the suits nor their wives would know the difference. Shuttled quickly through the checkout line—they kept things moving out here; this was a rich people's grocery, not like the frequently glacial ones Uptown—he headed back, his window cranked down, the evening wind drying the kitchen-sweat in his hair.

As he wound through the parking lot toward the valet area, the Pot O'Gold towered glowing before him, its lacy decks alight with imitation gas lamps. Despite the attempts to make it look like something from a nineteenth-century gambler's fantasy, it more closely resembled Rickey's idea of a 1950s-era floating plea-sure palace, overlit and slightly chintzy, the kind of place that made you aware of the threadbare rooms behind the "luxe" gam-ing areas. The kitchen was the only part of the boat he'd seen that didn't look like shit with a thin coat of gold paint slapped on it. The Soul Kitchen dining room was only just now being deco-rated, but Rickey could see that it too was going to have that un-mistakable slightly-down-at-the-heels casino look. He wondered why they had put so much money into the kitchen, then won-dered why the thought made him uneasy.

He didn't have time to worry about that now, though. To-night wasn't going to be hard, but it would be stressful. Impress-ing the owners and all that crap. Rickey wasn't used to worrying about owners and their opinions anymore; he'd gotten too used to being one. Well, maybe this would give him a fresh perspective.

•   •   •

Milford didn't realize he'd cut himself until he saw the blood flow-ing over his cutting board. He rinsed his hand, mummified the injured finger with a paper towel and some duct tape, threw away the gory basil leaves he'd been chiffonading, and started over again. He had to be careful or he'd really hurt himself tonight, one way or another.

Eleonora had called this morning. He hadn't talked to his sister since moving out of her house, but had been hoping to hear from her. The momentary spark of gladness died as soon as he found out why she was calling, though.

"Well, first of all, I done lost my job last week."

"What happened? I thought you was supervisor."

"I was, but they say guests been complaining about stuff stole out they rooms. Made out like I'm runnin some kinda theft ring."

"They know you're related to me?"

"I don't know." She took a long, shuddery breath, and Milford realized she was upset about more than the job. "See, when I told Ronald about it, he decided he's gonna make the rent." Ronald, fourteen, was her oldest child. "Got a toy gun from somewhere, pulled his T-shirt over his face, and tried to rob the corner grocery. The owner shot him."

Milford closed his eyes against the kitchen's sudden glare. "Is he dead?"

"No, praise Jesus. He in the hospital. Bullet nicked his spine—he probably ain't gonna walk again."

He had offered to go to her even though that would have meant abandoning his post and most likely losing his own job, but Eleonora wouldn't allow it. "I'll be awright," she said. "Pastor's here, and the rest of the kids. I just wanted to let you know."

As Milford hung up the phone, a bright bolt of pain went through his head. It felt like pure, undistilled anger, but what was he angry about? The Goodmans were a bad-luck family; their mother had always said so. He couldn't blame anybody in particular for Eleonora losing her job, and what had happened to Ronald was the kid's own fault, as much as Milford hated to admit it. In some ways, getting through his prison sentence had been easier than life on the outside seemed now. There, he'd had one hateful scapegoat, Clancy Fairbairn, to blame for everything. Things weren't that simple anymore.

· · · ·

It was 7:10 when Rickey walked back into the kitchen. Milford was slicing three different kinds of cornbread and tucking the pieces into napkin-lined breadbaskets. Rickey picked up where he had left off, dipping the spring roll wrappers in hot water to soften them before tucking in the ingredients and rolling them up into perfect little cigar shapes. He'd intended to do this earlier, but Milford was afraid they would dry out in the fridge. Neither of them had a whole lot of experience with spring rolls.

The smell of fresh mint and basil made Rickey think of Dr. Chau. He'd had two more acupuncture appointments, and each time the effects had seemed to dwindle more quickly. "You gotta get off that stuff!" Chau said vehemently when Rickey told her about the Vicodin. "Bad for your back, bad for your mind. All it does is mask the pain."

"Isn't that pretty much what anything does?" he'd asked.

"No. Best treatments change your body. Change your *qi*. Fix problems, not mask them."

Qi was a concept Rickey had trouble wrapping his mind around. Chau had explained it as an invisible cosmic force that flowed through his body and throughout the entire universe, which was a bit much for a Lower Ninth Ward boy with a New Orleans public school education. Rickey knew he wasn't stupid, but he hated anything that made him *feel* stupid, so he'd asked

Chau not to bring up *qi* again if she could help it. "Doesn't matter," she'd shrugged. "It's there whether you wanna think about it or not."

This reminded Rickey of those people who, if you said you didn't believe in God, responded smugly, *But He believes in you!* He guessed he must have shown Chau what G-man called his game face, because she dropped the subject of *qi,* but continued to nag him about the Vicodin. It wouldn't irritate him so much if he didn't know she was right: at some point soon he was going to have to walk away from the pills for good. No more excuses, no more waiting for the acupuncture to fix everything, no more maundering about the pain of the universe.

Abruptly he decided he would do it as soon as he was finished with Soul Kitchen. His need for the pills had gotten him into this troublesome venture, and he would wash his hands of both things at once. He finished the last spring roll, wrapped his fingers around the handle of his favorite chef's knife—the only thing he could think of to swear on at the moment—and made a silent, solemn vow to himself: *If I should go back on my word, may I forget how to use this damn thing.*

The four diners were seated at five minutes past eight, and the *amuses* went out at 8:15. Then they came right back in again, dropped and mangled by a casino-issue waiter more used to bringing people clean plates at the buffet. Of course Rickey's first impulse was to rip him a new asshole, but there was no point; they had six courses to go and he'd never see this guy again after tonight. It wasn't worth making an enemy over.

Instead, he grabbed the rice papers and pawed through his lowboy for the fresh herbs. There weren't any more cooked shrimp, so he picked the pieces out of the ruined dish and gave them a good rinse. All this took about a minute. He made eight more spring rolls on the fly, plated them up, and handed them to the waiter with a simple, "Try and hang onto this one, huh?" Hardly any time lost; the table wouldn't even notice the lag.

"Casino waiters got slippery hands from playing all them video poker machines," Terrance offered from the rear of the kitchen. "Or maybe just from playing with their own greasy dicks."

"That one's got any grease on his dick, he must've buttered his underwear," Rickey said.

"Buttered his *underwear*?" Terrance frowned. "That don't make no sense."

"I mean, it wasn't like he greased it up to stick it *in* anybody."

"Coulda stuck it in his fist."

"I guess you got a point there."

"Ahhhh," Terrance sighed. "Good to see the repartee here is just as witty and sophisticated as what I hear at Liquor every night."

"Liquor's not as witty and sophisticated as usual tonight, T, cause you and me aren't there."

"Yeah, you right."

"Will you two shut the fuck up!" Milford hollered.

Rickey turned and stared at him, then glanced at Terrance, who shrugged. Sure, the conversation had been stupid, but it was this sort of easy, meaningless banter that turned the kitchen into cooks' territory. He'd seldom been in a kitchen where it didn't exist, and he'd never had a chef tell him to cut it out, let alone someone who technically worked for him. "Uh, Milford," he said, "you OK?"

"Yeah. Fine. I'm fine. Let's just try to get some fuckin work done, can we?"

Even the slippery-handed waiter, who had been lackadaisical

when he first reported for duty, picked up on Milford's mood and began tiptoeing in and out of the kitchen as any decent waiter should. After clearing the soup course, he reported that Dr. Lamotte's wife had raved about the "excellent" caviar.

"What about Fairbairn's wife?" Rickey asked. "What's she like?"

"He the one with the fucked-up arm? Far as I can tell, his bitch be about one drink away from slidin out her chair."

"You talk like that at the table?" Terrance said.

The waiter straightened his shoulders, adjusted his bow tie, and spoke in plummy tones. "Certainly not, my good sir. My name has been Kevin. Allow me to tell you about our tempting specials this evening. We have an exquisite crawfish-and-rice-stuffed mirliton surrounded by a bed of creamed potatoes—"

"*Creamed potatoes!*" Rickey and Terrance hollered in unison.

"Man, you was doin all right until you got to that," Terrance told him. "Ain't nobody gonna serve potatoes with rice."

"I knew a chef who did."

"Remind me not to eat at his restaurant," Rickey said. "Hey, Milford, we're sending out the seafood course next, you wanna put the lamb in to finish?"

"I got it."

Course you do, Rickey thought, *and you wouldn't tell me if you didn't.* Glancing over at Milford's station, he saw a big stockpot simmering on a back burner. "What's that in the pot?"

"Just some gumbo for us. I thought we might be hungry ourselves after we get done feeding these assholes."

"Cool." Rickey meant it; he always looked forward to eating Milford's food. Despite Milford's evil mood, he thought the night was going pretty well. They'd be out of here in another few hours, and he could go drink with G-man. The thought carried him through the sofrito and the lamb, and then it was time for him and Milford to make their appearance at the table.

•   •   •

This had been one of Liquor's slowest Saturday nights of the entire summer, and after half an hour without a new table, G-man decided to shut down the kitchen at nine-thirty. The waiters finished up their tables, rolled some silverware, and trickled out in ones and twos. The dishwashers knocked out a last light load. The porter carried out a single bag of wet garbage, gave the floor a cursory mopping, and was gone.

"Y'all feel like having a drink?" G-man asked his two cooks.

Devonte peered at the display of his cell phone. "Naw, thanks, man, but I gotta go. My brother just sent me a text message sayin he in jail."

"How'd he text you if he's in jail?"

"Dunno, but I guess I better find out."

"I'll take a drink with you," Alain said.

Mo was gone too, and the bar was dim and still. She usually had a local jazz-funk theme going on the CD player—Kermit Ruffins, Los Hombres Calientes, and the like—but now all was silent except for the occasional faint clicks and hums of the small cooler. G-man fixed the drinks, a rum and Coke for Alain and a shot of bourbon for himself. They sat facing each other in one of the booths. The silence stretched out. The eye contact grew a little too prolonged. They both looked away and gulped at their drinks.

"So how'd you get into cooking anyway?" Alain said.

"Rickey. Well, my momma and my sisters taught me home cooking, but I never would've gotten into it professionally without him. We started out washing dishes when we were fifteen, at a Lower Ninth Ward greasy spoon called the Feed-U."

"Don't believe I ever been there."

"Nah, old Sal retired years ago. How about you? How'd you get started?"

"My momma and my sisters, same as you. Also my dad, my grammaw, my other grammaw, my Parrain, my seventeen aunts and uncles . . ."

"I guess Cajun families got a lot in common with Italian ones. You ready for another?"

"Another . . . oh, a drink. Sure, I'll take a refill. Let me get 'em."

Alain busied himself behind the bar. The bourbon shot he brought back was at least twice as big as G-man's previous one. G-man sipped it and found himself remembering the conversation he'd had with Rickey this morning:

- You want to start thinking about a new fall menu pretty soon?

- Yeah, sure. Why don't you make some notes and show 'em to me later?

- I thought maybe we'd kick around some ideas together. You know, like we used to?

- We will, G. It's just I got all this casino shit to deal with right now. Help me out here.

- I been helping you out. Least I thought I had.

- Yeah, yeah, course you are. I'm counting on you to keep Liquor going until I get through with this other thing. I couldn't do it without you. I'll be back soon.

- Good, I miss you . . . Uh, hey, you wanna mess around? I got a little while before I gotta be at Liquor.

- Nah, man, I gotta pick up Terrance, swing by Zanca & Sons and get some preserved lemons . . . I got a shitload of stuff to do.

And Rickey had kept getting dressed while G-man sat there thinking, *Yeah, news flash, I know you got a lot to do. Just take a few minutes and do me first.* It wasn't even that he was so horny, but that he felt disconnected from Rickey in a way he never had before. For most of their lives they had worked together when they could and spent almost all their free time together. Now Rickey had this whole other life that didn't really include him. Soul Kitchen and all the evil weirdness associated with it. The acupuncture, which was a good thing, G-man guessed, but it still freaked him out. And, of course, the pills. Rickey would come home after work, shower, and emerge from the bathroom already medicated. He'd lie in bed with his eyes half closed and his breathing getting shallower until he fell asleep. Sometimes G-man couldn't keep from reaching over and checking his pulse. Even when they had sex, G-man no longer felt Rickey was all the way there with him.

He'd been too embarrassed to say any of this earlier, and anyway you didn't pick a fight with somebody when he was about to go cook an important dinner. Instead he'd just wished Rickey luck and driven to Liquor by himself. By the time Alain arrived, he'd already finished most of the prep.

"You look kinda lost in thought," Alain said now.

"Who, me?" G-man made himself laugh. "I was just wondering if the Saints can go ten and six this year. What you think?"

"Well, I mean, there ain't never no hope for Saints D. I think it's gonna be pretty hard to stop our offense, though. I was going up against 'em, I'd blitz early, try to create lots of turnovers. Then I'd bring in extra defensive backs to crowd the line of scrimmage and make Brooks beat us with the pass." Alain saw G-man looking at him. "Aw, don't get me started—I played a little football in high school. Used to think I might coach one day."

"You were a South Lafourche Tarpon, huh?"

"Yeah, but not much of one."

"Is it true what they say about locker rooms?"

"I dunno, what do they say?"

"That you can get some action in there."

"Maybe in the porno movies. Not in Cut Off."

"Yeah, not in Cut Off . . . You finished with that?"

"Yeah."

G-man made the next round of drinks. The metal ice scoop was pleasantly cool against his hand. He wished he could roll it across his forehead. Why on earth had he brought up locker rooms? The weird tension that kept coming up between him and Alain had just about dissipated, and then that had to pop out of his mouth. He wondered if he really *wanted* the tension to dissipate . . . but that was a thought that needed to be pushed away before it could get a foothold. Maker's Mark in one glass, Bacardi in the other. Press the C button on the soda gun. Rack it and pick up the glasses, steady hands, no spillage. Back to the table, think of something to say quick, something innocuous—

But Alain was talking. "She got any limes back there?"

"I didn't see any. I think she cuts 'em fresh every day."

"Aw well, never mind."

"You want me to go grab one out the cooler?"

"Nah, hell, don't worry about it."

"I don't mind. Really, I gotta hit the can anyway." He didn't, but he needed a minute to collect himself. Things were getting screwy here, all kinds of unspoken signals flying around that he didn't understand. G-man took his drink with him and gulped it as he made his way through the unlit kitchen.

Limes. He flicked on a single light in the hall and entered the walk-in to look for limes. The cold air felt good on his face. He unbuttoned his jacket and ran a finger under the damp neck of his T-shirt. The limes should be right here on the bottom shelf.

He put his empty glass aside to look for them. Bending over, he felt a wash of vertigo like a deep ocean wave. How much had he drunk anyway? He'd lost track. He straightened up, rubbed his forehead. When he heard a noise behind him, he thought maybe Rickey had gotten here early. He turned, and of course it was Alain.

"I thought I'd help you . . ."

G-man just looked at him. He was suddenly so drunk, so dizzy, so *whatever* that he didn't trust himself to speak. As Alain approached, G-man knew he should raise a hand to fend him off, but couldn't quite manage it. He did take a step backward, but that only meant that his back was against the shelves when Alain got to him. Cold metal jammed into his spine, Alain's warm hands splayed on his chest, then sliding down his rib cage. Then Alain's mouth on his, only the second person he had ever kissed (or possibly the third—there had been an interval of drunkenness even worse than this, long ago when Rickey was away at cooking school). The smell of Alain, the taste of him, the way he used his mouth were all totally different, not better or worse than Rickey, just *different,* exotic, and for a long plunging moment G-man grabbed him tight and kissed back, unaware of anything else in the world. Then his personality returned, screaming at him. What the hell, WHAT THE HELL, *WHAT THE HELL WAS HE DOING.*

He twisted his face away, twisted his body away. "Quit it. Stop. I can't do this."

"I know you want to. You *been* wanting to."

"That doesn't matter. Quit it. *Quit it!*" He got Alain by the shoulders and held him at arm's length. They stared at each other, wide-eyed, breathing like racehorses.

"I just thought—"

"I know. I know. But I can't. And I'm not gonna." G-man let go, edged around Alain, backed unsteadily out of the walk-in. "I gotta go home."

"You're too drunk to drive."

It was true, G-man realized. Most people in New Orleans drank and drove a little more than they ought to, but you learned your limits. Right now he was over his. "Then I gotta go back to the bar."

"G, please, I—"

G-man never heard what Alain was going to say, never even saw the hand Alain extended toward him. He was already fleeing back through the dark kitchen, banging his hip on the steel countertop, heading full-tilt for the safe spot at the bottom of the bottle.

•   •   •

While Terrance busied himself arranging four perfect balls of lemon sorbet in four Chinese soup spoons for the palate cleanser, Rickey and Milford washed their hands, wiped the sweat off their faces, and went out to swan at the table. "I always hated this part of the job," Milford said.

"I don't mind it."

"No, I wouldn't expect you to."

They were still in the back passageway that led to the private room where Fairbairn, Lamotte, and their wives were dining. Rickey stopped walking. "Milford, I know you're pissed off about something and I'm not looking to start an argument, but can we clear the air here? We used to work pretty well together, I thought. Have you developed some kinda problem with me?"

Milford turned. "All I said was I'd expect you to like visitin tables, blabbin with people. You good at it like a head chef oughta be. What's wrong with that?"

"I don't know. By itself, I wouldn't make anything of it. But lately it seems like you always got something to say to me, and most of it isn't too nice."

"Aw, shit." Milford leaned against the wall and ran a big, scarred hand over his face. "You gotta remember I ain't had much chance to practice my manners over the past ten years. I preciate everything you done, Rickey. I preciate you takin me on at Liquor and I can't tell you how much I preciate you suggestin me for this job."

"But?"

"But you right, I got a problem workin with you."

"Well, what is it?"

"I can't say exactly. You just kinda grate on my nerves."

Apparently feeling this was sufficient explanation, Milford started walking again.

"Well . . ."

"Well what?"

"Is that all you're gonna say? I just grate on your damn nerves?"

"What else you want me to say? It's nothin personal, I just don't think our styles of cookin go real well together. But who knows, now I got my own kitchen again, maybe anybody'd grate on my nerves. Anybody I was s'posed to answer to, I mean."

"*Answer* to? I don't ever ask you to answer to me! One of my major conditions when I took this gig was that you got total creative control. *Answer* to! For Chrissakes, Milford!"

"Look, you axed, I told you. Can't help it if you don't like the answer."

"That's true," Rickey muttered. "That's true." It was as if Milford had hauled off and kicked him in the balls. For the first time, he felt more than a theoretical sympathy for Eileen Trefethen. He knew Milford had never laid a finger on her, but he thought maybe he'd just gotten a glimpse of why they had argued so much that a jury was willing to believe Milford had killed her.

There wasn't a whole lot more to say, so they continued on to the table. They entered the private dining room through a swinging door about thirty paces from the kitchen pass. Fairbairn, with his back to them, was gesturing expansively with his good arm and saying, "But that just goes to show why they can't handle the extra load," whatever that meant. Rickey was annoyed to see that the waiter hadn't cleared the last course yet. The empty lamb plates languished on the table, messy with sauce smears, bones, stray steak knives. Lamotte's gaze shifted to the two chefs, alerting the others to their presence.

"Well, well," said Fairbairn, "look who we have here. The creators of the exotic array."

"Little too exotic for you, Mr. F?" Rickey said. He found the guy creepy as hell, but he couldn't resist goading him a little every now and then.

"For my personal tastes, yes. For our future diners, here's hoping not. I understand the modern restaurantgoer is always looking for the next trend, the next sensation. You and Milford will certainly give it to them."

The two men introduced their wives. Trisha Lamotte seemed like a regular New Orleans girl: short dyed hair, plump arms, a big intelligent smile. Rickey wondered whether she kept Lamotte grounded somehow; ever since they had lurked in the bread nook together listening to Fairbairn and Milford discuss murder, Lamotte had struck him as a tad neurotic. Bitsy Fairbairn was well into her cups, just as the waiter had reported. She hung onto Rickey's hand too long and breathed gin fumes up into his face. "I knew you were a wonderful cook, but no one told me you were so *young* and *handsome*."

"You're barking up the wrong tree there, Bitsy," Lamotte said, making his wife roll her eyes.

"Bitsy's days of treeing her kills are long over, I'm afraid," said Fairbairn. "The only thing she preys on now is the bottle of Bombay Sapphire."

"Oh, Clancy."

Christ. Well, maybe it was some kind of routine they had; you never knew what went on inside somebody else's relationship. Rickey made all the appropriate noises, asked how they'd liked the various dishes, then signaled Milford, who was hanging back. "He's not a big ham like me, but this here is the real star of Soul Kitchen. That's mostly his menu you just ate." *All* his menu, really, but the suits might be upset if they knew how little Rickey was contributing for what they'd already paid him.

Mrs. Lamotte shook Milford's hand. She was the only one who offered to. "Wonderful meal. Just great. I don't know how you come up with it. Me, I'm hopeless in the kitchen."

Milford didn't say anything. *C'mon, man,* Rickey thought, *I know it's been a shitty night, but try a little.* Aloud, he said, "Milford's got a gift. He's probably the best cook I ever known."

"Did you go to school?"

"No ma'am. My grandmother taught me a lot of what I know and the rest I figured out myself, on the job."

"Isn't that marvelous," breathed Mrs. Fairbairn.

"Milford's learned so much over the years," her husband remarked to no one in particular.

Rickey saw Milford shoot Fairbairn a dark look. Hurriedly he said, "Yeah, us two worked together back in the day, when I didn't know anything. Now here we are again, and he still kinda makes me feel like I don't know anything."

"I'm sure you know a *great deal.*" More gin fumes. Rickey wasn't unused to lady diners breathing on him, but the fact that her husband was cosigning the checks for this place made it even more uncomfortable than usual.

"I do all right. I mean, I'm not running myself down. I just don't know as much as Milford. He's got it going on."

Rickey felt as if he were talking into a void. These people were hearing him, but his words didn't mean anything to them, and he knew Milford didn't want to hear it either. *You just kinda grate on my nerves.* Jesus. He'd tried to help Milford because he thought Milford deserved a leg up, not because he expected anything in return, not even gratitude. Rickey examined this conviction for a moment and found that, as far as he could tell, it was true. Still, had Milford really needed to say that to him? He'd asked, he reminded himself. Even so, it smarted.

"So you learned to cook from your grammaw, huh?" Mrs. Lamotte was addressing Milford, thank God; Rickey was sick of hearing himself talk. "Did she make Creole food, soul food, stuff like that?"

"She could make anything." At the thought of his grandmother, Milford's shoulders straightened. "Anything at all. One time in New York she had this Thai dish . . ."

As Rickey listened to Milford tell the familiar story, he watched the diners' faces. Dr. and Mrs. Lamotte had grease on their chins, but at least they looked interested. Mrs. Fairbairn was almost unconscious now, and Clancy Fairbairn looked bored, his little hooded eyes far away.

"You come from a big family?" Mrs. Lamotte said when Milford had finished.

"Yes'm, but most all of 'em gone now."

At that, Fairbairn seemed to perk up a little. He stretched, ran a hand through his silver mane. "That reminds me, Milford," he said. "How's your sister? Working hard, is she? Those kids holding up all right?"

Milford stared at Fairbairn. Fairbairn stared back, smiling just a little. Something passed between them; Rickey could see it. For a long, long moment, the two men locked eyes, and Rickey thought, *Oh, fuck, there's no good way for this to go.*

"You fixed it so she'd lose her job, didn't you?" said Milford. "Just to give me a little extra warning? Course you couldn't a known what Ronald was gonna do . . . but it ain't like you woulda cared anyway."

With that, Milford turned his back on the table and disappeared through the swinging door, down the passageway.

"Is he all right?" Mrs. Lamotte wondered.

"I don't know," Rickey said. "I got no idea what he was talking about. Do you, Mr. Fairbairn?"

"Certainly not."

Everybody stared at each other, but nobody wanted to meet anyone else's eyes. Only Mrs. Fairbairn was oblivious, rattling the ice cubes in her empty glass in an attempt to catch the waiter's attention. It was the most uncomfortable tableside moment Rickey had ever experienced. "Well," he said at last, "we got a couple more courses coming up for you folks—I guess I better get back too."

Rickey turned to go, but here came Milford back through the swinging door, the big stockpot of gumbo in his hands. Rickey tried to step in front of him. Milford dodged him easily, planted a foot on the edge of Fairbairn's chair, shoved him away from the table, and threw the steaming gumbo in his face.

The noise Fairbairn made was horrible, but it was soon drowned out by the women's screams.

"Jesus Christ!" Lamotte shouted. His fat fingers dug furrows in the tablecloth. Fairbairn was twisting on the floor, raking at his eyes.

Rickey grabbed Milford's arm, but now that Milford had dumped his scalding burden, the fight seemed to have gone out of him. Where the fuck was Terrance? Rickey needed some backup here. He tugged at Milford, and Milford moved a little, seemingly willing to be led away. "C'mon," Rickey urged. "C'mon, man, let's get you outta here." He jerked his head at Fairbairn. "Doc, can't you do something for him?"

Dr. Lamotte remembered his Hippocratic oath and scrambled to kneel next to Fairbairn. His wife handed him a half-full glass of ice water, and Lamotte poured it over Fairbairn's face, rinsing off some of the molten gumbo. Rickey didn't want to see what was underneath. Mrs. Lamotte was punching at her cell phone, dialing 911, Rickey hoped. There was no coherent thought in his head, just a constant yammering litany of *oh shit oh shit oh shit.* He tugged at Milford again, and Milford started to follow.

Only in his peripheral vision did Rickey see Fairbairn heave himself up off the floor and grab one of the steak knives the waiter had left on the table. "*Milford,*" he rasped through peeling, blistering lips.

Milford half-turned, pulling his arm out of Rickey's grasp. Rickey tried to get hold of him again, but before he could, Fairbairn stumbled forward and sank the steak knife into Milford's left eye.

18

FOR the twentieth time in an hour, Rickey highlighted G-man's name on the speed dial of his cell phone and hit CALL. For the twentieth time, G-man's phone rang and rang, then went to voice mail. Nobody had picked up at home or the restaurant either. What a magical night this was shaping up to be.

Beside him, Dr. Lamotte sat with his big ass wedged uncomfortably into a plastic police-station chair. Mrs. Lamotte was around here somewhere, maybe looking for a Coke machine; she'd said something about being thirsty. The station was near Joe Brown Park, where Rickey vaguely remembered having his sixth birthday party. His mother had made the cake herself; it was dense and dry, and she'd ended up in tears because none of the kids wanted to eat it. Or was his memory exaggerating that last part? He didn't know; his brain was on overdrive.

Terrance got to go home after the cops determined that he hadn't seen anything. He'd ridden to the casino with Rickey, so Rickey gave him money for a taxi. Turned out he'd been taking a piss when Milford came in and got the gumbo. *Lucky him,* Rickey thought without bitterness. Terrance had been involved in enough weird shit thanks to him, and Rickey wouldn't wish the fluorescent despair of a three A.M. police station on anybody.

A desk-jockey cop appeared at the doorway of the waiting room. "Uh, sorry to keep you folks waiting. We gonna be with you in just few minutes."

"You got any idea how Milford is?" Rickey said.

"Milford Goodman?" The cop looked at a sheet of paper on his clipboard, then back up at Rickey. "He was dead on arrival at Charity. I'm sorry."

Rickey closed his eyes, and he was back in the private dining room again, Milford's big body sagging against him, trembling horribly, sliding to the floor. His hands had come up to grope for the knife handle sticking out of his eyesocket, his fingers scrabbling in the blood and tears that covered his face; then he had jerked once and gone limp all over. Throughout it all, Rickey gripped his shoulder and talked to him, though he had no earthly idea what he'd said.

"What about Clancy Fairbairn?" Lamotte said.

Eyes back to the clipboard, and this time the cop didn't look up. "This says Mr. Fairbairn's at Ochsner with some pretty bad burns, but he's conscious and talking."

When the cop had gone, Rickey turned to Lamotte. "I just want you to know I'm gonna tell them everything I know, everything Milford told me. I'll leave you out of it if you want—say I was alone in the bread nook when I overheard them that time—but I'm not protecting his ass."

"Do you like your restaurant? Do you have family in New Orleans?" The doctor saw how Rickey was looking at him. "I'm not threatening you, I'm not! I know how these things work, that's all. People who talk about Clancy Fairbairn sometimes meet up with freak accidents."

"Yeah, Doc, I know it. But I got an ace in the hole named Lenny Duveteaux, an ace with a strong interest in not seeing me have an accident, and you know what? I think I'd tell 'em anyway. I'm tired of all you rich fuckers running things with threats and bribes and pills." Lamotte opened his mouth to protest. "OK, the pills were as much my fault as yours, but to hell with the rest of it. I'm telling them what Milford told me, and if anybody ever asks me to repeat it in court, I'm doing that too. I'd done it before, maybe I could've saved Milford's life."

"Well, it's your funeral."

"You know what? I really doubt it."

Lamotte just looked at him with frightened eyes, then took out a handkerchief and mopped his sweaty scalp.

"You're not gonna keep working with him, are you, Doc?"

The doctor said something inaudible.

"Huh?"

"I said, *I don't have any choice.* He's got too much dirt on me. If you're serious about testifying against him, just be glad you got out of his orbit before he got anything on you . . . and God help you."

Rickey was finally allowed to leave the police station around four in the morning, after repeating his statement twice to a cop who seemed distinctly unimpressed with it. They wouldn't give him a ride back to his car, and he'd given most of his cash to Terrance, so he had to bum a twenty off Dr. Lamotte. When the taxi dropped him off in the parking lot, he was as tired as he'd ever been. He couldn't wait to find G-man, get home, and swallow a couple of Vicodin. Then he remembered his vow: he'd give up the pills when he was done with Soul Kitchen. Well, he was sure done with it now. *If I should go back on my word, may I forget how to use this damn thing.* Rickey looked at his knife bag, then looked up at the Pot O'Gold. Even at this hour its tacky glitter was undiminished. Gamblers were still filing in, their pockets full of hard-earned dollars that would soon be thrown away. Rickey sincerely hoped he would never lay eyes on the place again.

They never got their last two courses. Even after all that had happened, the thought made him sad. He didn't care about the palate cleanser, but the mangoes had been perfectly ripe and gorgeous.

He got on the I-10 and turned on the radio. The late-night religious program was on WWL. He started to change the station, but something in the preacher's exhorting Texan cadence transfixed him. It wasn't a religious impulse, of which he had none, so much as a need to be reminded that he must endure pain. The guy was talking about Armageddon, Omega, Judgment Day. "You're not gonna have any more responsibilities after that last trumpet blows," he assured Rickey, "but that don't mean you're gonna be packing up and going to Six Flags. You got an eternity stretching out ahead, a whole eternity you gotta fill." Though he already knew that, Rickey kept listening until he exited the highway at the Claiborne Avenue off-ramp.

I'm tired of all you rich fuckers running things with threats and bribes and pills, he'd told Dr. Lamotte. That was right after he invoked his ace in the hole, Lenny Duveteaux, who'd probably bribed and threatened more people than Lamotte and Fairbairn put together. Lenny just happened to be better at it. What a laugh. There was no way to get by in this city without some kind of ace, some way to grab a little unearned power for yourself. Milford had never figured that out. The power had just kept grabbing him and grabbing him until it finally crushed him, and Rickey felt partly responsible.

Liquor was dark and still, but there were two cars left in the parking lot, G-man's and an old Mustang that Rickey thought belonged to Alain. He got a little flutter in his stomach as he unlocked the front door. You never knew what could happen in the middle of a New Orleans night. There was a single light burning in the bar, and Rickey smelled fresh cigarette smoke, which relieved his anxiety a little.

Alain was sitting at the bar smoking and drinking coffee. Rickey didn't see G-man. "What's going on?"

"I don't know what the matter is, Rickey. We was having a couple drinks just like regular, and all of a sudden he grabbed the tequila bottle and started going to town. I thought I better stay with him till you got here."

O magical, glorious night. "Where is he?"

Alain nodded at one of the booths. Rickey glanced at it, didn't see G-man, looked again and saw him curled up on the floor under the table, long legs sticking out.

He looked back at Alain. "Did you *say* something to him?"

"We was just talking."

"Talking about what?"

Alain didn't answer. After a minute, Rickey couldn't stand to look at him anymore. "Fine. Go on home. I'll deal with you later."

"Look, I'm sorry, maybe I should put in my notice."

"Maybe you should just quit right now. What goddamn difference does it make? My crew's shot to shit, who cares if I lose one more? This is the kinda effect you have on my co-chef, who the fuck needs you anyway?" He was done with Alain, didn't even hear him walking out of the bar. He kneeled on the floor, crawled halfway under the table, put his hand on G-man's leg and shook it. "G. Hey, G. C'mon, what's up?"

"Rickey?"

"Yeah, I been through the damn wars, but it's me."

"Rickey?"

"Yeah."

"RICKEY?"

"Yes! Jeez, keep it down, huh?"

"SEE? SEE?" G-man tried to sit up, bumped his head on the underside of the table, and fell back groaning. When he was able to speak again, he'd lost a little of the volume. "See? See? Look what happened. I'm sorry. This is why I gotta go to Mass, cause I'm so so so so bad."

"Aw, hell, G. You're not bad. I saw bad tonight and you ain't it. No, I'll tell you about it later, when you can understand me." Rickey crawled the rest of the way under the table and hugged G-man as best he could in the limited space. In doing so he dislodged a fifth of Jose Cuervo from the crook of G-man's arm, and it rolled away across the floor, empty. It probably hadn't been full to start with, but still, Jesus. "Look, whatever you did, I'm sure it wasn't much and I know I been a crappy boyfriend, co-chef, everything lately. It's gonna get better. I promise, it's all gonna get better. Do you need to throw up?"

"Yes."

As he held G-man's head over the toilet, Rickey thought about how once upon a time he would have taken Alain outside and kicked his ass if he'd come upon a scene like the one in the bar. Then he would have spent hours interrogating G-man, sloppy drunk or not. Now he knew without needing to ask that, whatever had started to happen, G-man had filled himself full of tequila so it couldn't. G-man didn't even like tequila; it just happened to be the liquor that would get you drunk the fastest and incapacitate you the most thoroughly. Well, maybe Rickey had figured out a few things over the years.

It took another hour, but he finally got G-man home, cleaned up, and into bed. That done, Rickey stood in the bathroom looking at the pill bottle in his hand. He opened it, tipped three pills into his palm, stared at their innocuous white facets for a long moment, and washed them down with a glass of water. Then he poured the rest of the pills into the toilet and flushed before he could think much about it. One dose to say goodbye. He didn't know if his vow would last forever, but he thought he could make it for now.

19

G-MAN took three days to recover from his hangover, and that only because he was young, strong, and an experienced drinker; a lesser man would have needed a week. He went to work, of course—*if you can stand, you can work* is the cook's adage—but for the space of those three days he wasn't much use to anybody. Rickey brought him chocolate spearmint snowballs and reveled in a rare mood of pure, inexplicable optimism. He knew he shouldn't feel that way in the wake of Milford's death, but he couldn't help it. He hadn't realized how much the pills and the consulting job had gotten on top of him until he didn't have to worry about them anymore. His back was sore, but the acupuncture appointments helped some. He didn't wake up queasy every morning and he could feel his mind beginning to clear. It was a little scary to realize how fogged in he'd been for the past several months.

When the *Times-Picayune* called, he just said "No comment." He'd had an awful lot of practice spouting that phrase over the last couple of years, and he was getting good at it. The paper's story on the "fight to the death" between Clancy Fairbairn (whom they hadn't yet exposed as Comus; perhaps they didn't dare go quite that far) and the exonerated murderer repeated several of the things Rickey had told the cops, though it didn't mention him as a source. Somebody had a mole in the police department.

He supposed he should worry about what Fairbairn would do to him—his statement to the cops had incriminated Fairbairn pretty severely—but he found that he could not make himself care. After everything he'd dealt with over the past three years, Clancy Fairbairn's machinations and Dr. Lamotte's dire warnings seemed like a joke, and not a particularly good one. Probably that was a foolish attitude, but he was unable to shake it.

A week after the dinner at Soul Kitchen, the U.S. Attorney announced his imminent investigation into Fairbairn's business dealings. Rickey didn't know if Fairbairn would ever see prison time, but he suspected Fairbairn's future influence might be severely limited in New Orleans. Of course, you never knew what could happen. Maybe it would all roll straight off his asbestos hide like the hot gumbo had apparently done.

Soon afterward, Milford's obituary appeared in the paper: *survived by his sister Eleonora Goodman, his beloved nephews Ronald and Vance, and his beloved nieces Chanella and Andrelean.* Eleonora had stayed conservative with the boys' names but gotten fancy with her girls. Milford's service was being held at the First Zion Holy Sword Baptist Church off Claiborne, and Rickey couldn't quite bring himself to go. He wasn't scared, but he didn't want to make Eleonora feel any worse than she already must. Instead he sent her a check for a hundred dollars toward burial expenses. A few days later he received a thank-you note in a small, crabbed hand. Lady might be prejudiced, Rickey thought—he had some idea of what had caused the falling-out between her and Milford—but she had manners.

He did return to Soul Kitchen once. It seemed cowardly and unprofessional not to at least go clean up his mess. The kitchen felt like one of those ghost ships where the crew has supposedly disappeared in the midst of everyday life, leaving pipes burning and glasses of ale half-drunk. Terrance had turned off the burners and shut down the hood, but everything else was just as the three cooks had left it. Looking at the four soup spoons of long-melted lemon sorbet beginning to crystallize, Rickey shuddered at the haunted feel of this place. It no longer seemed beautiful to him despite the exquisite design and top-of-the-line equipment; he now suspected that Clancy Fairbairn had never intended for the restaurant to succeed, and had only spent so much on the kitchen as yet another way of hiding dirty money. Most used kitchen equipment didn't have tremendous resale value, but for stuff this esoteric he could collect a pretty penny.

When Lenny asked Rickey and G-man to join him at the Polonius Room on their next night off, they almost declined. Rickey had had his fill of head games and power trips, and he wasn't interested in pouring Lenny into bed again. But Lenny persisted. "Come on, guys. This isn't about drinking, it's about food. They're doing some really crazy shit over there. Nobody's ever done anything like this in New Orleans before, and when Jaap finally gets fed up with the empty tables and leaves town, I guarantee you nobody ever will again."

"When Jaap leaves, they can just promote Tanker to executive chef. He'll be in hog heaven making his damn airs and deconstructions."

"I'm not so sure of that," Lenny said mysteriously. "Anyway, I don't think it'll happen. When Jaap leaves—or gets fired, whichever comes first—mark my words, the Polonius Room will go back to serving steaks and chops. They'll need to recoup their losses. You ought to experience this kind of dining while you have the chance."

"What do they call it, anyway?" Rickey asked. "Molecular gastronomy? I don't care about molecules, Lenny. I'm interested in food."

"It's about the food—just in a different way than you're used to. It's supposed to make you think in new ways about the chemistry of ingredients, the breakdown of flavors . . . Look, Rickey, it's not really my thing either, but I think it's worth checking out once. Or maybe it's too adventurous for you?"

Rickey was still suspicious of Lenny's sudden enthusiasm for molecular gastronomy, but he couldn't let that "too adventurous" crack go by. "Fine, make a reservation. Long as you're buying, that is. We're broke."

"Of course I'm buying. But why are you broke? I thought you just inherited a bunch of money."

Rickey glanced at a Shell Beach realtor's brochure that lay on his desk. "Uh, that money's kinda tied up at the moment."

"Hey, no problem, it's none of my business anyway. I just wanted to make sure you guys are doing all right."

"We're doing fine," Rickey said, and found that he meant it.

·   ·   ·

Years ago, when the Polonius Room was a normal restaurant, Rickey had applied for a job there. He wasn't hired, and he'd had no occasion to set foot in the place since. As he, G-man, and Lenny were seated tonight, heads turned and voices murmured at other tables. Not many people were eating here these days, but the ones who did were New Orleans' most hardcore foodies, and the three chefs had obviously been recognized.

When Rickey was here before, the walls had been painted with murals of famous figures from Louisiana history shopping in the French Market, partying in Storyville, dueling under the oaks in City Park, and other stereotypical New Orleans activities. Now the murals had been painted over with flat white primer and the walls were sparsely decorated with mystifying art. "What's that supposed to be?" Rickey asked the hostess, pointing at a blobby red painting that hung above their table.

"Oh, that's a portrait of Huey P. Long done in ketchup. The artist, F.X. Rodriguez, also works in blood, chocolate syrup, and dust. He wants the viewer to look more closely at the subject of his work and contemplate how the medium affects the meaning."

"So what's the connection between Huey P. and Heinz 57?"

"I'll bring you a brochure," the hostess said tactfully, hurrying away toward the safety of her leather-bound podium.

Rickey sniffed the air. "Nothing like the smell of old ketchup to whet your appetite."

"I'm sure he must've put some kind of sealant on it," Lenny murmured. "Check out the one across the room."

Rickey looked over and saw a huge canvas that seemed to depict a blurry image of the Eiffel Tower perched atop a giant egg. Upon further contemplation, he realized the "egg" was a naked female breast. "Jeez," he said. "I never thought I'd be nostalgic for the day when restaurants just decorated with those ugly-ass metal sculptures that could put your eye out."

They all ordered the Grand Narrative, which was billed on the menu as "The story of Chef Jaap's culinary life as told in a series of 10 small courses that will excite, challenge, and satiate all your senses ($90)." Lenny talked Rickey into getting the wine pairings ($75) that accompanied it. G-man ordered a gin and tonic, but asked the waiter to have the bartender make it as weak as a newborn kitten; he was still feeling a little delicate.

"Well," Lenny said. "This should be fun. I think it's good for us to step outside of our preconceptions about dining . . ."

His voice died away as the first course was set before them. It appeared to be a small tabletop hibachi covered with dried grass, wood chips, and little heaps of gray-brown powder. The waiter touched a kitchen lighter to the coals under the metal grate, and a cloud of eye-watering smoke billowed toward the ceiling.

"This is our Cajun Pu Pu Platter," the waiter explained. "On it you'll notice cattail greens, cypress chips, and filé powder. You don't actually eat anything on here; the aromas are intended to set the mood and get your digestive juices flowing."

He beat a tactical retreat as the smoke wafted toward him. Rickey fanned the air and stared at Lenny in horror. G-man sipped his drink, deciding maybe he didn't feel so delicate after all.

The next course followed soon after. "This is compliments of your friend Tanker," said the waiter, setting down what looked like three long wontons. "It's called Fried Water. He said you'd get the joke."

"Ditka," Rickey said.

Lenny looked up from poking at his wonton. "What?"

"When Mike Ditka came here from Chicago to coach the Saints, he talked a lotta shit about New Orleans cooking. Said we'd fry water if we could figure out how. I guess Tanker figured out how."

"Ow, dammit!" said G-man. He had just pulled off one end of his wonton, releasing a gush of scalding liquid that burned his finger.

"Sorry, sorry." The waiter held up a belatedly cautionary hand. "With some of these courses, it's better if you let me give you the chef's instructions for eating them before you dig in. In this case, just put the whole thing in your mouth and bite down. Can I bring you another one, sir?"

"No thanks. I'll take another drink, though."

"Very good."

They ate their Fried Water and stared at each other, speechless. It wasn't so much that no one had anything to say as that they didn't know where to start. While they were puzzling over it, another course arrived: three tiny monkey dishes, each holding two cubes of gelee, set atop glass bowls in which live Siamese fighting fish swam listlessly back and forth. The waiter took out a perfume atomizer and spritzed all the gelee cubes with some fishy-smelling substance.

"This is a nod to Chef Jaap's Dutch heritage. On the streets of Amsterdam the people eat *broodjeharing,* a sandwich made from pickled herring, chopped onions, and sweet pickles. Here we have onion and sweet pickle gelees enhanced with a touch of herring oil. The chef suggests you eat the whole thing at once, combining all the flavors."

"Does anybody ever try to eat these poor fish?" G-man asked, but the waiter was already walking away.

Rickey picked up the monkey dish and tipped the two cubes into his mouth. The flavor was indescribably foul and kept building up in layers: sugary sweetness, then onion, then a flavor like the oil at the bottom of a tuna can. He swallowed as quickly as he could and tried not to gag.

"Christ, what a face," said Lenny. "Maybe I'll skip this one."

"The fuck you will. You got us into this, now I want to see every goddamn nasty course disappear down that hairy gullet of yours."

"My *gullet* isn't hairy." Lenny gulped his *broodjeharing* gelee. "Oh, Jesus. Oh, fucking hell."

"I just can't wait to not eat this," G-man said.

"C'mon, dude, we're all in this together."

"OK, OK . . . shit. *Shit.* Where's my other drink?"

It arrived at about the same time the hostess dropped off the art brochure she'd promised. "'Dining at the Polonius Room is a complete synaesthetic experience,'" Rickey read aloud. "'Our art collection complements Chef Jaap Noteboom's groundbreaking cuisine in a manner that spans all mediums and delineates our interest in the horizons of gastronomy, the conflation of time, and the suggestion that things may not be what they seem.'"

"Things aren't what they seem, all right," G-man said. "When we came in here, it seemed like we were gonna eat dinner."

Rickey laughed, then grew sober again as the next course arrived at the table. "Here we have our Illustrated Muffuletta," said the waiter. "Chef Jaap has prepared olive oil and mortadella sorbets surrounded by Gruyère foam and sprinkled with dehydrated olive powder. On the outside of all this you'll find edible rice paper printed with pictures of a muffuletta in soy-based ink."

Indeed, the dish was wrapped in what appeared to be dozens of tiny, repeating pictures of New Orleans' classic Italian sandwich; the whole thing looked rather like an odd sushi roll. Rickey took a deep breath and popped it into his mouth. He was surprised to find that it was his favorite course so far; despite the goofy presentation, it really did taste a lot like a muffuletta.

"So what do you think?" Lenny said. "Has Tanker found his niche?"

Rickey shrugged. "You tell me. I haven't talked to him since we ran into each other in the grocery store a couple months ago. He always said he wanted to be doing more adventurous food than we serve at Liquor—well, he's sure doing it now."

"But do you think it's the best use of his talents?"

"It's not up to me to say how he should use his talents."

"Gentlemen—pardon me—your next course is another nod

to Chef Jaap's homeland. This is a hemp-infused Advocaat custard topped with a chocolate-covered raspberry."

The dish was served in a Japanese soup spoon that reminded Rickey of the never-served lemon sorbet at Soul Kitchen, but he soon forgot that as the essences of fresh raspberry, chocolate, and strong marijuana filled his mouth. "OK, he's shooting lights out on this one," he said, "but how'd he get away with it?"

"You can flavor a dish any way you want as long as it doesn't contain the actual illegal substance," Lenny told him. "Ever seen those fake versions of absinthe they sell in the liquor stores?"

G-man shuddered at the mention of absinthe. They'd ordered some of the real liquor from Spain once, hoping to feature it in a tasting menu, but everyone except Rickey had gotten so hammered on the stuff that the plan had been abandoned. Rickey had dodged the bullet due to his dislike for anise-flavored drinks.

The next course brought them crashing back to earth. The waiter called it "Oysters Rockefeller," but it was simply a soft blob of sodium alginate that looked for all the world like a bright green egg yolk, set aquiver in a square dish of tapioca pearls. When Rickey put it in his mouth, it burst softly, and the flavors of oyster, spinach, and Herbsaint gushed down his throat. It was all he could do to restrain himself from spitting the gooey mouthful back into the dish.

The "Oysters Rockefeller" was followed by "Crawfish Boil," a single crawfish, a potato cube, and a few dehydrated corn kernels encased in crab-boil-flavored gelee. After that it was back to the Netherlands for something called "Hodgepodge Injection": pureed white beans, carrots, parsnips, and brisket drippings layered prettily in a plastic syringe for the diner to squeeze into his mouth. The waiter said the technique was Jaap's way of building up successive layers of flavor. Rickey thought it was Jaap's way of serving baby food, but he didn't share this bon mot with the table; his own negativity had begun to depress him.

The sweet courses were ushered in by "French Market Soup," a thin liquid that tasted exactly and nauseatingly like a Café du Monde beignet, served in a delicate china cup that did nothing to improve it. The grand finale was "Bread Pudding," in which dishes of rum-soaked fruit were flamed tableside, then quenched by the ladling-in of brioche cubes that had been flash-frozen in liquid nitrogen. The meal ended as it had begun, in a cloud of billowing, choking fumes.

"Heads up," said Lenny as Rickey and G-man waved their hands in the air, coughing. Rickey looked up to see Jaap and Tanker approaching the table. They were clad in identical paper toques, white aprons, and spotless white jackets, the only difference being that Jaap's jacket was monogrammed with his name, his job title, and the restaurant's logo, while Tanker's was innocent of decoration.

"Jaap Noteboom," said the chef, shaking hands with Lenny, Rickey, and G-man—in order of perceived importance, Rickey supposed. His grip was overly strong, as if he thought he had to prove his culinary prowess by breaking a few bones in the other chefs' hands. Tanker didn't offer to shake, but stood slightly behind Jaap looking embarrassed.

"We hope you enjoyed your meal," said Jaap. "Nothing else like this in New Orleans. Eh?"

"Absolutely not," Lenny said. "I guess Chicago's the American epicenter of molecular gastronomy these days."

Jaap bristled at the phrase. "Molecular gastronomy? Do you have eyes like the microscope, then? Were you able to see the molecules in your food this evening?"

"No, it's just an expression—"

"A meaningless one! Molecular gastronomy. *Pah*. Yet another label invented by food critics to explain away what they don't comprehend."

Rickey couldn't stand it. "Actually, Jaap, the label was invented by a French scientist in the eighties. Before you or I ever picked up a knife, probably."

"Oh? And how do you know that?"

Rickey had done a search for "molecular gastronomy" on the Internet, but didn't want to say so. "I think I read it in *Gourmet*. Anyway, if you don't like the phrase, what do *you* call this kinda cooking?"

"I eschew labels. I call it the cooking of Jaap Noteboom. As it says on the menu, it is simply my Grand Narrative, my culinary story."

Rickey saw Tanker wince. He wanted to pursue the conversation a little further, but remembered that he was Lenny's guest; it wouldn't do to be openly rude to another chef on somebody else's dollar. Instead, he caught Tanker's eye again and said, "So how about you, Tank? You finally expanding your horizons?"

"Oh, infinitely," Tanker said. "Infinitely."

"Well," Lenny said, sounding a little helpless. No one seemed to know where to look. G-man reached for his drink and nearly knocked it over.

"I liked the muffuletta," Rickey said at last. "And the pot custard. That was real good."

"*Hemp* custard," Jaap hissed. "The dish is flavored with *hemp* oil."

"Uh huh. Well, it was tasty."

Jaap's eyes burned into him. Rickey smiled, picked up his wineglass, and drank the last few drops of something way too sweet whose name he couldn't pronounce.

"Tanker, if you want to talk to your . . . *friends* any more, that's fine. I'll see you back in the kitchen." Jaap turned on his heel and walked away.

"So," Tanker said. "Uh, you really enjoyed it? For real?"

Suddenly Rickey didn't want to be mean. "Well, it's not exactly my kinda thing, you know? I'll try anything, but I guess my tastes are a little more basic than this. I guess you must be learning a lot, though."

"Yeah, I'm learning a lot about cooking food nobody wants to eat."

Tanker's shoulders sagged and he looked away. Rickey suddenly knew beyond the shadow of a doubt that if he asked Tanker to come back to Liquor, asked him right here and now, Tanker would do it. He felt Lenny's shoe nudge his ankle under the table, and Lenny's intentions in bringing them here became clear. Rickey looked at G-man, but G-man only shrugged: it was Rickey who'd driven Tanker to quit, and Rickey would have to be responsible for inviting him back. And he wanted to. But that wall of stubbornness was still there, infuriating and impenetrable; he just couldn't make himself say the words.

"Well," said Tanker. "Thanks for coming in, anyway. I better get back to it. Guess I'll see y'all around."

"See you, Tanker," said Lenny. Then, when Tanker had gone, he leaned toward Rickey and whispered, "You fucking idiot!"

Rickey just looked at him. It was unusual for Lenny to lose his temper even in such a small way, but Rickey knew he deserved it.

After the presentation of a cart full of oddly flavored lollipops, truffles, and petit fours—most of which the chefs rejected, as none of them had a sweet tooth—Lenny paid the bill and they left the Polonius Room, a dejected, still slightly hungry little party.

"Who the fuck is Polonius anyway?" Rickey said in the elevator. "A king? A god? I never heard of them parading. Is it one of those krewes that quit when they had to integrate?"

"It's not a Mardi Gras krewe," Lenny told him. "It's from Shakespeare. Polonius was Ophelia's father in *Hamlet,* I think."

"Oh." At first Rickey felt stupid, but the more he thought about it, the more it annoyed him. "Well, what kinda dumb name is that for a restaurant in New Orleans? What the hell does Hamlet's father have to do with anything?"

"Not Hamlet's father. Ophelia's. That girl who drowned herself." Lenny sounded depressed. "I don't know what he has to do with anything."

"I bet somebody thought it was a Mardi Gras krewe," G-man said. "It does sound like one."

Simultaneously, they all lost interest in the subject. As they left the hotel and began walking back to Lenny's car, Rickey mused on the different ways in which one could respond to a bad restaurant meal. A spectacularly terrible meal could be almost fun. You could mock it, dissect it, feel superior to it. Under the right circumstances, you could dine out on a really bad meal for years; it could be told and retold an infinite number of times. Alternately, it made you angry; you thought about the money you'd spent, the rip-off factor, and got self-righteously pissed. As the great cookery writer Elizabeth David had said, a bad meal is always expensive.

Sometimes, though, a terrible meal was just sad. Tonight's dinner had been sad. Jaap Noteboom really believed in what he was doing, that much was clear even if he was a pompous fuck, but it just wasn't very good or very well-suited to New Orleans. When he thought of Tanker working in that ridiculous kitchen instead of at Liquor, Rickey almost felt like crying.

There was some kind of convention in town; the hotel garage had been completely full and they'd had to park several blocks away on Camp Street. As they walked away from Canal, the neighborhood grew darker and less populated. Up ahead, a skinny old black man sat folded on a stoop. By the way he watched them approach, Rickey could tell he was going to panhandle them, and as they drew abreast of him, he did just that. "Spare a little change so I can get somethin to eat?"

"Sorry," they said as one.

"Awright, God bless you."

The old man was half a block behind them now. Rickey's mind seized on the dissonance of the encounter and would not let go. With tax and tip, the three of them had just blown over five hundred dollars on an idiotic dinner that gave them virtually no pleasure. Yet when someone who was hungry asked for a little help, they told him no without even thinking about it. What was the problem here? What had gone wrong in his life, that things could be this way?

More importantly, could he fix it?

"Hang on," he told Lenny and G-man. "I can't go home yet. I got something to do."

"What—" said G-man, but Rickey was already turning, walking back toward the panhandler, pulling out his wallet. He had twenty-six dollars and thirty cents, and he gave it all to the old man, who couldn't get over his surprise. "Bless your heart," the guy kept saying. "Bless your heart."

"Thanks," Rickey said. "My heart probably needs it. Good luck." He didn't return to Lenny and G-man, but kept walking, a little faster, back toward the d'Hemecourt Hotel. The Polonius Room's kitchen had just closed; Tanker would still be there. If for some reason he wasn't there, Rickey would find him wherever he was and ask him to come back to Liquor. If necessary, he would apologize and even beg. He was sick of everything being so stupid and stubborn and senseless, and that went for himself most of all.

After a few minutes, Lenny and G-man caught up with him. They seemed to know where he was going. G-man put a hand on Rickey's shoulder and gave it a little squeeze. Lenny just walked along behind them looking satisfied with himself. Rickey didn't care. As far as he was concerned, they were all entitled to whatever satisfaction they could get in this world. Maybe there was even enough to go around.

EPILOGUE: ADRIFT ON BAYOU LA LOUTRE

NO kidding?" said Tanker, laughing. "Y'all really went to the Camellia Grill after dinner?"

Rickey nodded. They were in the kitchen at Liquor, and Rickey was trying to help Tanker get his dessert nook back in order.

"Yeah. After I barged into the Polonius Room and asked you to come back to work here, we all went and had chili cheese fries and chocolate-cherry freezes, and then Lenny dropped us off home. I mean, we really didn't get all that much to *eat*, you know? Those ten courses only added up to about twenty bites."

"I know. I kept telling Jaap we needed to either increase the number of courses or make them bigger, but he'd just get mad and start hollering about how New Orleanians are conditioned to want a big old plate of food. With cheese melted on top."

"Well, we kinda are, I guess. But we couldn't help it that night—we were still hungry."

"I know. It was a problem."

"Well, fuck him. Let him keep juggling his molecules."

"Actually, he says he's moving back to Amsterdam next year.

I guess they don't have any really freaked-out restaurants there, and he wants to open one."

"Good riddance. I'm just glad we got you back."

"Yeah, me too."

They glanced at each other and looked away again, embarrassed. When Rickey first got to know Tanker three years ago, he'd been so impressed by Tanker's cooking skills that he had almost had a crush on him—not a sexual thing, but one based entirely on food. He'd felt ignorant and tongue-tied in Tanker's presence and had had to work up the nerve to offer him a job. In the interim, they'd gotten completely comfortable with each other, but now it was like being back at square one. *Oh well,* Rickey thought, *things are still a hell of a lot better than they were a month ago when he wasn't here.*

"What time are y'all leaving tomorrow?"

"Early. We figure if we close and get the keys early, maybe we can do a little fishing."

"Jeez! You'll have the whole week to fish."

"I know, but . . ." Rickey shrugged. "I just want to."

"That's cool."

Tomorrow morning he and G-man would show up at a real estate agent's office to finalize the purchase of a tiny furnished camp in Shell Beach, a camp that—somehow, miraculously—came with a run-down flatboat and a slip to keep it in. Rickey was using most of his Dallas inheritance for the down payment. He wondered what it would feel like to write that check, which would have at least two more zeroes than any he'd ever written before. He thought it would probably feel good. Afterward, they'd continue on to the camp itself, where they planned to do absolutely nothing useful for a whole week. Tanker would be in charge of the kitchen while they were gone. Rickey had offered to close and give him a paid vacation, but Tanker declined: "I need to get back in the groove, you know? They never did let me do any desserts at the Polonius Room. Give me another week, I might forget how."

Rickey didn't feel the same trepidation he'd experienced when he left Tanker in charge before. Or maybe he felt it but had learned to live with it; he wasn't sure. The only thing he knew beyond the shadow of a doubt was that the restaurant business would grind him into little pieces if he didn't have a way of getting away from it once in a while. Shell Beach and the camp would provide him with that getaway. Of course, if anything bad happened, he was less than an hour away, and Tanker had sworn to call him if the least problem cropped up. Rickey had a feeling, though, that nothing would go wrong this time. It wasn't like him to be so optimistic, but he just couldn't seem to shake it.

•   •   •

"Dude," G-man said. "We own *property*."

Rickey just shook his head in mock disbelief. It was the only answer necessary, because they'd been saying variations of these words to each other ever since they left the real estate office twenty minutes ago. The verbal equivalent of pinching themselves, Rickey supposed. As recently as one year ago they would never have guessed that they'd be buying property, even if it was just a ramshackle fishing camp with a tangle of boating debris in the yard.

"Check it out," G-man said. "Our first time driving into Shell Beach as homeowners."

He turned the wheel and steered the car across the drawbridge. A few feet below, Bayou La Loutre sparkled in the morning sun. Rickey could hardly wait to try out that crappy little flatboat.

The camp had once been painted yellow. Sun, saltwater, and time had faded it to a sort of pale-piss color. To Rickey's eyes, though, it was gorgeous. He had thought it looked all right before, but the fact that he and G-man owned it improved its appearance a hundredfold.

"What's that on the porch?" he said.

They climbed the rickety wooden stairs and inspected the brown grocery bag someone had placed on the ancient welcome mat. Inside was a hideous lamp with a base made from a Saints football helmet and a shade fringed in black and gold. "Anthony B," said Rickey. "He must've drove down here to leave it when he heard we were buying this place. That dork."

"Maybe he's at his camp now. You feel like checking?"

"Later. Right now I just want to go in there with you and lock the door and fuck on that nasty-looking million-year-old mattress, and then I want to take that boat for a spin."

The first order of business was easily handled. The second proved a bit more difficult, as they couldn't get the boat's motor to turn over at first, but one of the guys from the marina showed them how to pour a little gas into the carburetor and it started right up.

"Which of us is gonna steer this thing?" Rickey said.

"You been steering all along. Why stop when you're on a roll?"

"OK, well, hang on to the cooler, because it might be a bumpy ride at first."

"Never bothered me before."

Rickey set the throttle on idle, shifted into forward, and maneuvered the boat slowly out of the slip. Once he got the hang of it, they might go wet their lines out on the lake, but for now he decided to just cruise up and down the bayou. Nice and easy. Nothing to worry about but the sun warming his head through his baseball cap and the prow cutting a straight line through the water.

In his pocket, his cell phone rang.

"Aw, shit."

"Please don't throw it in the bayou," said G-man.

"I won't. Just watch the throttle for a second." Rickey flipped the phone open and glanced at the caller ID. Tanker. Shit.

"What's up, Tank?"

"How'd the closing go?"

"It went fine. We're here. What's the matter?"

"Nothing. Nothing's the matter. I just called to tell you we're running a mackerel special for dinner. I know it's not the most popular fish in the world, but I think it's underrated."

"I agree. You called to tell me that?"

"Well, about that and today's mail."

"Tanker. Am I gonna have to drive all the way back to New Orleans just to kick your ass?"

"I got a letter from the Beard Foundation," Tanker said imperturbably.

"*You* got a letter?"

"Yeah. Apparently some crazy bastard thinks I should be nominated for something called the All-Clad Bakeware Outstanding Pastry Chef Award."

"At Liquor?" Rickey said stupidly.

"Yeah, at Liquor. You know anywhere else I been a pastry chef?"

"No, but I just thought . . . since you quit . . ."

"I guess they decided on the nominations before I left. Good thing I came back, huh?"

"Yeah," Rickey said. "Yeah, it is. Hang on a sec." He put his hand over the mouthpiece and gave G-man the news. G-man wanted to congratulate Tanker, and Rickey handed him the phone.

How the hell did we ever end up with so much good luck? he wondered. *What if something bad happens to balance it out?*

Then he thought of everything that had happened over the past few months, and he began to laugh. If the balancing hadn't already happened, the world was a crueler place than he was willing to believe. Still laughing, he dropped the throttle into idle again, shifted down, and let the boat drift. When G-man got done talking to Tanker, they could take off again, but for now it was enough just to sit here on the bayou, leaning back on his elbows, looking forward to grabbing a beer from the cooler, wondering where the fish might be and whether he would find them, listening to the thousand tiny movements of the shining water.

ACKNOWLEDGMENTS

Books are written in lonely rooms, but they have life-support systems that extend for miles—in the case of *Soul Kitchen,* all the way around the world. Thanks are due to Henry Barber; Leo and June Brignac of the Wateredge Beach Resort in Grand Isle, Louisiana; Bob Brite; Connie Brite; Ramsey and Jenny Campbell; Fr. Patrick Collum; Stephen Ellison; Neil Gaiman; Lorin Gaudin; Sue and Phil Gregory of Cassowary House in Kuranda, Australia; Benny Grunch; Irene Hardy; Mary Herczog; Peggy Hulin of the Old Castillo Hotel in St. Martinville, Louisiana; Aaron Jacks (from whom I first heard the term "molecular gastronomy"); Stephen King; Louis and Elly Maistros; Ti Martin; Darren Mckeeman; Lindsey Moore; Mindy Nunez; Greg and Sondra Peters; Chad Savage; Ira Silverberg; Heather Spear; Joseph Stebbins; Harry S. Tervalon; Carrie Thornton; Pete and Janis Vazquez; WYES; Hirut Yibsa and Germame Kassa.

Diners familiar with the American "molecular gastronomy" scene will notice certain similarities between Chef Jaap Noteboom's techniques and those employed by Chicago restaurants Moto and Alinea. Having enjoyed meals at both of these excellent restaurants, I can safely say that Chefs Homaro Cantu and Grant

Achatz are employing the techniques to far better effect than Chef Jaap.

As always, a separate and special thank-you to my most be-loved chef, Chris DeBarr, without whom there would be no con-tinuing adventures.